WHY DO EARLS FALL IN LOVE?

DEB MARLOWE

Copyright © 2021 by Deb Marlowe

All rights reserved.

No part of this book may be reproduced in any form or by any electronic or mechanical means, including information storage and retrieval systems, without written permission from the author, except for the use of brief quotations in a book review.

❦ Created with Vellum

Dedication:

*To Diane, who worried about the dowager Lady Chester.
No feisty old ladies will grow lonely on my watch, my friend.*

*Also:
To Gayle and to Lori. I blended your ideas for an annoying
footman and Old Alf was born!*

CHAPTER 1

"There he is. It's Lord Whiddon. Just there, by the pillar. And yes, of course, he is frowning."

Miss Charlotte Mayne looked out across the ballroom to the spot her friend indicated. The other young ladies in their group did the same. Lord Whiddon. Something stirred in her, just looking at him. It was no wonder they all watched him. His was not the highest title in the room. His fortune might not be the largest—although the matrons whispered that it was plump enough. But saints be praised, he was certainly one of the most beautiful men of the *ton*.

Beautiful. It was the right word. The sort of word you used to describe an ideal. The most stunning landscape. The most elegant settee. A breath-catching portrait. A perfectly proportioned stallion.

He put all of them to shame.

"Why is he not *dancing*?" Her cousin, Miss Harriett Mayne, sounded aggrieved. "He never dances."

"He does," Lady Mary Twynly corrected. "He always limits his choice of partners, though, to the wives of his friends."

"Yes, but then he frowns at them across the room. Why?" asked Miss Winthrop.

"And why does he not dance with us? Any of us?" Harriet complained. "He even avoids a simple introduction, at least to any of the young, unmarried ladies."

"He avoids us as if we are plagued," Lady Mary declared. "Are we so frightening?"

"Yes, of course we are. One of us might fall into his arms or kiss him madly in the midst of a quadrille. He would be compromised and forced to marry," Miss Winthrop said with a giggle.

"You jest, but I believe that is the crux of it. He has no wish to marry. That is what my mama says," Lady Mary said. She leaned in closer. "Even the servants gossip of his reluctance. I heard the attendant in the retiring room call him Lord Unwavering."

"Lord Unwilling," quipped Miss Winthrop.

Charlotte looked to him again as they all giggled behind their fans. She had the uncharitable thought that he might be right to avoid them.

"You are very quiet, Charlotte," Harriet said a bit sharply. "What do you think of Lord Whiddon?"

"I think he looks unhappy," she said simply.

Purposefully, she turned away from the handsome earl. Lord Whiddon's woes might be intriguing, but she had her own to consider. Her time, and her chances, were limited. She had managed, against all odds, to get to London for the Season. She had to make the most of the opportunity. She had to find a husband. A generous and understanding husband. Everything depended on it.

"Excuse me," she murmured to the young ladies. "My aunt is signaling me." She nodded and headed toward the ballroom entryway, where Aunt Bernadine beckoned her.

"Mr. Helden is coming through the receiving line now,"

the older woman whispered. She took Charlotte's arm and pulled her along with her. "We must see you situated so that when he spots you, he sees you at your best." She scanned the crowd as she went. "Ah, yes. Perfect."

Charlotte followed as her aunt moved toward the buffet set in an alcove at one side of the room. She nearly bumped into Bernadine when she stopped to address a tall gentleman moving in the other direction with a glass of champagne.

"Lord Treyford!" her aunt trilled. "How wonderful to run into you."

"Miss Mayne! What a delight to find you here."

Charlotte stared. *Lord Treyford*? Her aunt knew the infamous, world-traveling, treasure hunting earl?

"I'm thrilled to have the chance to thank you in person for the Nafran coin you sent. It is a highlight of my collection."

"It was the least we could do, considering the help you gave us in sorting that old cache. I'm impressed you not only could identify so many, but knew their value, as well. Your help was much appreciated."

"It was my pleasure. I do confess to being surprised to see you, though. I didn't think you fond of these sorts of gatherings."

"I promised my brother I'd come. And I might say the same of you, Miss Mayne. I didn't think you often came to London?"

"Nor do I, but this year I am presenting my niece." She waved a hand toward Charlotte. "May I make her known to you?"

Thoughts of Mr. Helden faded as Charlotte made her curtsy. She could not resist adding, after the pleasantries were exchanged, "Oh, but I so enjoyed your book, my lord!"

He grinned. "My thanks. I am glad to hear it."

"England must feel so tame, after all of your fascinating

travels and discoveries. Will you and your countess be off again, before long?"

"We are settled here until my wife is released from her confinement." His mouth quirked. "Chionne's people insist this one is a boy. They were right about the first being a girl, so I put up no argument. And she insisted he should be born on English soil."

"Congratulations to you both," Charlotte said. She peered up at him hopefully. "Will your wife find time to write another installment in her thrilling series of adventures?"

He laughed. "Fear not, there will be at least one more. Chionne spent the voyage back here penning the latest book. It won't be long before you'll be able to read it."

"That is good news, sir." She grinned back. "Thank you."

"Ah, Mr. Helden, good evening," her aunt said as the gentleman approached. "My lord, do you know Mr. Helden?"

Introductions were performed and then the newcomer looked to Charlotte. "What good news are you remarking upon, Miss Mayne?"

"Lady Treyford's next book is to be released soon."

"Ah," Mr. Helden said in bland response.

Lord Treyford grinned. "Not a fan of romantic, peril-filled tales, I take it?"

Mr. Helden made a face and shook his head.

"Oh, then perhaps you would enjoy Lord Treyford's own book," Charlotte told him. "It is filled with tales of his travels and of the artifacts he has uncovered."

"I'm not a fan of reading in general," Mr. Helden admitted with a shrug. "I prefer reality."

Charlotte exchanged an alarmed glance with her aunt. Did the man not realize he might insult the earl? Did Mr. Helden think Lord Treyford had invented his travels and accomplishments?

And then she considered further, for she dearly loved to

read, as did the rest of her household—her aunt and both of her siblings, too. What would it be like to live with a man who did not? Sighing, she brushed away her worries. Mr. Helden might not be ideal, but he was the only gentleman who had paid her any sort of marked attention. She couldn't afford to be put off by such small concerns.

Except, they didn't feel small.

"Do you travel much, Helden?" the earl asked.

"No, no. I like the comforts of home." He brightened. "Unless, of course, I am after one of my birds. I once traveled all the way to a tiny isle off of Northumberland to obtain a roseate tern."

Aunt Bernadine blinked. "What did you do with it, once you'd got it?"

"Why, I had it stuffed, of course. I took my own taxidermist with me, in fact, for I wanted it preserved right away and in the best condition."

"Your own . . . taxidermist?" Charlotte asked weakly.

"Oh, yes. It takes a precise set of skills to do a truly good job of it, you see, and so many in the profession are lacking. When I found a really skilled man, I snapped him up. I hired him to work for me nearly exclusively and set him up with a workshop and a home on my lands."

"Goodness," Aunt Bernice said, pulling out her fan. "How do you keep him occupied?"

"Very easily, madam," he assured her. "My collection has grown quite impressive."

No one asked for clarification of his collection.

He started in anyway. "It's birds, you see. Fascinating creatures. Except for the quick, odd, unpredictable way they have of moving." He shuddered. "I much prefer them stuffed and posed. I have over two hundred specimens. I prefer them in lifelike poses and settings—"

"Oh, listen to that. The musicians are starting up again."

Lord Treyford bowed. "You must excuse me. I am promised to my sister-in-law for this set. So lovely to have met you, Miss Mayne." He nodded. "Helden."

The earl departed and Mr. Helden looked around at the set forming. Rubbing his hands together he lifted his brows at Charlotte. "Shall we, Miss Mayne?"

"Well, here you are, Charlotte!" Suddenly Harriett was at her elbow. "And Mr. Helden! I was afraid you would not arrive in time to claim your dance. You do recall asking, when we all met in the park?"

"Oh. Yes. Of course." He looked to Charlotte. "You'll save me a set, Miss Mayne?"

"Of course, I—"

She stopped, gasping as Harriett thrust her glass at her and cold liquid slopped over the rim and down the front of her gown.

"Oh, dear. How clumsy of me. Do forgive me, Charlotte. I only meant for you to hold it for me."

Harriett set the glass on a passing waiter's tray and held out her hand for Mr. Helden. He took it and she swept toward the dance floor with a swish of her skirts.

Charlotte blinked after them.

"Here you are." Aunt Bernadine pressed a kerchief into her hands. "Spiteful cat," she muttered.

"She doesn't want him," Charlotte said indignantly. "She just doesn't want me to have him."

"She's just like her mother," her aunt sighed.

"Harriett is Harriett and we must deal with her," Charlotte said, low. "But he—" She stopped and grimaced.

"I know. Good heavens, but the man does not improve upon further acquaintance." She squeezed Charlotte's hand. "Go and clean yourself up, darling. We'll find someone else." She smiled. "You are entirely too pretty and too kind to continue unseen."

"I don't think the gentlemen are looking for my sort," she said in despair.

"Some of them surely must be. And if they are not . . ." Aunt Bernadine shrugged. "We will contrive." She straightened her shoulders. "We will be fine, dear Charlotte. We've done well enough so far."

They had indeed contrived, so far. But they wouldn't for much longer. Anne, Charlotte's younger sister, would be fifteen soon. She was a darling. So sweet and bookish and smart and kind. If Charlotte didn't marry someone well connected, Anne would never meet anyone beyond their village of Hoverstoke. Anne needed a scholar, or at least someone who could look beyond the borders of their small hamlet. Someone to stimulate her mind as well as her heart, to carry on conversations about the subjects that fascinated her. And George! Her brother had an always-empty belly and two hollow legs beneath it. Feeding him was worry enough, but what of his future? He was an active, curious boy and starting to go a bit wild. But there was no money to send him to school, or to perhaps buy him a commission when he grew old enough.

No, they would not be able to contrive forever. Charlotte needed to marry well—and that meant someone kind and willing to interest himself in her family.

She doubted Mr. Helden was that gentleman. "We'll keep looking," she told her aunt. "There is still time."

"Plenty of time," Aunt Bernadine said encouragingly. "In fact, I'll go and speak to Lady Tremaine and make sure we are invited to attend her riverside garden party next week, while you go and get yourself in order."

They parted ways and Charlotte started toward the ballroom doorway. As she squeezed through the crowd along the wall, Mr. Helden and Harriett danced past. Her cousin sent her a look of malice—and victory.

And Charlotte was suddenly filled with hot, molten fury. Harriett! That girl had everything that she did not—a doting mother, an indulgent father with the family title, wealth, a fine wardrobe, an accepted and expected place in London society—and still, she begrudged Charlotte's every crumb of success or happiness.

Wicked girl!

Her fists clenched. Her color must be high. Abruptly, she turned on her heel and headed for the door to the terrace. Her bodice could dry just as well in the clear, fresh air as in the retiring room.

She realized her mistake the moment she opened the door and a couple pushed in past her, frowning and coughing and waving their hands before their faces. Still, she stepped out, too irritated to face anyone inside.

She immediately began to cough. *Ugh.* What was that vile smell?

She stopped, frozen.

It was Lord Whiddon. He stood at the far edge of the terrace, blowing clouds of evil smelling smoke from a cheroot.

She nearly choked on it. She should follow the couple back inside before her gown took on the horrid scent, but her blood was up and so was her temper. She crossed to the far side of the open terrace, as far away as she could contrive. Whipping out her fan, she waved it to direct air away from her.

He glanced over, smirking, and turned away to ignore her.

She tried to do the same, but good heavens, he was hard to ignore. Even in the filtered light from the ballroom, his figure loomed large. Long, long legs, slender hips and a torso that broadened considerably into a fine set of wide shoulders. Standing there, strong and aloof, he seemed the embodiment of this house, of Mayfair, of London Society itself.

Ideal. Yes. But also hard and possibly dangerous.

At first, she only cast quick glances in his direction, but he paid her no mind, and she began to watch him in earnest. He kept his gaze turned skyward. Until he took a long drag on his cheroot and then held it out before him, frowning at the thing.

Fascinating.

Had she made a sound? A movement toward him? Suddenly he was watching her. His eyebrow raised. His eyes, showing green even in the dim light, were shades warmer than jade, yet just as sharp and glittering.

"I chose this blend of tobacco to drive people away," he said casually.

She raised her chin. "Yes. I worked that out, all on my own."

"And yet, here you still are." The words were rude and dismissive. But the voice? It sent a shiver fluttering through her. Dark, smooth and textured with just the slightest rasp.

"Apologies, but I was so very busy cataloguing all the other ways you were telling me to go away."

That gave him pause. The brow went up again, expectant. And his fingers began to beat a rhythm against his thigh, one finger at a time.

Fascinating.

"Your stance," she began. "The pointed way you gave me your back. The stiffness of your spine. The way your shoulders have lifted high." She shrugged. "That's all I meant."

"I had no idea I was communicating in so many ways." He stared. "And no idea why you did not heed any of them."

"Oh, I was about to." Her lip curled. "That thing truly is vile. But then I saw you partake of it . . . and I was caught."

"Caught? By?"

"By what you were saying with that cheroot."

He blinked. "What was I saying?"

"I'm trying to figure that out." She tilted her head and ran a bold gaze over him. "You pulled it into your lungs like it was going to bring all the answers to the mysteries of the universe with it—and then you looked at it as you exhaled—as if you were disgusted and perhaps a little despondent that it did not."

"The hell you say," he said blankly. "I've never looked despondent a day in my life."

She lifted a shoulder. "You might think so, but most people have no idea about the messages they send with the position and movement of their bodies. It's a whole other language, and it is fascinating. I've made somewhat of a study of it."

He gave a grunt of disapproval. "Bad enough that you should take up such a hobby. Hardly fitting for a young girl. Worse still that you should speak of it openly." He blew another cloud. "Are you not on the marriage mart? Such talk will do you no good there."

"I am," she said with a sigh. "But that is why you are likely the *only* person I can discuss it with. For I must marry, and you will not."

His shoulders relaxed and came down a bit. She refrained from pointing it out.

"Oh, well. Good," he said. "As long as you realize my stance on such matters." He shuddered. "Marriage is a pit, waiting for you to fall into it. And once you're in, you are trapped in the farce. Oh, it might be well enough in the beginning, but eventually it all sours and there you are, putting a good face on it in company and wallowing in your misery when alone." He straightened suddenly and frowned. "But wait. You already knew how I felt? How did you know it?"

"That you don't wish to marry? Everyone knows it. It is what they say when they speak of you." She laughed a little. "Presumably because of speeches like that one."

He didn't respond and she examined him closely. "My lord, did you not know? You have *nicknames*."

"Do I, by God?" He glared at the crowd through the windows. "Damnation, but the lot of them are worse than I thought—and that is no small achievement." Abruptly, he shifted his gaze and pointed the glare at her. "What are they? These nicknames? Wait. No." He held up a hand. "Don't tell me. I don't wish to know." He tossed his cheroot over the balustrade. "What about you, my bold young miss? Do you have a nickname?"

She laughed. "Heavens, no. I've scarcely found anyone interested in knowing my real name." She glanced toward the windows herself. "But I suspect I had better get back inside before people notice I am out here with you—or I might gain exactly the wrong sort of notice." Closing her fan with a snap, she gave him a nod. "Good evening, my lord. I wish you the best of luck with your . . . avoidance."

She'd just reached the door when he spoke. "Hold a moment. You don't wish to miss a chance to have at least one more person in Society to know your name, do you?"

Her mouth twisted. "Much good it will do me," she said as she turned and gave him a very correct curtsy. "I am Miss Mayne, my lord. It has been very, ah, interesting, to make your acquaintance. Good night."

CHAPTER 2

Whiddon downed the rest of his champagne and exchanged it with another as a footman eased past. Two society events within a few days? It was not his idea of time well spent. But his attendance tonight was mandatory, he'd been informed, so it might as well be well lubricated.

In truth, he wouldn't have missed this event, even without the marching orders delivered by his friends. It was an evening to celebrate the dowager Lady Chester, and he was more than passing fond of the old girl. The new Countess of Chester was throwing the party to celebrate the publication of the dowager's new book—a new story in *The Lattimere Legends*.

The scandal broth had heated to a boil when the *ton* discovered the dowager countess was the long unknown authoress of the popular tales. They were all here tonight to savor a taste of the latest brew. And bless the new Lady Chester, for she was giving them plenty to gossip about.

She'd themed her party around Intrepid Women in History and arranged the décor and even the canapés around the idea. Instead of a long table of *hors d'oeuvres*, she'd had smaller tables set up throughout the public rooms of the house, each with a portrait of a famous—or infamous—lady and a themed bite of food to go with it.

So far, he'd had a severe looking Flora MacDonald watching him sample a mash of root vegetables piped into the shape of a white rose, and he'd gazed upon a sensual portrait of Cleopatra as he chose from a selection of pyramid shaped pasties.

He came up beside his friend Sterne. "Wait. What is that you've got?"

Sterne held up an intricate crown of pastry layers baked with jam rubies showing through and pearls of cream adorning the tips. He popped it in his mouth and gestured over his shoulder. "Queen Elizabeth's table," he said, once he'd finished chewing. "Delicious."

Whiddon pushed past him and went to scoop up a handful of the delicacies. Coming back, he found Chester had joined Sterne, as well.

"Ah, those are good," Chester said when he saw his hoard. "But I'd stay away from Boudicca if I were you. I heard the debate about her offering, during all the planning. There was much talk of brown hares and minced rabbit, but Julia put her foot down. Last I heard, they were debating between old Celtic dishes of either eggs or parsnips."

"Noted," Whiddon said. "I'm happy enough with these." He crunched down on another crown.

He relaxed a bit, safe in the company of his closest friends. Until Sterne narrowed his eyes at him. "You look fagged. Like you are burning the candle at both ends." He pursed his lips. "And was that a bit of a limp I noticed, when you came back over here?"

Whiddon shrugged. "I'm fine."

Chester stiffened and stared at him. "You've found another one, haven't you?"

He sighed and nodded.

"Another of the refugees?" Sterne asked.

Both of his friends looked concerned.

"This one has done well. Found him at a decent sized warehouse. And he reportedly has a house in Soho."

"You approached him alone?" Chester was annoyed. "We told you to take one of us with you."

"Be glad I didn't, or you'd be as sore as I am tonight."

"What happened?" Sterne asked.

"This one knew me. I tossed the purse onto his desk and he just looked me over and asked if I had his mother's pearls. He sighed when I told him I did not and weighed the purse in his hand."

"And found it wanting, I suppose," sighed Sterne.

"He must have. He had his men take an extra strip or two out of my hide before they tossed me out."

"Hell and damnation." Chester was seriously annoyed. "No more. No more making atonement for your nasty father—not without taking one of us along. Swear it, Whiddon. Promise, here and now—do you hear?"

"Fine. Fine."

"I'll have your word on it."

"Fine. I promise. Will that make you happy?" he asked.

"Yes," Chester said, but his arms were still folded as he glared.

"I said I promise. Now stop glowering before one of your wives begins to ask questions. Especially you, Chester. It's your event. You must look at least as happy as your Julia. Her first soiree is a raging success, if you judge by the sheer number of people crowded in here."

"Yes, well, you know Julia—she's likely judging the success of the night on how many of these people recognize the importance of the featured women."

They all exchanged less-than-hopeful glances. Both of his

friends then looked away and he followed the direction of their gazes.

"Who is that? There with Penelope and Julia?" Both of their wives were standing in a corner, involved in an animated discussion with an older woman.

"That's Miss Mayne. She is apparently quite an expert on old coins. She heard Julia talking of Boudicca and mentioned she has a gold coin from one of the old Celtic tribes from that time."

"Then Penelope barged in with ideas of how the Roman systems of commerce changed the Celts—and they were off."

"And so were we," Chester said wryly.

"Miss Mayne?" Whiddon asked. "I thought she was a young miss, on the hunt for a husband?"

"That's the niece. The elder is a spinster aunt, bringing the girl out. You've met her? The younger one?"

"Briefly. Ah, there she is now." He pointed with his chin as the girl from the other night joined the ladies.

"I'm just shocked you remembered her name," Sterne marveled, eyeing him closely.

"Probably would not have, had you not just said it out loud." Whiddon shrugged and turned his attention elsewhere, determined not to get caught staring at the chit.

Bad enough that she kept intruding on his thoughts these last few days. It wasn't her looks. He told himself that he could surely find thick, honeyed locks and smokey blue eyes on any number of other debutantes. But the willowy form and the graceful way she moved? Even when she was fanning his foul smoke away, she had moved with a fascinating fluidity.

And that was the rub, wasn't it?

He only pulled out his stinking cheroots when he found himself in desperate need of a bit of solitude. It all pressed in on him at times, the forced cheer, the cut-throat maneuverings beneath the gaiety, the constant vying for position.

He retreated from it, occasionally, behind a literal smokescreen.

It was usually effective, too, chasing away persistent mamas and determined chits in irritation and disgust. That is, until Miss Mayne stood defiantly in the opposite corner, poised gracefully while she blew his vile smoke back at him.

He grinned every time he thought of it.

She was pluck through, that one. No simpering or fawning from her. She took the disdain he tossed at her and flung it back with a bit of her own.

He didn't like how much he'd enjoyed it.

He didn't like how often he'd thought of it, since.

He was *not* going to seek her out tonight to see if she would do it again.

"How long do I have to stay tonight?" he asked Chester. "In order to stay in your lady's good graces?"

Chester clapped a hand on his shoulder. "Frankly, I think she's amazed that you showed your face. Grateful, too, for your support, Whiddon." The earl glanced over at his wife. "But if you really wish to turn her up sweet, then stay on and dance a set or two."

He made a face. But he didn't leave. Though he did half hide between his friends and a pillar covered in greenery and boughs of apple blossoms. It was the perfect vantage point from which to surreptitiously watch the younger Miss Mayne as the evening wore on. She seemed to have several friends amongst the young ladies. Both Penelope and Julia seemed friendly and welcoming to her when their paths crossed. But only a few gentlemen approached her, and she did not seem to be dancing much.

It took him a while to discern the why of it. At first, he thought the young bucks must be blind as well as stupid.

How could they ignore such a girl amidst the usual standard fare of debutantes? But once she joined a group of young ladies, he saw a pattern emerge and he realized that Miss Mayne was the object of a subtle game of interference.

The perpetrator was another young girl. She was dressed in a gown of a garish peachy-orange and she was very, very good at subterfuge.

It all appeared quite natural. A gentleman would approach or be drawn into their group and he would innocently converse with or admire Miss Mayne. Who could not? In a slip of ivory silk with an overskirt of violet lutestring, she drew a man's eye. Especially the bodice, where the lutestring was heavily embroidered with matching silk and pearls, and where it met beneath the girl's bosom and showcased her fine curves.

But each time, the gentleman's attention would be diverted, drawn away by the orange gowned girl, either to herself or to one of the other young women. It appeared, even from afar, that this girl steered the conversations. Inevitably, the gentleman would be enticed away to the dance floor, or to the refreshment tables, or to another group.

Their crowd shrank steadily until Miss Mayne was left alone, standing against the wall.

Whiddon was struck with a spike of empathetic fury. By all the demons in hell, but he hated a stacked game. He despised a cheat. He loathed nothing more than a charming smile that hid a knife aimed at your back.

He knew firsthand the damage that decay could do when it hid behind a sparkling façade.

He'd straightened, trying to decide what to do about it all, when a murmuring at the front of the room turned into a rumble that made its way back through the crowd.

"It's the King, himself!"

"He's here!"

"He's come!"

Beside him, Chester straightened. "By all the—"

"Hurry, man!" Sterne urged. "Find Julia and go and meet him!"

Chester took off through the crowd.

"Well, well," Sterne mused. "Julia's success is guaranteed now."

The king appeared in the doorway. There was a shifting in the throng as some of the guests pushed forward to get a closer look or better access. Two of the king's attendants stayed at his side as several others moved into the throng.

Whiddon looked back to Miss Mayne, but she'd been joined by someone . . . was that Treyford? Back in London? The two conversed easily, as if they were acquainted.

"Why do you suppose he chose to show up tonight?" Sterne asked. He nudged Whiddon and indicated the monarch's slow progress into the room.

"He's a fan of *The Lattimere Legends*," someone said from behind them.

Whiddon turned. "Stoneacre." He bowed. "Did you arrive with the king? It's been an age, man."

"I did. Whiddon. Sterne. It's good to see you both. And in answer to your question, His Majesty heard about the reason for tonight's soiree. He was thrilled with the idea of talking to the dowager countess about her tales, and especially the scandalous truths behind them." His mouth quirked. "And of course, Chester has always been a favorite with him."

Sterne laughed. "Chester is everyone's favorite. He can't help it. It's in his nature to be charming. So, tell us, has the Privy Council kept you busy? And what mischief have you and that beautiful wife of yours been up to?"

Stoneacre spoke of their current efforts to flush corruption from some city and parish workhouses.

Whiddon listened. He liked the man and respected the work he and his wife did at Half Moon House and beyond. But he could not stop his gaze from wandering back to Miss Mayne.

Treyford was still with her. They had been joined by her aunt and also by the girl in the orange dress.

"Where is Tensford?" Stoneacre asked at last. "Has he not come to Town for the Season? I know Hestia would love to see Hope."

"No, they did not wish to bring the baby out of the country while he is still so young, and Hope would not be separated from him," Sterne told him. "At least, that is how Tensford tells it. I don't think he would leave his son either, truth be told. They are besotted."

"As well they should be," Stoneacre said easily. "And Keswick still has not returned from Ireland?"

"No," Chester said on a sigh. "He writes of plans to start this new horse breeding venture often, but he keeps putting off his return."

"It is his bridal trip." Stoneacre grinned. "I'm sure he's finding plenty to keep him busy."

They spoke then of other acquaintances, but Whiddon noticed that the king had laughed and bowed over old Lady Chester's hand. As the rotund monarch turned away, his attention was caught. He appeared to notice Treyford. His face lit up.

Stoneacre had noted the monarch's interest as well. "Is that Treyford? Home again? Well, now. The earl and his travels are another point of interest for him. He'll be doubly glad he attended tonight."

The king had begun to move toward the Earl of Treyford —and the rest of the group around him. The crowd parted before the royal personage and soon enough he'd reached his destination. Whiddon was too far away to hear what was said, but the earl bowed, and the ladies sank into deep, respectful curtsies.

He saw it happen. A flash of movement in peach silk. Suddenly, in mid-curtsy, Miss Mayne tilted forward and sprawled on her hands and knees before the king.

The deceitful chit had pushed her!

Whiddon was moving, even as the first gasps of horror erupted. He arrived as the murmurs grew in the crowd and Treyford helped Miss Mayne to her feet.

She was as red as a beet. "Please, your majesty. I do offer my apologies. I don't know how—"

The king waved a hand. "Pray, do not think on it." His smile twisted into a grin. "You are hardly the first young lady to fall at my feet."

Everyone around them tittered dutifully and the girl grew impossibly redder.

"Your Majesty," Whiddon bowed. He turned and offered another to the girl. "Miss Mayne. Pray do excuse me, sir, but I believe the young lady promised this set to me."

The girl blinked at him. The music had stopped when the king arrived.

"Oh, yes. I should like to see some dancing, at that." The king waved his hand. "Do begin again, if you please. I shall watch as I chat with Treyford."

The musicians hastily returned to their instruments. Miss Mayne looked as if she might object. Whiddon took her hand and pulled her close. "I don't care if you sprained your ankle or broke your leg in that fall. If you have any hope of salvaging your reputation, you will dance."

CHARLOTTE, still in a haze of embarrassment and fury, let herself be led away. She was still reliving her humiliation. So much so, that she barely noticed when Lord Whiddon led her onto the dance floor. She didn't come to herself until he took her hand and placed his at her waist.

"Oh! A waltz." She blinked rapidly back into the still-humiliating present.

"Yes. Thanks be to the gods, for it will allow us to speak. But first—relax."

She gave a bitter laugh.

"You must. Listen to me. You must act as if nothing happened. Nothing of consequence. You must smile and enjoy our dance. Everyone will be watching."

Heat rose again from her chest and climbed upward. She kept her eyes fixed firmly on his neckcloth as the music started and they began to move. She could not bear to glance aside and see the sea of faces waiting, watching and whispering.

"Relax!" he ordered again.

She tried.

"Good. Now, I should like to know who that chit in the orange dress is to you."

Charlotte's lips pressed together. "She's my cousin," she said tightly.

"Surely not!" She sensed his surprise in the sudden tension of his shoulders. His broad shoulders, she suddenly realized. Her hand rested there, and she registered the heat and hard strength beneath her fingers.

"I'm afraid so."

"She pushed you!"

"Yes. I am aware," she said flatly. "She was behind me. Could I have seen her, I would have read the signs and known she was up to something."

"Ah, yes. Your study of unconscious messages."

"You may laugh, but I am very familiar with all the ways

Harriett signals ill intentions." Her tone emerged darkly, but her patience was at an end.

That silenced him. "What is the relationship?"

She frowned. "I just—oh. How are we related, you meant? Her father, Lord Burchan, is my father's elder brother. Or was, I should say, before my father's death."

"You are Lord Burchan's niece?"

"Yes." She was beginning to recover. She was *waltzing*. Her first waltz, although she'd been given permission by the patronesses of Almack's weeks ago. And with Lord Whiddon. His hand felt like a brand on the curve of her waist and she was keenly aware of the small, heated universe that existed only between them as they moved in elegant twirls across the floor.

"I thought you were being brought out under the guidance of your aunt, the other Miss Mayne."

She looked up into his face at last and let her sudden amusement show. "Have you been inquiring after me, my lord?"

He shot her a quelling look. "I didn't have to. I heard someone else talking about you."

She risked a glance at the other dancers. "If only more of them would speak *to* me, instead of *about* me."

"Smile," he ordered. "Don't frown at them. You must at least look like you are enjoying yourself."

Startled, she stared up at him again. And it struck her abruptly, how kind it had been of him to rescue her like this. Against his own inclinations, to be sure. She'd seen his fingers tapping their rhythm against his leg as he spoke to the king. A sure sign of his tension and distaste. She should not waste his sacrifice.

And more, he was right. Did she want everyone to titter and whisper about her fall? Or did she wish it to become only the prelude to the talk of her of her dance with the elusive Lord Unobtainable?

"Thank you," she whispered. Then she obeyed. She smiled up at him with all of her frazzled nerves and fervent gratitude.

She felt his sudden tension again, beneath her fingers, but there was no sign of it in his expression. She let herself relax a little more. Good heavens, but he was a fine dancer. She didn't have to think at all. She just enjoyed the feel of his hands on her and gave herself over. It felt as natural as . . . as the air moving in and out of her lungs. She gave a little shiver at the warm rush of pleasure it gave her.

"I'm thinking back," he said. "I did attend the ball Lord Burchan threw to launch his daughter, at the beginning of the Season. It was Lady

Chester's first society event, and we all went to support her."

"That was kind of you. She seems a lovely person."

His lips thinned a little. "So she is, I'm sure."

What was it her friend Lady Mary had said? He danced with his friends' wives, then glared at them across the room?

"Granted," he continued. "I spent most of that evening in the card room, but I don't recall seeing you there."

"No. You would not have. My aunt and I had only just arrived in London. We were scarcely settled in our lodgings and not yet ready to go into company."

"Lodgings. Separate lodgings?"

She nodded, puzzled.

"Why is your uncle not bringing you out, from his home, under his care?"

"Because he does not wish to, I presume." He watched her, as if waiting for her to admit to some crime, or some defect of personality, and it irritated her to no end. "And since he is a man, and a gentleman of fortune and title besides, that is the end of the matter. He does not wish to."

"Putting aside the matter of your uncle and what he could or should do, I have to ask you—is that what you believe? That men like your uncle—like me—are free to do whatever we will?"

She nodded. "Or whatever you will not."

He snorted.

"Do you deny it?"

"I do." He shrugged beneath her hand. "I will agree that I have more authority and opportunity than any woman and more than most men, but there are obligations attached. Serious and binding duties that balance against the advantages. And the notion of utter freedom?" His expression darkened. "No."

She held silent as he maneuvered them through a crowded section of the dance floor. When his attention shifted back to her, she asked the question that had been building.

"What constrains you, then? Is it duty that is so important to you?"

He laughed. "Is that the answer you expect? Honor, duty, propriety?"

"Would it be the truth?"

"No."

She waited.

He drew a deep breath. "I care for a handful of people only, Miss Mayne. But they are dear to me, indeed. My younger sister, my friends. They would be adversely affected if I threw off the shackles and did just as I wished."

"What would you do?" she whispered, fascinated.

He grinned, but it was a bleak, caustic thing. "If I was completely unfettered?"

She nodded.

He laughed. "Oh, I would enjoy myself. The pranks I would play! I would recruit my friend Chester and we would pour blue ruin into the lemonade at Almack's and watch all the biddies get tipsy. Chase greased pigs through Kew gardens. Bring a monkey to tea at all the highest sticklers' homes."

She laughed.

"But more than that—I would speak a thousand truths. I would start small, upsetting apple carts here in London, exposing lies and deceits. I would shine the light on the corruptions that hide beneath polite veneers. I would tell the world about Lord Lowell's trophy room. I would turn back Mr. Moore's sleeves the next time I found him at a gaming table and show everyone the cards he hides there. I would stop in the green room at Drury Lane and tell that soprano that her high notes are flat and her vibrato uneven, and that everyone knows she beds the manager to keep her starring role. I would sit down with Lady Drummidge and tell her that she is the only one in London who does not know about her husband's mistress, who dresses him in ruffles and nappies."

Her mouth dropped open.

But he was not finished. His eyes were shining. "I would rent a grand, fast horse and pound through the fashionable hour at Hyde Park, scattering timid debutantes like leaves, and then I would point his head out of London, and I would ride hell for leather for—" He stopped. Glanced down at her.

"For?" she prompted.

"For the seaside."

She knew that wasn't what he'd meant to say.

"I would crash into the dens of a smuggling ring or two, send the ones who could be convinced of their wrong-doing back home and see the rest press-ganged, so they could repay some of the patriotic debt they've incurred." He threw back his head and smiled. "I would get on a ship and travel to a quiet island in some warm sea and swim in the surf beneath the moon and the wide, dark sky."

He looked down, then, with the air of a man who knows he's said too much. "What would you do, Miss Mayne?"

She blinked.

"Utter freedom," he urged. "What would you do with it?"

"My sister," she began.

"No. You. No consideration of others, remember? What would you do—for yourself?"

"I—" She flushed suddenly. She didn't know the answer. "I cannot . . . I've never . . ."

"You've never let yourself even ask the question?"

For the second time that evening, mortification flushed through her. Was the unhappy, curmudgeonly Lord Unwilling looking at her with pity?

His gaze sharpened. "You must marry. Those were your words, when first we met. Why? Why must you?"

She couldn't tell him. She wouldn't. But then she breathed a sigh of relief. She didn't have to. The music was ending. She took her hands away from him and clapped along with the other dancers and turned back toward the spot where she'd left her aunt.

His jaw set, he led her away, off the dance floor.

"What a lovely dance," her aunt said, welcoming her back.

"Thank you, Lord Whiddon," she said. She meant it, too. Yet she could not quite manage to meet his gaze directly.

He nodded at Aunt Bernadine. He gave her a correct and very formal bow. Then he was gone.

"Oh, my dear." Her aunt gripped her arm.

"Where is Harriett?" Charlotte asked grimly.

"Gone. Completely chastised. *Did* she push you?"

"Of course. Do you think I toppled over on purpose?"

"Don't be too cross, dear. I think the king must have seen

it! After you were off, he turned to one of his men and made a very cutting remark about reminding the palace chef to strike oranges from the menus at the palace, as he'd quite gone off on the color."

"He didn't!"

"He did. Everyone knew what he meant by it. Harriett nearly melted. Several people heard it. Word had spread across the ballroom almost before you danced across it!"

"She'll be furious," Charlotte whispered.

"She'll be lucky to hold her head up in company," Aunt Bernadine corrected. "She left in tears."

Charlotte's stomach dropped. She was already in her aunt's and her cousin's bad graces, just for getting herself to London for a chance at a Season. They would blame her. She knew it.

"Should we . . . go and check on her?"

"No, dear. I'm afraid you are going to be far too busy."

"Busy?"

"Lord Whiddon's attention has been noticed. Others will follow. Brace yourself," her aunt whispered.

Behind Charlotte, someone cleared a dainty throat. She turned to find Miss Winthrop there. "Charlotte, dear, if you don't mind, my cousin is begging for an introduction."

"Of course." Charlotte summoned a smile for the young man at her friend's side.

Beside her, a gentleman bowed to her aunt. "Miss Mayne, how do you do this evening?"

"Lord Norwell!" Aunt Bernadine said. "Good evening."

"Perhaps you might make me known to your niece?"

Charlotte had not a moment, after that, to spare a thought for Harriett. But she searched in vain, for the rest of the evening, for another sign of Lord Whiddon.

CHAPTER 3

"Sir. Lord Whiddon. Sir."

Whiddon groaned and buried his face into his pillow.

"You'll want to wake up, sir."

That caught his attention. His valet wouldn't say such a thing lightly. "Why?" he asked, lifting his head.

"Lord Chester and Mr. Sterne have sent 'round a message. They've gone to breakfast at the club and will stop in here afterwards to collect you. Do you recall an appointment with them?"

Squinting into the morning light, Whiddon considered. "Oh, yes. Tattersalls. We're to look over the latest crop, in search of good bloodstock for Keswick's new stables."

"I've drawn a bath for you, sir. If you get up now, you can be ready and intercept the gentlemen outside."

With a groan, Whiddon sat up. His head had surely swollen several sizes larger than normal. He rested it in his hands a moment and winced at the military beat drumming in his temples. What had he done last night? Oh, yes. The

Caradecs' salon. The artist and his unusual wife always hosted a wild evening.

"You don't wish for the water to grow cold, sir."

He stumbled into the dressing room and sighed in relief and pleasure as he sank into the steaming water. "Thank you, Chapman. You are a prince among valets. I'm sure I don't pay you half enough."

"You pay me very well indeed, sir," his man answered a bit smugly. "But I am well worth it. Should you doubt it, I will allay your fears by telling you that I stopped at *Le Cygne* for those crumpets you like. I shall put them over the fire to toast while you bathe. The coffee is already brewing."

The hot water had eased the pounding in his head. Whiddon sank down further into the heat and thought he could indeed enjoy a crumpet or two. "Bless you, Chapman."

His valet truly was a godsend. It was not in the normal realm of duties for a manservant to see to breakfast, but then, this was no usual household. The townhouse was in the fashionable part of town, it was true, but inside it bore little resemblance to its neighbors. The kitchens were in a deplorable state and the rest of the house was little better. But it would take a great deal of work to set it all to rights, and honestly, Whiddon secretly cherished the idea of his father arriving in Town and finding the place in such a state. Just the thought of his reaction was enough to stay his hand.

And so, Chapman maintained Whiddon's suite of rooms and his own comfortable quarters next door. He existed in an uneasy truce with the few other servants and he saw to it that he and his master both ate decently, at least semi-regularly.

"Your green coat with the buff breeches, sir?" Chapman asked when Whiddon finished bathing and sat down to eat. "Or the blue?"

The blue was decided upon and later, while tying his

neckcloth, Chapman cleared his throat. "About that other matter, sir. The one you asked me to look into?"

"Yes. Have you found something on the Comte de Perette?"

"No. That one has proved difficult. I am following up on a lead, though. A possible family member." He pursed his lips. "I meant the other matter, sir. The girl."

Whiddon stilled. His heartbeat ratcheted up a bit, and he hoped the valet could not see it. "Yes?"

"I have gleaned a bit of information. Several of Lord Burchan's footmen tend to patronize a certain tavern, I discovered."

"Well done, man. What did you find?"

He wanted to know the Mayne girl's story. He didn't ask himself why. She interested him. She was different. He wanted to know why. And he had no wish to suffer the endless questions and pointed teasing that were sure to result if he asked his friends what they knew.

"The elder Miss Mayne is the present baron's elder sister. The younger is the daughter of his deceased younger brother. She and her siblings live with the spinster aunt."

"Burchan supports them?"

"Barely. The girl apparently received a very small inheritance after her mother's death. The aunt has a small allowance. According to the servants, they live humbly in a small village, a good piece away from any of the family holdings. Also, according to one of the footmen, the baron is tight-fisted when it comes to money, except when it comes to his own comforts, or to those of his wife and daughter. The servants are not high on his list of priorities and yet they still come in above his sister or his nieces and nephew."

"So, he's not sponsoring her come-out at all?"

"Not a bit."

Whiddon couldn't help but wonder why. "Is there more

to it than his nip-farthing ways, I wonder? Has the girl somehow blotted her copybook?"

"Not according to his people. She's all a young lady should be, and more popular with the baron's servants than his own daughter."

Well, they weren't alone in that. That spiteful girl held no interest for him at all. But Miss Mayne . . . he'd been across that ballroom and trying to ameliorate her humiliation before he'd had time to even think about it. What was it about her that fascinated him?

The smoke in her blue eyes had cleared when she'd smiled up at him, during that dance. Her whole face had brightened. His hand had tightened on her nimble waist and his fingers had itched to explore the rest of her generous curves. But it was something else altogether that hooked him and would not let him go.

She held her own with him. No looking away or casting her gaze down. No demurring to his opinion or simpering at his harsh wit or any of the usual wiles that females sought to use against him. She stood toe to toe with him in a way that no one did, save for his closest friends. Damnation, she'd even somehow got him talking about himself—and that was something Chester, Sterne, Keswick and Tensford had to work at.

He needed to be more on his guard with her. He needed to keep the upper hand, or he'd have to avoid her altogether.

He wasn't sure avoiding her would be possible. Very privately, he acknowledged that he wasn't sure he wanted it to be.

"How on earth did she come up with the blunt for a Season, then?" he wondered aloud. "They are renting a house, I gather. That comes with its own expenses. And she and her aunt would need wardrobes—and not the kind you wear in a small village. And all of the smaller expenses—the servants, the subscriptions and tickets and carriages and vails and everything that go along with it all."

"The footman I spoke with speculated that the older lady sold something from her collection of old coins."

"Ah, I did hear of the aunt's expertise."

Chapman finished sliding him into his coat and glanced at the clock. "The gentlemen will be here soon, sir."

"Oh. Yes." He smoothed his coat and took up his hat. "Thank you for making those inquiries for me, Chapman. Anything else I need to know?"

"That's all I heard, save for one thing, concerning the girl's father's demise."

Whiddon paused.

"He was struck down by a carriage. There are whispers that it could scarcely have been an accident."

"Ah, well, we are hardly in the position to judge anyone for dubious deaths in the family, are we?"

"I suppose not, sir."

"Thank you, Chapman. You've done well."

"Of course, sir."

Whiddon set off downstairs. He paused as Old Alf shuffled to open the door for him. "What's that . . . odd . . . smell, Alfred?"

The footman glanced around. "Ah." He nodded toward a bundle of fur in a corner. "I believe it's the cat, sir."

"Has the cat died, Alf?"

The old man moved over to peer down at the animal. "Not yet, sir. He must be sleeping off a rat."

He shrugged. "Fine, then. Carry on."

He stepped outside and caught sight of his friends coming down the street. Good. Perfect timing.

∼

CHARLOTTE HELD HER BREATH, then gave a little jump of victory as her bowl edged past another and settled close to the jack.

"Good show, Miss Mayne!" Mr. Rostham grinned good-naturedly. "How on earth did you come to be so skilled at bowls?"

"It comes of having a twelve-year-old brother." She smiled up at the young gentleman. "I have to keep sharp or risk losing to him every single match."

"Yes," he said wryly. "Twice is enough for me. But I'm shocked you deign to play with your brother. The devil knows my elder sisters moved heaven and earth to avoid me when I was that age."

She raised a brow. "And did that have anything at all to do with your own behavior, I wonder?"

He laughed. "I did enjoy tweaking their curls and pinching them in church."

Her mouth twisted and she waited.

"Very well! I may also have been known for hiding a favorite ribbon or sticking burrs in bonnets."

"Remind me to keep you away from my brother, sir," she said with a grin.

"And so I will," he said easily. "Now, enough of my sins. Shall we go and find some champagne?"

She looked around at the beautiful expanse of Lady Tremaine's riverside lawns, and at all the people gathered upon them. "I'd far rather have some of the lemonade," she confessed. "It's warm in the sun."

Mr. Rostham offered his arm, and she took it as several young people decided to follow them from the bowling green. Their chatter rang out, happy and carefree, and she let it wash over her with a sigh of gratitude.

What a difference from the first few weeks of the Season. Then, she had been acquainted with only a couple of gentlemen and a few of the young ladies. Now it seemed her name was on everyone's lips—and mentioned with pleasure and approval, as far as she could tell. She'd met scores of people in the last week. Their parlor had been awash in flowers and filled with callers. Last night at the Loverton ball, she'd danced every set.

It was all due to Lord Whiddon. That dance had been a mission of rescue and it had nicely done the trick. Her fall had become infamous, but all sympathy lay with her. As for Harriett—for the first time in her life she was feeling the consequences of her casual cruelty. Some were kind enough to ignore the talk, but others gazed at her with disapproval or pity.

Charlotte tried to speak with her cousin but had been rebuffed. She decided not to worry over Harriett and to enjoy her new acclaim. She doubted it would last. Something else would come along to occupy the *ton*, but she hoped she would have found some lasting friends by then—and perhaps a viable suitor or two.

Mr. Rostham might be one of them. Young, carefree and the heir to a viscount, she had the feeling that he'd strayed into her orbit only because of her new notoriety. But she'd surprised him a time or two, and he'd seemed to enjoy it. He'd been flatteringly attentive over the last few days. But he *was* young. She wondered if he was just enjoying himself, or if he was truly ready to choose a bride.

It was a worry that she could tie to all of the newly enthusiastic gentlemen about her, but if she was going to be honest with herself, she had to admit that the greatest flaw in each of them was that they were not Lord Whiddon.

She flushed, just thinking such a thing. Thankfully, she could attribute her high color to the heat of the day. But it was true.

Whiddon was reclusive and curmudgeonly, but he also

smoldered with an intensity that called the hairs on her nape to stand on end and set her every nerve to tingling. He was frank in a way that appealed to her and showed nary a blink when she responded in the same way. He was handsome, gruff and completely tantalizing.

And utterly unavailable.

She knew that. She did. He could not enter into her plan to marry well and save her family's future. She accepted the fact, but it did not stop her from watching for him in the street, in the park, or wondering, when the bell rang, if he would be the next caller admitted.

He never was, of course. She didn't truly expect him, and she hadn't spotted him even once since he danced with her—and saved her.

"Oh, look there." Mr. Rostham gestured. "Lady Tremaine is bringing out the ices."

A line of maids and footmen were carrying out trays of sparkling dishes and placing them beneath one of the beribboned tents.

"Shall I fetch us one?" Mr. Rostham asked.

"That would be just the thing. Thank you."

"Any flavor preference? If there is a choice?"

"I am partial to strawberry," she admitted.

"Noted." The look he gave her appeared more serious than his usual countenance. He gave her hand a squeeze, then left her.

She stepped into the shade of a tree and let her gaze drift across the party. She'd never imagined such an elegant outdoor event. The lawns were wide and sloped gently down to the river. Potted topiaries fluttered with ribbons matching the tents. They had been placed strategically, showcasing seating areas, a small platform for the musicians, and the bowling green. Down by the water they flanked the wide pier and the spot on the bank where small boats were launching onto the water. She hadn't yet been out in one and wondered if Mr. Rostham would suggest it.

"Miss Mayne!"

She glanced behind her. "Mrs. Sterne. How lovely to see you."

The lady drew abreast and looked around. "What a perfect day the countess has for her party. It all looks so beautiful."

"Indeed. She's thought of everything, it seems."

"I heard it will only improve this evening. Lady Tremaine has apparently hired men from Vauxhall to light up the evening, as they do in the gardens. She's planning fireworks, as well."

They spoke for a while about the workings of such an undertaking. Mrs. Sterne was scientifically minded and always so interesting. Charlotte was grateful for her friendship and Lady Chester's as well. They were both kind and nearly as new to London Society as she was. They were also both married to two of Lord Whiddon's closest friends. Perhaps one or both of them might know where the earl had got to.

And perhaps she should stop thinking about him and get on with the business of finding a husband.

"Oh, I had wanted to speak to you about something," Mrs. Sterne said suddenly. "I do recall that you said you are fond of painting."

"Oh, yes." She felt a pang. "I do enjoy it, especially oils, although it has been some time since I had the chance to pursue the hobby." She'd begun lessons with watercolors as a child and had advanced to oil lessons. How she'd loved the smell, the colors, and the feeling of sharing her views of the world, just with the stroke of her brush. But all of that had ended with the death of her parents.

"We are attending a showing at a gallery in a couple of

days. I was wondering if you would care to come with us? The gallery belongs to a friend, Mr. Caradec. He teaches classes for passionate and talented young artists who might not have the money or connections to be admitted to the Royal Society."

"Mr. Rhys Caradec?" Charlotte breathed. "I greatly admire his work."

"Wonderful! Then you will come?"

"Thank you so much. I should love to."

Suddenly Sterne stepped around the tree. "There is quite a crowd gathered, vying for ices." He smiled at his wife. "That means no one is currently waiting for a boat. Shall we go out on the water, my dear?"

"Oh, yes!" But Mrs. Sterne hesitated. "That is, perhaps we should not leave Miss Mayne on her own."

"No worries," her husband countered cheerfully. "Whiddon can take her out, as well." He looked over his shoulder and Lord Whiddon came around the tree behind him.

Charlotte's startled gaze flew to his—and there it was. The *zing* and spit and sizzle of . . . connection. It was an awareness, a burn, a field of friction that existed only between the two of them.

"Penelope. Miss Mayne." He nodded.

"Lord Whiddon."

"You won't mind taking the young lady out in one of the boats, will you?" his friend asked him.

Whiddon's gaze held hers. It was still there, that aura of . . . promise. It had sputtered into life on that terrace and crackled higher on the dance floor. It hung between them still, but was dimmed by the hesitation she saw in his manner.

"Oh, no need to worry over me," she said brightly. "I am

waiting on Mr. Rostham. He's bringing me an ice. You two go on and enjoy the breeze on the water."

Sterne glanced at his friend, then nodded and took his wife's hand. Looking proud and content, he led her away.

Charlotte steeled her spine and glanced back at the earl. Sunshine carved light furrows in his chestnut hair and turned the sharply turned edges of his face into a study of light and shadow. She swallowed.

"I must take this opportunity to thank you for that dance, sir, the last time we met. You pulled me from disaster and saved my Season. In fact, you improved it immensely. I truly am grateful." She glanced away. "I must make the most of my chance here."

Nodding, he leaned against the tree. "I'm just glad it worked. I don't think your cousin bears me the same good will, though. She glowered at me as I came in, both she and the small but malevolent group around her, too."

"Yes. They give me the same dark looks. Honestly, though? I'm just glad I got to witness the first time Harriett has had to face a bit of disapproval for her behavior."

"A *bit* of disapproval?"

"Well, she hasn't been completely shunned, after all. And her parents, of course, do not blame her for her sudden unpopularity."

His brow raised. "They blame you?"

"And you, as well," she told him. "I am sorry, but it is true."

"I shall bear the weight of it," he said dryly.

"I would avoid her, if you can. She can be quite unpleasant when crossed. And more than a little vengeful."

"That sounds like the voice of experience."

"Yes, experience gathered at each dreaded childhood visit. Now, enough about Harriett. I am glad to have the chance to speak to you. I have been wanting to ask you about your archery skills."

"Archery skills?"

He looked blank and she grinned. It was so incredibly satisfying to stump him.

"Yes. How are they?"

"My archery skills? Nonexistent."

"Oh, dear, now that is a disappointment."

"Oh, I am sorry to hear those words from you, Miss Mayne." It was Mr. Rostham speaking, as he approached them. He came empty handed, she noticed. "Whiddon," he greeted the earl and turned to her. "I must apologize. I fear I let myself get distracted. I was speaking with a friend as we waited, and I missed our chance at an ice." He shrugged and gave her an apologetic smile, then looked to Whiddon. "But at least I am not alone. How have you disappointed the lady, sir?"

"With my lack of expertise with a bow and arrow, it would seem."

"Why?" Rostham looked around. "Are they setting up targets? I hadn't heard. But I warn you, Whiddon, do not try to compete with Miss Mayne. She's a ringer at bowls and a threat to a man's masculine confidence."

Charlotte stilled as Whiddon ran a flagrant eye over her, tracing a leisurely path down and back up again.

"I think my masculinity is up to Miss Mayne's every trick."

She suppressed a shiver, even as something inside her trembled, then opened up to let loose a stream of chaotic feeling. Thrill and more than a hint of craving and . . . caution.

Lord Unobtainable, she reminded herself.

Hiding any sign of the turmoil he called up so easily, she rolled her eyes at him. "Very funny, I am sure, my lord. Now, if you are through sharpening your wit at my expense, I must tell you I lament your answer. Is it true? You don't have *any* expertise with a bow?"

"Never touched one in my life."

"Well. That's an opportunity missed."

"I'm a crack shot with a pistol. Does that redeem me?"

"No." She shook her head. "That won't do at all."

"I tried my hand at archery when I was a lad," Rostham interjected. "My cousin still likes to keep her skills sharp. She hosts an archery club for ladies at home in Sussex. Perhaps I can speak to her and arrange an afternoon's shooting?"

She gave him a warm smile. "Oh, that would be lovely," she said appreciatively. "What fun. You must be sure to invite Lord Whiddon so he can try his hand at it."

"Of course," Rostham assured them.

Charlotte glanced over to find the earl had fixed her with an intense stare.

"You were discussing art with Penelope earlier?" he asked. "Did I hear you say you are a painter?"

She flushed. "No, no. It is something that I once enjoyed, but I haven't actually painted in quite some time." She hurried on before either of them could ask why. "I do enjoy art so very much, though. It is one of the joys of coming to London. There seems to be some great piece around every corner."

Whiddon snorted.

"Very true," Rostham agreed. "I am fond of a good history painting myself. The battle scenes, especially, capture the imagination."

The weight of the earl's gaze lay heavy upon her again. "I would wager Miss Mayne is a fan of portraiture."

"I am," she admitted. "I'm terribly apt to wander in people's houses, gazing at their ancestors."

"A trait you share with Penelope," he said wryly.

"I admit, though, that I am also fond of lithographs and

prints, especially if they are a study of character. Or of a place."

The earl raised a brow. "Such as the *Costume of Yorkshire?*"

Her mouth dropped open. "You know it? Yes, that sort of thing exactly."

"*The Collier?*" he asked. "It makes me wonder. He seems quite cheerful for a miner. Not to mention, quite clean."

"But isn't that what is fascinating? Is there such a man, so cheerful and content? And what of *The Leech Finders*? How sanguine they look—utterly nonchalant about wading into the water for such an endeavor. I confess, I am filled to the brim with questions!"

They both grinned. Her heartbeat tripped and stumbled. Wasn't there always something about shared mirth that heightened intimacy?

"My father has a Stubbs in his study." Rostham clearly wished to be included. "I could arrange for you to see it."

Gathering her wits, Charlotte smiled at him. "How kind you are, Mr. Rostham. That sounds delightful."

The young man smiled in relief.

Whiddon straightened suddenly. "Since I have neither a Stubbs nor any talent for archery, I must strive to impress you in other ways, Miss Mayne. I'll start by taking Sterne's suggestion and show off my prodigious rowing skills." He nodded towards the river's edge. "Sterne and his wife are returning. Shall we go down and take their boat out?"

Charlotte hesitated. She wanted to agree—far more than she should. But shouldn't she stay and encourage Rostham? On the other hand, a bit of competition seemed to be spurring him to some effort. Perhaps it might persuade him to view her as a serious candidate for his bride? He was kind, cheerful and easy to get along with. Not to mention in line for a significant title. He joked about his sisters, but he didn't seem the sort who would expect her to abandon her siblings.

She would do what she must to stir him up a bit and would not mind if it was the thought of a rival that did it—even if she knew that Whiddon would never think of himself so.

Making her decision, she nodded. "Oh, of course. Thank you, my lord. I've been wanting to go out. Will we see you later, Mr. Rostham?"

"I look forward to it." He bowed and watched them leave.

But the thrill that shivered through her did not come from success at her stratagem. No, the tingle that traveled from her arm to race up her spine came from the heat of Whiddon's touch as she took the earl's arm.

She did her best to suppress it.

Unobtainable.

She repeated the word in her head like a chorus.

CHAPTER 4

Miss Mayne tucked her hand into the crook of his arm, all trusting confidence and joy in the day. Her eyes were a far more interesting and complicated shade of blue than even the sky. There was a bit of silver mixed in there that stole his focus and kept him looking for more. He'd stared at her furtively even before he and Sterne had approached her, and he'd done it openly once they'd been left alone. She wore white today, a flimsy, gauzy wisp of a gown that he approved of—almost as much as he favored the dark blue sash tied beneath her bosom. It outlined her curves and darkened her eyes.

Lord, he was a fool.

He should have stayed home. His own interest in the girl was unwelcome and unwise enough, but now he knew why Sterne had pressed him to join his party today. His friends had seen and heard of his rescue of the girl—and now they were reading more into it than it warranted.

Why did marriage have to be so contagious? He knew Tensford had been forced by circumstance to look for a bride, but then the rest of his closest friends had fallen, one by one. Even Chester, by God! And now, in the time-honored tradition of the newly married, they were trying to drag the rest of the male species into the same trap.

And it was so often a trap or a trick. He'd seen it first-hand. It was why he found himself watching his friends—and especially their wives—with suspicion. Those four men were his true family. He hated the idea of any of them hurt or taken advantage of.

The fact that they all looked besotted and seemed to be living blissfully was a relief—but it also wracked his nerves.

When would the blow come? Upon whom would it fall?

And with all of that in mind, why the hell was he still mucking about with Charlotte Mayne? She'd stated unequivocally that she was looking for marriage, and he was determined to avoid the state completely.

He supposed his lingering curiosity was partly to blame. He understood that her finances, and her churlish family, meant that this might be her only chance at a Season. But there was a desperate tinge to her determination. He wanted to know what could frighten a bold, confident girl like her.

She was laughing with Penelope now, as Sterne and his wife climbed the short bank up from the water. He was forced to admit that Charlotte was the rest of the reason why he was flirting with danger. He admired her humor and he ease with which she shared it. Not to mention her long-legged grace and the way she looked with the breeze pressing her gauzy gown against her and setting the ends of her blue sash to fluttering.

He had to tread carefully here. He could satisfy his curiosity and bask a bit in her spritely, enticing and slightly vulnerable company, but he could not raise any expectations, either with her, with his friends, or with the rest of Society.

Ignoring the pointed look Sterne tossed him, he moved to the edge of the bank to assist her down. He stopped abruptly, though, as something caught his attention. "What on earth is that smell?"

"Oh, watch your feet, my lord," Miss Mayne cautioned. "I believe the smell is rising from the line of linked fuses that will be used to light the lamps at dusk. Penelope says they use whale oil and seal blubber in them. That's the smell you've noticed."

"Ah." He nodded and stepped over the trail of fuses to scramble down. "The Thames does have its own host of odors, but that was one I've never encountered before."

He saw her safely into the boat and stepped in as a footman helped to launch it. Taking up the oars, he began to row them out as she sat smiling, her face turned into the rays of the sinking sun.

"What was that nonsense about my archery skills?" he asked gruffly, to distract himself from the lovely picture she made.

She shaded her brow with a hand and smirked at him. "I had an idea to add to your list."

"List?"

"Of pranks. Misdeeds. The things you would do if you were free of consequences."

"Oh. That list."

"Yes."

"Am I to skewer someone? Someone you don't care for, I presume?"

"No." She paused. "And yes."

"Pick one."

She laughed. "Well, you see, there are still a few high sticklers who will not receive me or my aunt."

"No!"

"Yes. Even though my aunt debuted with some of them, herself."

"They are probably some of the same stick-in-the-mud

ladies who will not invite me into their drawing rooms, either."

"Even better. I thought it would be incredibly funny if you invaded their sanctuaries dressed as a cupid. You could shoot them with arrows padded in red velvet and announce you've come to fill their cold hearts with love."

"I—" He stopped, torn between horror and laughter. It sounded just like one of Chester's plans. He could picture it so clearly in his head.

"That's twice today!" she crowed. "Oh, I am going to make it a goal to flummox you speechless at least once at each encounter, my lord. It's great fun and terribly satisfying."

"Cupids are *naked*," he said with gruff disapproval.

"Not all of them," she countered. "Some wear charming, short tunics slung over one shoulder. Of course, I would never recommend you go into a drawing room *nude*."

"Of course, you would not." He rolled his eyes. "In any case, my list is quite rounded out. It's your list that needs filling. It makes more sense if *you* traipse about as a cherub—and please, do warn me ahead of time, for I'd dearly love to see you in such a get-up."

She gave him a twist of a grin. "Ah, well. It was worth a try."

He merely looked at her for a long moment. "Painting," he said softly.

"What's that?"

"Painting. That should be on your list."

A look of longing crossed her face. He left off rowing. The current took them up and set them drifting slowly along. "Not grand portraits. Not for you. You'd do the sort of character studies you mentioned. A dirty chimney sweep with a cheeky grin. A wistful wallflower watching the dance. A maid sneaking around the corner to toss back the dregs of sherry left in the glasses."

She blinked at him. "How do you know that?"

"Because what a painter chooses as his subject says as much about him or her. And because you can *see*, Miss Mayne. In a way that many others do not."

She sat quite still a moment, then gave a shaky little laugh. "Well! Now *you* have struck *me* speechless. I suppose you've taken up the challenge and will try to match my number." She leaned over and dipped her fingers into the water. "You are still behind one for the day, then. And I scored another on that terrace, the first night we met."

He lifted a shoulder. "I believe I canceled that one out when I practically dragged you out onto the dance floor at Lady Chester's soiree. You were uncharacteristically silent at the start, if I recall."

"Fine, then." She still didn't look at him, but watched the small wake trailing behind her fingers. "That leaves me one ahead, still."

They drifted into a shadow cast by a grove of elms in the curve of the river. The temperature in the shade noticeably changed. The sun had begun to sink below the tree line. He should get them back. But he didn't pick up the oars. He frowned instead and studied her.

"How goes the hunt?" he asked abruptly.

Straightening, she shook her fingers, sending droplets flying. "Hunt?"

"For a husband. Are you still set on pinning one down?"

She met his gaze, her shoulders stiff. "I am."

The thought of it bothered him. She was different. Funny and proud and clever. A challenge. She needed someone man enough to appreciate her.

"Don't settle for a puppy like Rostham." It popped out without conscious thought. He instantly regretted it.

Her brow raised. "I thought it was marriage as an institution you disapproved of."

"It is. It's nothing like so many debutantes think it, all flowers and smiles and dances and stolen kisses. All that lasts a very short time indeed, and then you are shackled for life to a person who never showed you his true self." He snorted. "I don't think Rostham is old enough to even know his true self."

"That all may be true. Perhaps the romance masks the truth. Or perhaps it makes what is necessary more palatable. And for the majority of us, it is a necessity." She considered him closely. "You were the one who spoke of the duties and obligations that restrain us," she reminded him. "Do you think that women carry no such burdens?"

"I suppose I hadn't thought of it."

"Well, then."

Mulling it over, he took up the oars. She'd mentioned a sister, hadn't she? And Chapman had said 'siblings.' He wondered just how humble their village home might be. As the eldest sister, she might take on the responsibility for bettering her family's circumstances—especially as it looked as if her uncle would not.

Well. He could certainly relate to such a view. And he had to respect both her integrity and her wishes.

But it was a damned shame.

Dusk was falling quickly now. Lady Tremaine's home loomed ahead as they navigated the curve in the shoreline. The footman waited where they'd left him, and the other boats were already back and tied in.

Suddenly, Miss Mayne leaned forward. "Oh, look. The workmen are getting ready to light the fuses." She placed a hand over his and suddenly the cool air felt warm again. "Might we stay here a moment? See the lighting from this vantage?"

He nodded. They waited. Shadows lengthened as Lady Tremaine's guests laughed and drank champagne, unaware of the men scurrying at the edges of the lawn and near the clustered topiaries. The boat was drifting again and Whiddon took advantage of the moment and let his gaze linger on her rapt expression and taut anticipation.

Suddenly, the first topiary lit up—and others followed suit at a surprisingly rapid pace. The edges of the lawns also glowed.

Even from here they could hear the company exclaim as the whole party took on a multi-colored, magical glow.

"How beautiful," she sighed.

"Something's gone awry with the ones at the pier and down by the boats," he pointed out. "They haven't lit up." The workmen were converging near the shore from all directions.

He started rowing again and maneuvered them in to where the footman waited. Standing, he reached to take her hand.

She gripped his tightly. "I . . ." She let out a sigh. "I just wanted to thank you, Lord Whiddon. For everything."

They both stood a moment, moving with the slight sway of the boat. It felt oddly like a goodbye, he realized with a twinge of regret. But he understood. Their goals were incompatible.

"It has been my pleasure, Miss Mayne," he said lightly, but he knew she understood he wished her well.

He helped her onto the shore and the footman moved off, once they were disembarked and the boat was tied off. Without waiting for them, the servant moved to consult with the men clustered around the still-dark topiaries.

The lights were pretty, but they also made the unlit area they stood within feel darker and more isolated. He led her a few steps away to where the bank was smaller. "Be careful as you climb," he warned her. "Here. Take my hand as you go up."

She did and stepped up easily. "I wonder where my aunt—Oh!"

He saw it happen and everything looked like it occurred in oddly slow movements. Her foot was raised as she stepped over the edge of the bank to the lawn, but at the same time, the line of fuses raised up from the ground. They caught her foot, tripping her. She gasped and windmilled, trying to keep her balance, but she lost the battle and toppled backwards.

Whiddon didn't think. There was no time. His body had already reacted. He dove, caught her and rolled with her locked tight in his arms—right into the Thames.

It wasn't deep. They came up sputtering and sitting waist deep in river water. She scrambled away, in a panic, wiping her eyes. "What? What just—? My shoe! I've lost my shoe!"

He looked frantically up towards the bank, but miraculously, nobody had observed them. The area here still lay in darkness. The footman and the workmen were still huddled around their problematic lamps.

"Shh." He tried to quiet her, but she was splashing about, searching for her lost shoe.

"Who is looking? She peered toward the shore as she climbed to her feet. "C . . . can you see my aunt? How bad is it? Are they staring?"

Reaching out to take her arms, he realized she was shivering, likely as much from reaction as from the chill. "Miss Mayne," he said low. "Miss Mayne. Charlotte!"

Hearing him use her given name caught her attention.

"Do be quiet. No one has yet realized what has happened."

"Oh. That's g . . . good."

"Yes." He helped her to stand. "Now, listen. Let me get you back onto the lawn, then I will sneak along the edges and around the house. I'll have a servant fetch your aunt to you here. Stay here, near the boats. You can say you came back, for a bit of lost jewelry or your gloves or something. You tell them you lost your balance in the boat and fell into the water. Do you hear me? Can you do this?"

"Y . . . y . . . yes." She pushed back a hanging lock of wet hair.

"Good. Your aunt can whisk you home. Then we will both make it through this unscathed."

"Y . . . yes. It's a good plan." She was recovering now. "Thank you."

"You are welcome. Fine, then. I'm off." But he didn't let go of her arms. He just stared down at her, faint in the dark. But even in the dim light, he could see her eyes were huge and her gown was clinging to her.

He didn't mean for it to happen. One moment he was letting her go and the next he'd pulled her in against his chest and pressed his mouth to hers.

A hundred sensations struck him at once. Soft, cold lips. Warm, wet curves. She tasted of lemonade, sweet and tart together. When was the last time lust had rushed him so hard? His pulse pounded. His groin tightened.

And she was kissing him back. Arching into him, she pressed closer. Sweet and warm, her lips yielded to his and when he ran his tongue along the seam of her mouth, she opened to him. Yes, she was his equal even in this, giving even as she took, her mouth soft and demanding at once. Sweet, merciful heaven, but it shook him, because it felt so . . . necessary. As if he'd been wandering, waiting for this moment, for this passion, for this touch. He'd been going through the days and months and years of his life alone, not even knowing he was reaching out for something or someone, until she reached back and grabbed him. With this kiss.

Something in the region of his chest, long asleep, suddenly sat up and took notice. *Her?*

Yes.

No.

He pulled away. She stared at him in shock.

He searched for something to say as his face hovered over hers.

"I believe that makes us even, now."

She blinked.

And suddenly, the topiaries along the pier and near the boats lit up. Their dark refuge disappeared. They were caught, frozen, and bathed in light.

From the bank came a loud, theatrical gasp.

"Charlotte!"

It was the hateful cousin. She looked horrified, but triumph lived in her eyes. "What in heaven's name are you doing?"

CHAPTER 5

Charlotte did not say a word as she was hurried into Lady Tremaine's home, wrapped in blankets and escorted quickly out to her carriage.

She kept her silence all during the long ride home, while Aunt Bernadine *tsked* and worried and, at last, stopped asking questions.

She held her tongue as they arrived, and she was ushered into a hot bath and bundled into warm nightclothes and a heavy wrapper and perched before the fire to dry her hair.

Not until the maid left and she was alone at last, did she let her composure crumble. Bending over in pain, she fought the keening that had lodged in her throat. But then she straightened and vented her fury by pounding it out on the arm of the chair.

The tears started then. She let them fall, silent and hot, full of embarrassment and despair. They seemed without number, falling endlessly while she stared unseeing into the flames.

"Oh, my dear."

How long had her aunt been there in the chair across from her? She didn't know.

"Shall I leave you be?" Aunt Bernadine whispered.

"No. I hate the silence. It reminds me of Father."

"Oh, my dear." Her aunt's tone sounded impossibly sadder, now.

"What on earth is wrong with her?" she cried out.

"I certainly do not know." Bernadine hesitated. "Do you really think she arranged it?"

"If you had seen her face, you wouldn't doubt it." Charlotte's gut twisted at the recollection of unholy glee in Harriet's eyes. "Well, it doesn't matter now. She's got her revenge. Everything is ruined." Charlotte dropped her head in her hands. She'd seen the looks on all of the faces tonight. The turned heads and the whispers behind hands and fans. Her Season was over. There would be no chance of contracting a marriage now. One fall in a ballroom was bad. In front of the king, no less. She'd barely survived that. A second fall, into a river? And being caught in the wet and dripping embrace of a man sworn not to marry?

Whiddon would suffer the consequences of the gossip for a bit. The incident would enhance his reputation of being a bit of a rogue. He would be forgiven in a matter of weeks, likely. But her?

She would be shunned, and for her, the situation was permanent. There would be no callers, no invitations, ever again. Women would sniff and cross the street to avoid her. Men would turn away, or make other, humiliating offers.

"There's nothing left," she said flatly. "No other respectable alternatives. No one will even hire me as a governess or companion, now."

Bitterness and steely determination joined the fury in her chest. Harriett, that spoiled brat, would not win. Charlotte would find a way to support her family, to see them thrive the way they were meant to. Her mind drifted, searching, trying to come up with ideas she hadn't already tried or discarded.

"Surely not all hope is lost," Aunt Bernadine ventured. "We must wait and see what Lord Whiddon intends to do."

That penetrated the fog in her brain. For a moment her mind went back to that kiss. Good gracious. That kiss. Girls whispered of how it felt, how it was done, but she'd always been a little unbelieving. Truly? Tongues? But no, she'd been wrong. And that kiss had been a revelation, full of surprise and pleasure and so much *wanting of more*.

She should be glad of that kiss. Glad it was the sort to make your knees go weak and your mind go blank, and your mouth turn hot and insistent.

She should be glad, because it was likely the only one she'd ever get.

Charlotte abruptly stood and went to the small dressing room attached to her bedchamber. She pulled out a portmanteau and placed it on the bed.

"What are you doing?" Bernadine asked.

"Packing. I shall write in the morning to cancel our lease and see if we can get a return of part of the rent."

"But, Charlotte—"

"It's over," she said flatly. "Why do you think they call him *Lord Unwilling*? Lord Whiddon does not believe in marriage. He will not be riding in to rescue us. He will not offer for my hand."

There was no time for grief, for mourning lost chances or even for railing at her hateful cousin. She must be practical. She must see to her own rescue and that of her family.

Just like she had always done.

∼

Whiddon went to his club for breakfast. It didn't take long for Chester and Sterne to track him there.

"I've sent for Tensford," Sterne said, taking a seat.

"Well, that was a waste. He won't come." Chester took another seat and signaled for a porter. "It's not as if Whiddon is going to marry the chit."

"You don't know that," Sterne objected. He cast a sideways glance in Whiddon's direction. "I know that marriage is not precisely your favorite word."

He raised a brow. "Come now, Sterne. Marriage is not a word. It's a sentence."

Sterne rolled his eyes.

"You left it wide open," Whiddon told him.

"Yes, I did. I can't fault you for walking through with that old joke." His friend's tone grew serious. "But have you truly considered the situation? You may well have to marry her."

"Why should he have to?" Chester scoffed. "Who is to say that the girl didn't plan the whole debacle, just to trap him? She shouldn't be rewarded for such duplicity."

"She didn't plan anything. I don't believe it." Sterne looked nearly green with remorse. "In fact, I was the one who suggested that Whiddon should take her out in the boat. I am sorry," he said directly to Whiddon. "I apologize for my part in it. But I don't think you believe such a thing of Miss Mayne, either."

"I don't." He calmly sliced a sausage.

"Her uncle may very well insist that you marry her and salvage her reputation," Sterne said glumly.

"He hasn't. He won't. Pass the jam, if you please?"

"There! You see!" Chester said, triumphant. "If her uncle doesn't press her case, why should Whiddon worry?"

"There are other considerations," Sterne told him.

"What are they? Do you think Whiddon will care if a bunch of old hens cut him? Half of them do so already—and me along with him. He knows *we'll* never abandon him—and what more does he need?"

"Thank you, Chester," Whiddon said sincerely. "I do know that none of you will toss me away, and it means everything to me."

It was true. Their friendship was the most solid rock in the foundation of his life. It steadied and sustained him. For years it had given him comfort and confidence.

Just now, it was giving him one very good reason why he *might* marry Miss Mayne.

It was the thought that she didn't have any such support system that swayed him. It hardly seemed fair. She was a very good sort of girl—likely superior to him in many ways—but she didn't have anyone to fall back on.

She had her aunt. The small, selfish part of him argued the point. But the rest of him knew the aunt was not enough. She could not prevent the girl from sliding into a life of isolation and ignominy.

Only he could.

If he could get past his horror at the thought of marriage.

His stomach soured.

If only he hadn't kissed her.

But, oh, what a kiss.

He set down a slice of toast and stood, making sure no crumbs had lodged in his neckcloth.

"Where are you going?" asked Chester.

"I'm not exactly sure. I suppose I'll figure it out as I go."

CHARLOTTE WAS FINISHING the letter to the landlord when Bernadine burst into the small study. "He's here! Whiddon is here!"

Her heart jumped. She reminded herself sternly that this

was Whiddon they were talking about. "No doubt he's come to make his excuses."

"Now, don't give up hope so easily," her aunt admonished. "And don't be sour, dear. This mess is not his fault. He's as much a victim in all of this as you are."

It was true. She sighed.

"I had him put in the parlor. Pray, do not keep him waiting!"

Charlotte looked around the snug room, filled with dark covered books and heavy furniture. It was gloomy in here without the fire going. "Send him in here," she said. "It's a fitting place to deal with bad news."

Bernadine slumped a little. "Very well."

Charlotte left the desk and moved to throw open the curtains. She took the seat facing the door, settled her hands in her lap and waited.

Whiddon walked through the door alone, without announcement or ceremony. He closed it behind him.

She stared. "Perhaps you should not—"

Her words trailed away as he came to stand before her, serious and unsmiling. "Tell me about your sister."

"I . . ." She was taken aback. None of her imaginings of this moment had gone quite like this.

He tossed his hat onto the desk and took the opposite chair. "Tell me. How old is she?"

Charlotte drew a deep breath. Goodness, she had to admit, she had not given him enough credit. Casting her mind over their few encounters, she knew the sum total of personal information she'd revealed was small enough—and still, he had managed to distill the situation down to the truly important.

He waited for her answer, his green eyes fastened on her face, his strong jaw fixed. He looked implacable, like he'd been carved from stone for the express purpose of sitting here and waiting for her to comply.

"She's fifteen," she said on a sigh. "Anne. She's quite brilliant. Her French is impeccable, as my mother taught us both, and my Aunt Bernadine is well able to keep us learning and practicing. Anne also speaks German, though, because her mind is hungry to learn. She discovered that the squire's agent is from one of the German principalities, and she bribed him into giving her lessons."

"Bribed him?"

Charlotte smiled at the memory. "She showed up at his office with a plaited stollen loaf. Herr Adlung was delighted and declared it just like his mother's. She offered to make it regularly in exchange for lessons."

"She's not afraid to take action, then. Like her sister."

Charlotte flushed. She could feel the heat bloom in her cheeks. "My lord," she protested. "I hope you don't think that I had anything to do with—"

"No. That's not what I meant." He waved a hand. "Please, continue. Your sister?"

She narrowed her eyes at him. "She's taught herself how to navigate by the stars, the way that sailors do. She is fascinated with the Herschels's work, and with anything to do with ancient Egyptians. She is not, however, interested in men. Not yet."

His eyes widened and he gave a sudden snort of laughter. "I didn't mean that, either." Sobering, his eyes widened. "Her future will be affected as much as yours will, with this scandal."

Her shoulders slumped. "I was trying to assure her future, to make it possible for her to eventually meet the right sort of young men. Now, she'll be as tainted as I am."

"And I've heard mention of other siblings?"

Slowly, she nodded. "My brother, George. He is ten."

"And? What is he like?"

"Hungry."

He laughed. "Yes, I am familiar with that stage. I myself have been known to devour nearly a whole apple cake in one sitting."

"And were you sick afterward?"

"Horribly. How did you know?"

"Because George once ate nearly half a joint of mutton. He was so miserable afterwards, we could not be angry with him, even though it meant the week's stew had no—" She stopped abruptly.

Whiddon leaned forward, his gaze intent.

She looked away.

"There's not enough money for meat for your table?" he asked quietly.

"Of course, there is," she protested.

"Once a week?"

She pressed her lips together.

"Once a month?"

She did not want to answer.

"Let's be honest with each other today, Miss Mayne."

He was right. No matter what the outcome, this was the time to be honest, so they both would know what they were getting into . . . or not. But it was a blow to her pride.

"Every fortnight I balance the village butcher's books." Her chin lifted high. "In return, he gives us a nice joint. We have learned how to make it last."

"Thank you for telling me." He sat brooding for a moment, and she thought he was going to comment further on her shameful admission, but instead he asked, "How is it that you have managed a Season? Your aunt has paid for it?"

"Yes. She had a decent income, once. A small bequest from her mother and a quarterly allowance, and she lived at the estate where she grew up. But when her father passed and my uncle inherited, his wife did not wish her in the household. My uncle moved her into a cottage and felt justified, as she was not responsible for rent, in cutting her allowance in half. We manage, with her income and the small amount I have from my own mother's will, but there is nothing for extras—"

"I hardly call decent food an extra."

"The worst part is that there is nothing to see to Anne and George's futures. They deserve so much more. It wouldn't even take much to set them each on a better path. I thought that if I could find a decent and kind man for a husband . . ."

"Yes, I see. You took the chance. I commend you, but it must have been a dreadful expense for you."

"Aunt Bernadine sold one of the most valuable specimens of her ancient coins. It was bad enough that she'd not been able to add to her collection since she took us in, but I thought that if I was successful, I should be able to get her coin back, once I was married."

"It was not a bad plan, considering your circumstances. So, you sold the coin, gambled all and came looking for a husband, leaving Anne to her books—and George? Is he a budding young scholar as well?"

She held her expression steady, though this was nearly as painful a subject. "Heavens, no. George is all action, I'm afraid. He can scarcely sit still long enough to finish his lessons. He is full of curiosity, energy and industry, but he needs focus."

The earl sat back. "You worry for him."

Perhaps it would be better if he left her here today. It might not be easy to live with so perceptive a man. "Yes."

He let loose a long sigh. "I know the feeling, exactly. I worried for my brother, as well. He was a little wild at that age and only grew more so."

"Yes. That is one of my fears," she confessed. "George, he

is so active, so restless. What will his future be? He needs a man's influence, the guidance of a steady, kind hand."

"Well, that is no point in my favor, I'm afraid."

She frowned. "I don't know what you mean."

He stood and went to the window. "Honesty, Miss Mayne. It's important to me. My father, you see, came to London as a young man, when he was ready to seek a bride. My mother was in her second Season. Beautiful and lively, she was the toast of the *ton*. He wooed her, won her, and took her home to Devonshire—where she proceeded to live miserably."

"Why?"

"Because she was a social creature. She pined for people, gaiety, friends and activity. But Broadcove is quiet and rural, with only a small village nearby. My father had promised they would return for the Season. They didn't. She'd thought she could host house parties—he wouldn't allow it. In short, he lied. He wanted her and her money. He lied to get it and he never cared if she was unhappy."

Turning, he looked at her with a bleak expression. "I will never do that. I will not make a promise that I cannot or will not fulfill. And I tell you now, I am not the sort of man a boy should look to for guidance."

"I'm sure there are those who would disagree with you."

He gave a bitter laugh. "Not even my friends would tell you such a whopper."

She watched him closely. "Perhaps your brother would disagree."

His expression instantly shuttered. "My brother is dead."

"Oh." She was horrified to have been so forward. "I do beg your pardon."

He lifted a shoulder. "You could not know."

"You mentioned you have a sister."

He looked at her, questioning.

"It was during our dance."

"Oh, I had forgotten. Yes. My sister lives in Hertfordshire with my aunt and uncle," he said absently before abruptly turning toward the window again. "You know my views on marriage."

"Yes." She studied his back and those impressively broad shoulders. They already carried burdens aplenty. He would surely be reluctant to take on hers as well. "It's why I didn't expect you this morning."

His head turned. "A wise outlook. I wasn't sure, myself, if I was coming. My friends have succumbed. One by one they have mated and married, and I, knowing their deepest secrets, aware of their backgrounds, have marveled at it. I don't understand it. I don't trust it. I've vowed it would not happen to me."

She had not even realized how hard she'd been grasping that last hope until it slid from her gasp. "I understand."

"No, *I* understand, at last. I've been thinking all night. It was a foolish fancy—the idea of freedom that you and I discussed. My own thoughts were foolish as well. I thought I could escape the net, vowed to try. But there are considerable obstacles. My father's constant carping, for one. It's only grown worse since my brother's death. His despair makes sense, for my cousin, next in line after me for the marquessate, is a damned bounder and estranged from the rest of the family. It is my duty, I suppose, to keep the title and estates and people free from his hands. And now my closest friends have begun to pressure me, as well. And Society as a whole, of course, has its own expectations. I can only anticipate such encouragements will increase, from all directions."

He turned around, his face grave. "And now there is the fact that your cousin has put us—but mostly you—in a hell of a mess."

Charlotte straightened. "You saw it, too? It was there, in her face, wasn't it?"

"Oh, yes. She orchestrated it. It was clear. And we will deal with her in time. But for now, we must forge our way forward."

She was unexpectedly warmed by his use of *we* in that sentence.

"What happened was no fault of yours, my lord. I cannot expect—"

"Honesty, Miss Mayne. I kissed you." He shook his head. "I should not have done it. If I hadn't, I would have been across the lawn when those damned lights came back on, but there you were, wet and vulnerable, with your eyes shining like stars, and it felt like we were parting ways."

"I rather think we were, were we not?"

"I made the mistake, and now we must both pay for it."

"Since you asked for honesty, I must point out, I did kiss you back."

Was he *flushing*? She stared, her hopes rising again, utterly unable to look away.

"In any case, here we are."

"In a hell of a mess, as you said."

"Yes."

Suddenly, he pushed away from the window and paced to the desk, then to the door and back again. "The thing is, I find I like you, Miss Mayne."

"I like you, as well," she told him.

"You've wit and character and a sense of fun and you are damned pretty. I like you better than any other woman of my acquaintance."

"Thank you." *I think.*

"And yet, I still cannot quite reconcile myself to the idea of marriage. I'd make a damnable husband. I am solitary and cranky and set in my ways. I do what I want without consulting anyone, and I like it that way. I don't want to change my life. I cannot imagine dancing attendance on a wife, even you, Miss Mayne. Knowing me, I'd likely forget your existence from one minute to the next."

She had no idea how she was supposed to respond.

"And so, I have an . . . unusual sort of proposal to put to you."

"Oh?" She held her breath, hardly knowing what to expect.

"We could marry, but it would be in name only."

"In name only?"

"Yes."

She frowned. "We would not live together?"

"I do not see that we must."

"Forgive me, my lord, but if you marry me and then just send me home to Hoverstoke, then my reputation will be just as damaged as if you walked away now. All of Society will assume I am an adventuress who trapped you unwillingly. You would be praised for doing the right thing and I would still be vilified. And my sister and brother will be painted with the same brush."

He'd stopped his pacing. "Well. Yes. I hadn't considered it from that angle." He looked about the pokey room. "You won't want to live here. I suppose you would have to move into my townhouse, then. But we must agree to the idea of separate lives."

She took a deep breath, thinking hard. "I believe many Society marriages are run just that way. But you did mention the necessity of . . . heirs."

His gaze drifted over her. Suddenly, her heartrate picked up. A shiver ran through her. The air between them warmed with . . . something intoxicating.

"Yes. Perhaps we can postpone that bit. For a while. After

all, there's no hurry. And it might go more smoothly if we wait until we are otherwise settled."

She nodded. Her mind was racing nearly as fast as her heart. Images and impressions flashed in her mind. His scorn, shifting to interest at their first meeting. The urgency in his face when he asked her to dance. The feel of his shoulder under her hand. The way his face lit up when she made him laugh, out on the river. And the surge of desire when his lips touched hers and her body pressed against him.

He approached her. She looked up and knew suddenly, everything she wanted from him. Warmth, closeness, tenderness. Love? *Oh, this was very bad.*

"Well?" he asked. "What would you say to such an arrangement?"

"I would say . . . I have questions."

He raised a brow.

"What of my siblings?"

"What of them?"

"We are a family. A *close* family. This is the longest I've ever been away from them."

"They will not stay with your aunt?"

"Well, yes. They will."

"Was that not always your plan?"

"It was, but I shall need to see them. To visit Hoverstoke occasionally, and to have them visit me."

"Well, then." He looked like the was thinking hard. "I suppose they can visit." He frowned. "I'm not good at that sort of thing. I waver between flippant and ill-tempered when I'm in company and most people are just relieved to see the back of me. I'm tempted to instruct you to leave me out of it, but you did say you hoped for a male influence for your brother."

Frowning, he sat back down in the chair across from her. "I've been trying to make you understand the truth about me.

My own family is *not* close. I'm not sure I know how such a thing even looks, let alone happens." He sighed. "I may have a title and money, but I'm a bad bargain when you weigh in the rest. But I do have one thing of value, and that is my circle of friends. They are good men, real gentlemen and my true family. I am sure they would be willing to help. Sterne will teach your George about science and culture. Keswick can teach him how to ride and all about horses, if he ever returns from Ireland, that is. Chester, well, we may have to watch Chester around him, but if the boy likes dogs, Chester will thrust a puppy on him, and it will be the animal perfectly suited for him. And George might find a friend in Chester's ward, Charlie. And finally, Tensford will bore him to death talking about farming, but he'll take him out hunting for fossils and show him how a true gentleman cares for the people he's responsible for."

Everything he said made her wonder more about him. He'd been nothing but—well, *mostly* kind to her. And if his friends were such paragons, why would they tolerate him if he was as surly and antisocial as he claimed? Her instincts were telling her that there was a bit of a mystery here, but also that Lord Whiddon was a far better man than he suspected.

But could she risk her future—and her family's—on the hunch?

Suddenly, the image of her father flashed in her mind. Not the smiling, caring father of her youth, but the man who had returned, wounded from the wars. The man who increasingly sat silent, who drifted, always distant and far away.

Did she wish a husband who would be the embodiment of that distance?

Did she have a choice?

She dragged in a deep breath. "It all sounds perfectly

reasonable, and I am so very grateful for the offer. I told you that first night that I had to find a husband. Now you know why I've been so determined. To answer your question, I would agree to such a proposal."

Something lightened in his face, but he only gave a brisk nod.

"But I do have another question."

"Yes?"

"We agree now to live nearly separate lives, but what if one of us changes our minds?"

"Divorce will only land you back in the scandalbroth you are trying to avoid."

"I agree. But what I mean is—what if one of us decides he or she wants . . . more?"

"More?"

"More out of the marriage."

He reared back a bit. "Truly, I cannot picture it. I'm a solitary man. There are difficulties with my family. I don't like many people." He snorted. "I can count them on one hand."

"Who is the fifth?"

"What's that?"

"Your four close friends and . . . who else?"

"My valet," he admitted.

"Oh."

"Six, now. If I count you."

Something in her melted a little. "I am flattered." And she meant it.

"I will not change my mind," he said gently. "I urge you to decide now, if what I offer is enough."

Her mind was whirling. It already wasn't enough. But she would have to learn to live with it. Or find a way to make him see how much better things could be. She closed her eyes. She was gambling with her heart. But she was making things better for Anne and George, and even Aunt Bernadine.

This was always the sacrifice she'd been planning to make.

She opened her eyes. Nodded. "Very well."

"Fine, then." He stood. "I'll see about getting a special license. It will be better if we do this quietly, without a big fuss. And quickly."

"Thank you, my lord."

He sighed. "You'd better use my name."

She waited, expectant.

"Gabriel Nicholas Ogden Harris. You can see why everyone just usually calls me Whiddon."

"I like Gabriel." She smiled at him. "You will wish to talk to our family solicitor soon, as well."

"Will I?"

She stiffened. "I do have a dowry. A bit of one. Two hundred pounds a year. I know it doesn't sound like much to an earl."

"Ah. Your money, and you couldn't touch it, all this time?" He grinned. "I'll wager it drove you crazy."

"Not my money, precisely. But, yes. It's driven me mad. A hundred times I've plotted what I could do if I could have got my hands on it."

"I'll have them turn it over to you. You won't much need it, but it seems only right. I'll see that you are given pin money. The household accounts should cover the rest."

A wave of relief washed over her. Gratitude soon followed. Even if this marriage turned into a colossal failure, she would not be left in the same straits, with no choices. She knew she could do quite a bit for Anne and George with that annual income.

"Thank you again, my—" She stopped. "Gabriel."

She stood and he hovered awkwardly a moment before

he reached for her hand. Bending, he touched his lips to her bare skin—and they both froze.

Did he feel the same, stirring need in his belly?

"I'll be in touch."

As he left the room, she sank back down into her chair.

She was going to try. She *had* to try.

But she must go about this very, very carefully.

CHAPTER 6

Whiddon had a great deal to accomplish in a short amount of time. He asked Sterne to see about arranging the special license, but he took Chester with him to see to the next necessary and distasteful task. This proved wise on two fronts, as Chester's large form could be quite intimidating, and as the exercise also served to ease his friend's doubts about Charlotte Mayne.

It took all day, but at last the fruit of their labors were condensed to a sheaf of papers folded into a wallet and tucked into a pocket of his coat. They drank to their success, and the next morning, Whiddon took the wallet with him when he went to meet Lord Burchan's solicitor and man of business.

Mr. Charrings was prepared for him, and as Whiddon brought along his own man of business—who was notably *not* the family solicitor and not likely to report his doings to his father—things were proceeding quickly.

Until Lord Burchan arrived.

"Whiddon." Sneering, the baron took the seat Charrings

vacated. Ignoring the other men, Burchan raked him with a disdainful gaze. Whiddon took great pleasure in returning it.

"I didn't think you'd actually marry the chit," Burchan drawled.

"I suspect thinking is not your strong suit," he returned.

The baron gaped. "What's that you dare to say, you insolent pup?"

Whiddon merely lifted a shoulder. "Why would you think so, after all? You did not contact me to force my hand or even ask my intentions. You have not even stopped in to check on your niece, have you?"

"Fine sentiments, coming from the man who dishonored her," the baron spat.

"Dishonored? I kissed her. I admit it. I should not have, perhaps, but it was not planned or malicious, nor should it have proved fatal to her reputation. All of those charges I lay at your daughter's feet."

Lord Burchan straightened. "Do not dare to speak of my daughter."

"Oh, I shall not. However, my betrothed may choose differently." He shrugged. "The choice will be up to her. Either way, she'll have my full support, and if she does choose to reveal your chit's wickedness, she'll have the written proof I've gathered to back up the truth of the tale."

"Poppycock. You've ruined my niece. And I've half a mind to refuse to hand over her dowry." The baron's mean eyes narrowed further, as if in threat. "But I'll be damned if I will let you besmirch my daughter's name."

"Oh, you'll be damned," Whiddon agreed easily. "But it will come from your own actions."

"Now you think to threaten me?" the man blustered.

Whiddon sat back. He gestured to the two men of business, still shuffling their papers, their heads down. "Why don't you tell us, Burchan, what your cook served for dinner last night?"

"What? You've gone mad."

"No. I'm merely curious. How many courses? Five? Six?"

Burchan stared.

Whiddon waited.

"Was it more? Did you entertain last evening, gossiping about your own flesh and blood?"

"No, damn you. We dined quietly at home."

Whiddon raised a brow.

"Three courses. Four if you count the pudding."

"I do count it. And did you have a joint? Fish? Perhaps a roast chicken?"

"All three," the man answered belligerently. "What of it?"

"I just believe it makes a remarkable comparison, when I think of how your sister, along with your nieces and nephew, have had to regularly scrimp and struggle to put food on their table. When I shudder at how they have been forced to barter to afford meat, and just twice a month."

Burchan stilled. "Nonsense."

"Is it? Indeed? Mr. Charrings would know, I'd wager. Are you the one, sir, who sees to the payment of the baron's sister's allotment?"

"I am, sir." Charrings did not look at his employer, but held Whiddon's gaze.

"And what is the quarterly amount that Lord Burchan thinks sufficient for his sister?"

"It's not your—" The baron tried, but his man had already answered.

Whiddon's own man looked up in surprise.

"A paltry amount indeed." Whiddon raised his brows. "And when you combine it with the small bequest that Miss Charlotte Mayne receives from her mother's estate, then I should guess that their entire household receives less per quarter for all their expenses than your cook alone likely spends in a week."

"You've no business—"

"No, sir!" Whiddon stood. "It's you who have no business calling yourself a gentleman! Not when you've turned away from both honor and duty and neglected the family who depend on you." He tilted his head. "I will give you a chance to redeem yourself, though. You will authorize the release of Charlotte's dowry and you will double the amount of Miss Anne's."

"Double it?" the baron objected.

"Yes. And you will bestow an inheritance of the same amount upon Mr. George Mayne, to be granted when he reaches his majority."

The baron rolled his eyes. "And why should I do so?"

"Because they are your family, your brother's children. Is that not reason enough?"

Burchan only sneered. "Yes, my brother who might have married to advance the family, but instead pleased himself and took up with some military man's daughter." He tossed his head. "And what if I do not throw good money after bad, as you think you can bid me? Will you refuse to do right by my niece?"

Whiddon shook his head. "No. I am not so low a worm as you. But if you do not do just as I've requested, then I will tell anyone who will listen of the circumstances in which you've left the lot of them. I will expose your skinflint ways and your neglect, and I'll leave the *ton* to compare it to the lavish lifestyle you and your wife and daughter enjoy. I will listen as whispers of your dereliction of duty fly through every drawing room in London. And I will watch as true gentlemen refuse to sit at your table or to see you at your club. As invitations dwindle and your daughter's prospects disappear." He leaned forward. "And I'll enjoy it."

"Damn you," Burchan whispered.

"You will see to it, Mr. Charrings?" Whiddon thought he caught a glimpse of approval in the man's eye when he nodded.

"And you have the papers ready for my signature?"

The men pointed out all the spots where he needed to sign. He bent over the desk and signed them all, giving the last one a flourish.

"Well, then. Good day to you all." He took up his hat. "I expect Miss Mayne and I will be married tomorrow." He cast a glance askance at the baron. "You will not be invited."

Whistling, he left the offices and set off to see his betrothed.

∽

CHARLOTTE PAUSED, a stack of folded shifts in her hand. She could not stop staring at her wedding dress.

She could not stop marveling that she possessed a wedding dress.

Whiddon had left her yesterday morning and she'd sat, stunned, while her aunt rejoiced and sang his praises. Scarcely an hour had passed before another knock sounded on the door. In had swept Lady Chester and Mrs. Sterne. They brought smiles, chatter and a large box.

"It's terrible of us to intrude just now, but we've heard your news and we felt we must come and congratulate you." Lady Chester gripped her hands and squeezed.

"And we've come to offer help, as you must have a hundred things to do." Mrs. Sterne lifted the box. "Also, we come bearing gifts."

Charlotte had tried to protest, but the ladies would not have it. "Our husbands are all exceedingly close. As close as family. The wives have created a sisterhood of sorts and we are thrilled to welcome you as our newest member."

Hugs, well wishes and first names were exchanged, and they took seats in the parlor.

"I had a feeling, that night at my ball," Julia, Lady Chester, confessed. "Whiddon watched you quite intently all evening, and then, when he asked you to dance!" She fanned her face. "It quite reversed the outcome of that unfortunate incident."

"Sterne quite agrees with you, Julia. He says he's never seen Whiddon show such an interest in any woman," Penelope confided.

"We know the circumstances are . . . unusual," Julia confided. "We just want to be sure you are . . ."

"Willing?" Charlotte asked.

"Well, yes." Julia reached for her hand. "You are, are you not?"

Charlotte clutched her for a moment. "You are both very sweet. But yes, I am very happy to be marrying Lord Whiddon." She glanced between the two women and decided to be upfront. "Perhaps happier than it is wise for me to be."

The ladies exchanged glances. Penelope leaned in. "Whiddon is going to be a tough nut to crack, Charlotte dear, but we are exceedingly happy to hear you would like to make the attempt. And to that end . . ." She pulled Charlotte to her feet and drew her over to the box, which had been placed upon a settee.

"I had this made up for an event at Court. The queen was to present Sterne's uncle with a commendation for his contributions to the natural sciences. However, we were at Greystone beforehand and the newest little Tensford decided to make his appearance right at the time we were set to leave. Of course, we stayed. Sterne would never leave Tensford at such a time and I wished to do all I could for Hope. We missed the event, therefore, and this gown has never been worn. I would be honored if you would wear it at your wedding."

She removed the lid from the box and Charlotte gasped. "Oh, my. Oh, I could not."

It was a gown fit for a princess. The ivory underdress was trimmed in tightly woven gold lace. The bodice and open skirts were of a rich, dusky blue, with gold dangles at the short, puffed sleeves and elaborate gold embroidery adorning all the edges.

"You can," Penelope insisted. "I believe we are a similar size and there should be only the smallest adjustments to make." She smiled warmly at Charlotte. "Truly. We want to help."

"It is perfect for your coloring," Julia added. "Goodness, what it will do for your eyes."

"Whiddon will not be able to take his eyes off of you," Penelope predicted.

That made her hesitate a moment—and that was all the opening the two ladies needed. In minutes, a seamstress was called in from where she waited in the carriage.

"Not fair," Charlotte objected, but the women laughed and dragged her upstairs and she was soon being fitted in the gorgeous gown.

Her aunt sent up tea and crumpets and tiny, apricot tarts and Charlotte had quite a wonderful afternoon, full of laughter and camaraderie, quite unlike any she'd ever experienced before. By the time the sun began to sink behind London's sooty skyline, she was possessed of a stunning wedding dress and two new, fast friends.

As she'd drifted off to sleep last night, she'd thought Whiddon hadn't even married her yet and still, he'd given her so much.

She'd awakened this morning and sat down to write Anne and George of the news of her engagement. Once that was done, she'd set herself to packing. Whiddon had said they should marry 'quickly' and she had a suspicion that his notion of such a thing meant very soon indeed. Yet still, when she was tucking away the lone sketch pad she'd brought with her, she could not help but sit at the desk with it.

Soon she had a page full of doodles. A fine set of eyes that made her long for her watercolors and myriad shades of green. A broad back and a thick head of hair surrounded by a cloud of smoke. A strong pair of hands upon a set of oars. When the page was full, she shook herself out of the fog she'd drifted into and flushed a little. Quickly, she tore the page out, crumpled it up and tossed it into the fire.

"A message for you, miss." The maid bobbed a curtsy and left as Charlotte took the missive. Thick vellum unfolded to reveal strong, bold handwriting.

She sighed. Lord Rostham had sent her a note of congratulations. It ended very sweetly.

I CONFESS, *I've been thinking incessantly about how things might have gone differently, had I brought back that ice, that day on Lady Tremaine's lawn, or if I had taken you out on the river myself. I am very glad, indeed, though, to hear of your impending marriage and I am thankful that the situation came out well for you. If ever you need a friend or any sort of help, Miss Mayne, I hope you will call on me.*

IT WAS VERY KIND OF him. But now was the time for looking forward. She went back to packing. There had been mention of a special license yesterday afternoon. She supposed it made sense. Whiddon would want to get the ceremony over with, with as little fuss as possible, so he could move on with his life.

His separate life. Alone.

Well, they would see about that.

She heard the knock on the door downstairs and hurriedly closed her trunk. Ducking to look into her mirror, she smoothed her hair, then ran lightly down the stairs.

The footman was closing the parlor door. "Lord Whiddon has—"

"Yes. Thank you." She breezed past him, entering with a wide smile on her face.

Whiddon turned away from the window.

"Good morning my lor—" she stopped herself. "Gabriel." Her heart beat out a happy, thrumming rhythm.

The ease in his manner faded. He tightened, visibly gathering himself in. "Charlotte," he said stiffly.

Goodness. It was but a moment's transformation, but it was profound. Was that all it took to spook him? A light, happy greeting? A smile set him to shoring up his defenses?

Oh, she did indeed have her work cut out for her.

She dampened her own enthusiasm, stilled and reached for a detached demeanor. "How are you today?" she asked calmly—and saw relief flash behind his eyes.

"I am well, thank you. I have news. And something for you."

"Please, sit. Will you have tea?"

"No, thank you. I won't stay long. But I thought you'd like to hear about my meeting this morning."

He explained and she had to remind herself to rein in her enthusiasm. "Double Anne's dowry?" she asked. "And a sum for George, too?" There was no curbing the flood of gratitude she felt, but she directed it down into the grip she tightened on the arms of her chair. "Thank you. Thank you so very much."

He shifted in his seat. "Yes, well. It's less worry for you that way, and frankly, it's the least that Burchan can do." He cleared his throat. "There is another matter."

She watched as he pulled a wallet from his coat, taking out a set of papers and smoothing them over his knee before offering them to her.

She took the papers, a question in her gaze. Examining the top one, she read it over—then covered her mouth with a hand. "Oh! How did you . . ?"

"I had help. Lady Tremaine summoned the work crew who set up her garden lights and Chester intimidated them until the culprit confessed. It's all true. Signed and witnessed. Proof that your cousin bribed the workman and arranged our mishap. The question is, what do you want to do with it?"

"What do you mean?"

"You have options. You could give the information to the papers. They would love to create a scandal out of a jealous girl's machinations. You could confront her yourself. Or you could just tease her with your knowledge and let her suffer in doubt about what you might do." He shrugged. "I did tell her father I had evidence. It's probably making him insane, wondering."

"I don't know." It wasn't triumph she was feeling, only sadness over her cousin's baseless enmity—and a bit of confusion. Honestly, she should be grateful to Harriett for setting this marriage in motion, but saying so would only send Whiddon into a tailspin.

"I thought perhaps you would like to go to the art gallery this evening," he ventured. "Sterne said that Penelope invited you. Society will attend. Likely Harriett will, too, if you should wish to make use of the evidence."

"Must I do anything with it?"

"No. It is entirely your decision. But I would recommend

keeping the evidence safe, just in case you need it in the future."

"I will." She hesitated. "Penelope said that Sterne meant to obtain a special license."

"He has." Whiddon's expression had gone flat. "Chester insists that he will host the wedding in his townhouse. It will be tomorrow afternoon, if that suits you?"

It suited her. It thrilled her. It scared her almost as much as the idea of no wedding at all. She couldn't admit to any of that, though. She just nodded, instead.

"You don't wish to attend the gallery showing tonight, then?"

"No. Although I hate to miss the art, I'll be happy if I never have to see Harriett ever again." She gave a vague wave of her hand. "I have a few matters here still to arrange. Also, it might prove awkward to go out, to see people . . . before . . ."

"Before. Yes. Well." He abruptly stood and took her hand, bowing low over it.

A great shiver went through her, threatening to unravel her completely. She knew he felt it, too. It was a mutual arousal that fed her body's responses, but it was the carefully built wall he tried to hide behind that touched her heart.

"Tomorrow, then," she said softly.

"Yes." He'd shuttered everything behind those variegated green eyes, but she knew it was there. "Tomorrow."

CHAPTER 7

Whiddon, standing next to Chester in his friend's formal parlor, felt more uncomfortable by the minute. He longed to stick a finger beneath his collar and loosen his cravat. He didn't dare, though. Chapman had scrubbed, polished and coiffed him, then dressed him in his finest. From somewhere he had unearthed a magnificent waistcoat embroidered in navy, silver and gold. Whiddon didn't dare mess with the eminently presentable version of himself that his valet had created.

He eyed the crowd nervously. A crowd! Where had Chester dug up so many people in such a short time? Chester's grandmother, the dowager countess, winked at him from where she was already seated. He grinned back and continued to shift nervously. When were they going to start? He wanted it over with, already.

A commotion sounded outside the parlor. Perhaps his bride was running, thinking better of linking her life to his, before it was too late. He was surprised to feel a pang of loss at the thought.

The parlor door opened, and a gentleman strode in.

"Tensford?" Whiddon's jaw dropped.

His friend, covered in road dust, stubble and a general air of weariness, strode right up to him and engulfed him in a hug.

"What in the—? How did you get here so quickly?"

"I left Hope and the baby at Greystone and changed horses every chance I got. Did you think I would miss this?" Tensford clapped Chester on the back and grinned as Sterne came up, as well. Sobering, he looked at Whiddon. "So. I assume the girl was in some sort of trouble?"

"They were both in a spot of trouble," Sterne confirmed. "But yes, she'd already stirred up Whiddon's protective instincts."

It might have been a curse, having friends who knew him so well. It would have been, if he didn't care for them so much. It was a jolt, though, hearing Tensford put the simple truth into words. He'd been attributing the situation to her manner—confident and funny, with a lashing of vulnerability, and to his lack of discipline—he pushed away the memory of that eye-opening, wet, warm and incredibly unwise kiss—but he should also remember that it was his protective instincts that led to that moment. And he should force himself to recall the sort of havoc those tendencies had wreaked in the past.

His anxiety ratcheted up another notch. Here presented another reason to make this a marriage in name only. A union of civility. Polite discourse. Distinct and separate lifestyles.

He'd need an heir, of course. Eventually. But it could wait. There was no hurry. He would put it off, give it time—time for him to become accustomed to her presence. Until she was safe and secure and in no need of his overprotective sense of justice and caretaking. Until she was just another attractive distraction in the background of his life, like a painting or a sunrise over the Devon sea.

The door opened again. Penelope Sterne slipped inside, bringing Miss Bernadine Mayne with her. She looked at Chester and nodded, and his friend took him by the arm. "Come. It's time."

He stood, nerves aflutter, before the vicar. *Parson's mousetrap.* His heart beat wildly for a moment, and then the door opened again.

Everything inside of him seized, grinding to a halt. Surely that was not the same drenched girl he'd kissed just days ago?

Her hair was done up in an elaborate coiffure that swept up her thick locks but left a cascade of curls to tease her nape. Her skin glowed in the candlelight, as luminous as the gold trim on her gown. The bodice and skirts were of a shade that made her eyes look like blue smoke. Her expression was set, determined. She looked regal, remote, and utterly lovely.

Music swelled. Chester had hired a trio and stuck them in a corner. Charlotte's steps kept time and her gaze fastened on him and stayed there as she moved forward.

He was frozen. A statue of ice, caught forever in a flow of longing, panic and good, old-fashioned lust. Surely he would shatter if he moved. But she reached him, and he took her hand and he stayed in one piece. Together they turned to face the clergyman, who stepped forward and began to speak.

Whiddon didn't hear a word. His mind was awhirl. It was going to be quite an adjustment, getting used to having her in his orbit. The difficulty hit him anew each time he saw her. But he would do it. He would learn to not catch his breath when she stepped into a room. He would somehow train all the hairs on his nape not to stir and stand at the sight and scent of her. Not to mention certain other parts of him, lower down. Not even an audience at his back and a parson ahead had discouraged his . . . interest.

He slammed abruptly out of his reverie and back into the present. Had she just *nudged* him? During their wedding ceremony?

He frowned down at her.

She tilted her head toward the vicar.

His frown deepened. He didn't like the light in here. He could scarcely find the silver flecks in her eyes.

"Pick one," she said, low.

"Excuse me?" he whispered.

She jerked her head toward the vicar again. "Last chance. Time to choose."

His gaze remained fastened on her face. Her lips were pink and as fresh as the rose petals in his mother's garden.

"Will you? Or won't you?" she asked.

"What?"

The vicar cleared his throat and asked his question again.

He started. "Oh. Yes. I will."

He lost the rest of it again. He must have put the ring on her finger. Hadn't he? He came back to himself when the kissing was mentioned.

"You don't have to," she said reassuringly. She turned her cheek toward him. "Just a peck will do."

Damned if it would. Did she think he wanted to hear his friends hooting about the chaste and sisterly peck he gave his bride, for all the rest of his life?

God's teeth, no.

She was his. His bride. He'd gone and done it and he wanted to mark it. To claim her. This once. He would kiss her now and be done with it, at least for a while.

Reaching out, he pulled her close. Her cheeks flushed and he turned her to face him so he could kiss her properly.

Mistake. This kiss wasn't proper. It was a rush of heat and longing. Damnation, he'd thought the kiss in the Thames had been a shock. He'd caught her by surprise then. This time she was expecting it—and she threw herself into it. The press of her lips set loose a shockwave of other sensations, other emotions. It was just a fancy, was it not? That the passion sweeping through him was igniting a thousand small explosions inside of him? That each flare of rough, possessive yearning illuminated more of his soul? Bared his empty spots, his secrets, and his shameful desire for *more, deeper, farther*?

Opening his eyes, he released her. Stepped away.

She blinked. Slightly unsteady on her feet, she stared at his mouth.

The vicar made a pronouncement.

Whiddon turned, bracing himself for the onslaught of well wishes and congratulations. People surged forward and surrounded them. He let the crowd sweep them apart.

He looked over at her once, smiling and conversing coherently, although her eyes still held the daze that he felt himself.

Resolute, he turned away. Someone made a quip. It was Mr. Simon, from the British Museum. He laughed and let his friends clap him on the back. He did not stare after Charlotte.

His bride.

His wife.

He would begin as he meant to go on. He would grow used to her. She would become commonplace. He would become more . . . indifferent.

Best to start now.

HER WEDDING WAS LOVELY. She felt beautiful in her new gown and rich with well wishes and new friendships and connections. Bless Lord Chester for his skill in navigating the guest list, because she met only smiles and encouragement and congratulations.

She felt a rush of nerves when Lord Chester's grandmother cornered her. The older woman was notoriously blunt. But the dowager merely handed her a flute of champagne. "Gird your loins, girl. Whiddon won't be an easy husband for you. But I've been watching you, and I think you are up to the challenge."

"Thank you, my lady."

The countess leaned in closer to her. "Most men put their virtues on display for the world to see and hide away their faults." She shook her head. "Whiddon does the opposite. It makes him devilishly hard to know. To truly know." She gave her a direct stare. "Make him show you, girl, and you'll both be better for it."

Charlotte thanked her for her advice. She knew she had a challenge before her, but she was so hopeful it would be worth it, in the end. Today, she'd stepped into that parlor and blanched a bit at the sea of faces that had turned toward her. But she'd caught sight of Whiddon and felt a rush of pleasure and gratitude—and trepidation.

He was as tall and sleek and as tawny as a great cat. Her breath had literally caught at the sight of him waiting for her. For a brief, wonderful moment, she'd thought she'd glimpsed the same sort of awe in his expression.

It had quickly passed. He'd been woolgathering during the ceremony, scarcely paying attention at all. She, on the other hand, had been deeply conscious of what they were doing and intimately aware of him beside her. His scent—soap and sandalwood and the faintest twinge of his terrible cheroots. His large, powerful form, looming close. His strong hand taking hers. His fingers, long and deft as they slipped on the ring.

And that kiss. Better not to think of that while she was meant to be socializing with wedding guests, but the memory hovered at the back of her mind, along with the question—would there be more, tonight? She smiled and conversed and tried to decide what she wanted the answer to be.

Oh, who was she fooling? She was filled with a yearning hope for more. But was that wise?

His attitude suggested it was not. He didn't object when the crowd separated them. He never glanced her way again until dinner was announced, and he took her arm to lead her in. He laughed, green eyes shining, when he saw that Julia had placed them together at the head of the table, but he seemed entirely unfazed at the close contact, while she was beset by smoldering awareness. She twitched and flinched at each brush of their arms or touch of their thighs—and he continued to laugh and trade quips with his friends.

Charlotte began to worry. The first course arrived—white soup served with baskets of soft, fluffy rolls—but she was too preoccupied to taste it. Had she exaggerated Whiddon's interest in her? If she couldn't keep his attention while she was dressed so finely—and on their wedding day—then how could she hope to entice him into a deeper relationship?

Her husband—how odd that sounded—was listening to Lord Chester tell a humorous tale about a cricket match. Good natured debate broke out about it, until a dispute arose over the final point. Exasperated, Chester tossed a roll at Whiddon.

Without conscious thought, Charlotte reached out and caught it. Whiddon's reaction was a split second behind hers and his hand closed over hers and bore it down to the table.

He couldn't hide it, then. Not from her. His fingers

spasmed. His breath hitched, and next to her, his whole body tightened. His heated gaze flew from their clasped hands to her face.

A tidal wave of relief swept over her. She hadn't been wrong. He was just as affected as she was.

He just didn't wish to be.

He snatched his hand away and she flashed him a brilliant smile. "I'm counting that as a score. I've managed to flummox you on our wedding day," she said in a low tone. Raising her voice, she tossed the roll back to Chester. "Perhaps you should add me to your team, my lord."

He looked skeptical. "Women don't play cricket."

She shrugged. "Today is a new beginning. Perhaps we'll break new ground."

Strategy. That's what she needed. She would map a plan to happiness the way a cricket team captain planned a win.

"Hear, hear!" Chester said, lifting his glass.

"To the bride," Sterne chimed in. "And to new ground."

"To the bride!" Everyone echoed the toast.

Feeling immensely better, Charlotte drank and smiled back at them all.

CHAPTER 8

Whiddon managed to remain calm for the rest of the evening. *Treat this like any other dinner, just another social evening to be tolerated.*

It did the trick. He endured, made it through dinner and port and conversation in the drawing room. He and Charlotte were toasted and teased and sought out by everyone. He held onto his façade and maintained his usual distance. He nearly convinced himself that perhaps marriage was something he could navigate.

Until Chester's wife, Julia, stepped in close. "Your bride is beginning to look a little glassy-eyed, my lord. I'll take her upstairs to change. Why don't you send for the carriage?"

He stared at her.

"Tell them to wait for you at the gate at the end of the garden." When he still didn't respond, she smiled at him. "Take your wife home, Whiddon," she said gently.

He realized abruptly that he'd made a miscalculation. Worse, he'd failed to connect the factors of the day's events and arrive at the sum realization.

He was going to have to take Charlotte home.

To his home.

Tonight.

His mind raced, searching for an answer to this conundrum. He hadn't yet found one when Julia beckoned him and bade him slip quietly out with Charlotte.

"I don't think she's up to the fanfare—or the innuendo, of a public departure," Julia said with a smile.

Neither was he.

Charlotte came down the stairs. She wore a simple, navy carriage dress and carried a bandbox. He took it from her. Meeting his gaze, she flushed a little.

He frowned, looking closer. Had she been crying? "Is something wrong?"

She shook her head. "Aunt Bernadine came up while I was changing. She's going home in the morning, to reassure the children."

He understood. She was saying goodbye to her closest confidante and embarking on a new life. With him. He'd cry if he were in her shoes.

Julia led them into a study and out a glass door onto a terrace. "Down the stairs and through the garden. The gate is unlocked. Your carriage should be waiting."

"Thank you," Whiddon managed to get out. "For everything, Julia."

Her face softened. "You are welcome. Congratulations, to both of you." She engulfed Charlotte in a hug. "We'll talk soon."

He took his bride's arm, thinking she did look a bit fatigued. Leading her down the flagged path, he held the gate for her, then the carriage door. When she was settled, he hesitated, standing outside. "I just had a thought. Perhaps we should spend the night at a hotel."

She blinked. "Why?"

"It might be more suitable."

WHY DO EARLS FALL IN LOVE?

"More suitable than beginning our marriage in the place that will be our home?"

He hesitated.

She let her head fall back and held out her hand. "I would like to see my new home. Would you mind?"

He sighed and nodded up at the coachman. "Home." Climbing in, he settled across from her. She was relaxed against the squabs, but he sat rigidly. "There's something I should tell you."

She sat a little straighter. "Yes?"

"I've been so busy, between your cousin, the settlements, and making arrangements for the ceremony . . . I forgot . . . I failed to make arrangements at home."

"I'm not sure what you mean?"

"There are issues. With the house. With the staff."

She frowned. "Staff? Do you mean a maid for me? The woman Aunt Bernadine and I have been using came with the rented house. I knew I would have to make arrangements for a lady's maid. Penelope and Julia have offered to help."

"It's more than that."

"Oh?"

He shifted in his seat. "Well, it's to do with my father, mostly."

"Your father is in London?" she asked, surprised.

"No. No. He keeps to Broadcove in Devon almost exclusively."

She waited.

"He and I don't get on, you see."

"Yes. You mentioned that your family is not close."

"It's worse than that between me and my father. We actively antagonize each other, I'm afraid."

"That is . . . sad."

"You'll understand, if you ever have the misfortune to meet him. He's insufferable. He plays at being king of his fiefdom at Broadcove. Head of the family. Landowner. Village leader. Magistrate. He has near absolute authority and power and he revels in it. He insists on perfection. No, worse, he insists on the *appearance* of perfection, but he will not work at actually achieving it. It makes me insane."

"I don't understand."

"He likes everything neat, polished, and shiny. His bride was beautiful and fashionable, no matter if she was miserable. His children must be well behaved, well educated, well mannered—but again, he could care less if they are happy. Broadcove must dazzle the eye, inspire envy, intimidate the unworthy, but it's all on the surface. Yes, the marble glows and the art is spotlessly dusted and the brass shined, but the piping is in disrepair and the attic leaks and there is too much damp in the cellars—but he won't go to the work and expense of fixing such issues because they cannot be seen."

"Oh. Yes, that would be frustrating."

"It's infuriating."

"But what does it have to do with the townhouse?"

"You'll see."

For a moment, he thought she would tease him for more answers, but she seemed to reconsider and just leaned back against the seat again. Folding his arms, he sat silently for the rest of the short journey.

They pulled into the square and the carriage stopped before the house. It lay dark and quiet. No one emerged to greet them.

With a sigh, Whiddon wrenched open the door himself. He helped Charlotte down and escorted her to the door. It remained closed—and locked, he found, when he tried to enter.

He sighed again and pounded on the door. He had to thump several times before he heard the lock turn and the door creaked open.

A lad, slim as a rail and apparently perched on the threshold of his own manhood, gaped at him. "Your lordship?" he croaked.

Whiddon didn't recognize him. A stable lad, perhaps? One of the gardener's boys? "Why are you answering the door?" he demanded.

Still gripping the door, the young man stepped back. He glanced aside. "Old Alf's out . . . he's under the weather."

Whiddon stepped in, pulling Charlotte with him. A candle burned in the footman's alcove just to the right. It clearly illuminated the empty stool and the substantial form lying stretched out along the base boards. She sucked in a breath and pressed close to Whiddon, shrinking away from the inert body. "Is he—dead?"

He bent over his prostrate footman. "Drunk," he declared. Straightening, he glared at the boy. "Where is Hurley?"

"He's . . . ah, with the rest of the staff, downstairs. They are all celebrating, sir."

"Celebrating?"

The boy darted a glance at Charlotte. "Your nuptials, sir."

Across the entry hall and down the main passage, the green baize servant's door crashed open. "Did ye send 'em on their way?" A maid hung out of the door and craned her neck in their direction. "Did ye tell 'em today's the day his nibs got hitched?"

The lad didn't answer. The girl stumbled into the passageway, squinting at them. "Who is it, then? They cannot —" She gasped suddenly and reared back. "Yer lordship! But —what? What are you doin' here?"

"I live here," he answered sardonically.

Hanging onto the wall, the maid stepped forward. "But today was the day you was meant to be marrit! Never say you peached on the poor girl?"

He rolled his eyes. "I won't say it, as I did not *peach* on her."

"But what have ye done wi' 'er, then?"

He shot Charlotte an apologetic look. "I married her. And then I brought her home."

The girl froze. She was close enough now for the candle to illuminate the look of horror on her face. "Ye never did such a thing, surely?"

"Married her? Or brought her home?"

"But . . . we thought ye must be settin' off on a bridal trip! Ye never brought her 'ere without a word to us? Without a warnin'? Our new mistress?"

Whiddon merely gestured toward Charlotte.

The maid moaned and sank down, sliding her back against the wall until she sat on the floor.

Charlotte cleared her throat. "Excuse me," she said clearly. "But *what* is that smell?"

The boy at the door at last closed it. He glanced about and then crossed over to a corner of the hall. Peering down, he said contemplatively, "I think the cat's died, at last."

The maid groaned.

"A dead cat? In the entry hall?" Charlotte's voice raised an octave. "A *dead cat?*"

He shrugged. "Flummoxed, are you? I think I just evened the score." When she raised an indignant brow, he turned to the waiting servant. "Remove it, please."

The boy grinned. "I'll get a shovel."

"Give it a burial," Charlotte told him firmly. "Do not just toss it in a midden heap. Give it a bit of the respect it clearly missed in life." She pushed away from Whiddon and carefully leaned over Old Alf's inert form to snatch up the candle. In the light it shed, he could see her make a face as she set it down again and wiped her fingers. Shooting him a warning look, she moved to shine the light into the adjacent parlor.

Whiddon let her go, hoping she wouldn't find anything but dust and shrouded furniture. She stepped in, looked about, then turned to march down the main corridor. He saw the maid cover her face when Charlotte stopped at the first door.

Gingerly, she turned the nob. Thrusting the candle in, she peered inside, but choked and backed out, closing the door quickly.

"Is that the library?"

"It is, ma'am," the maid whispered.

"What, precisely, is *that* smell?"

"Some o' the books, here and there, might be . . ."

"Yes?"

"Bloomin' wit' a bit of mold." Her head hung in shame.

"I see."

Charlotte said not a word. She just came back and stood before him. The candlelight caught the silver in her eyes as, with a wave of a hand and an arched brow, she asked the question.

"It would drive my father mad, you see," Whiddon said defensively.

"Your father? The man who never comes to London?"

"Yes, well. There's no saying he might not become exasperated enough to come to Town. To deal with me."

She sighed. "And if he did . . ."

"He'd throw a fit."

She closed her eyes. "We will discuss this. At length. But for now, I think I'd just like to go to bed."

He took the candle from her. "Come along, then."

She walked silently by his side while he led her upstairs, all the while trying to recall what the condition of the countess's rooms might be. For the life of him, he could not remember what they looked like, but he knew where they were.

"Here we are." He stepped in and she slowly followed. He winced as he heard the rustle of movement retreating from the light. He raised the candle. More shrouded furniture, a curtained bed, the smell of stale smoke and fetid air.

"No," she said distinctly. "Absolutely not."

~

CHARLOTTE BIT her quivering lip and refused to cry. She was tired and unexpectedly forlorn at the changes in her life and the challenges still to be faced. She certainly hadn't expected a filthy house, an inebriated staff and a dead cat to greet her upon arrival. Good heavens, why must it all be so difficult? She permitted herself a few moments pitiable despair, then dragged in a breath and drew herself together.

Turning to face Whiddon, she watched him evenly. "Where do you sleep?"

He looked startled. "Why?"

"Where. Do. You. Sleep?"

She recognized his suddenly shallow breathing and the widening of his eyes as the first signs of distress. He was distressed at the thought of sharing even something so small with her. She sighed.

"Through here," he said, relenting.

They had connecting doors. She liked the idea.

This was his bedchamber. It was dark, the fire unlit. They truly hadn't expected him back tonight. Whiddon moved about, lighting lamps and candles and the room brightened around her. It was done in cream and beige, with touches of dark wood and deep greens. It was also clean, orderly and comfortably appointed. She could see a sitting room beyond, and another door, closed now, that she guessed was a dressing room.

The sound of an opening door and hurrying feet

preceded the breathless entrance of a servant. He was a man of middle years and trim physique. He looked rumpled and utterly astonished. "My lord! We did not expect your return this evening! You made no mention . . . We thought . . ." He stumbled to a halt when he noticed her at Whiddon's side.

Her husband sighed. "Charlotte, this is my valet, Chapman. Chapman, make your leg to the new countess."

"My lady." Looking mortified, the servant bowed deeply.

"I am happy to meet you, Chapman. Lord Whiddon speaks highly of you." She looked around. "You have the keeping of these rooms?"

"Yes, ma'am."

"Then you are clearly a treasure." She looked about again. "I should like to consult with you tomorrow. After breakfast, if you don't mind. But for now, will you track down my portmanteau and have it brought in here?"

"In here?" Whiddon asked.

"In here," she said firmly. She watched Chapman expectantly.

"Of course, my lady. Shall I also send up one of the maids?"

"No, thank you. Just the portmanteau, then we would like to be left to ourselves until the morning."

"Very good." Bowing again, he left the same way he'd come.

"Your rooms," Whiddon began.

"Are uninhabitable. I heard the rustling when we entered, the same as you. I will sleep here tonight. It looks as if it is habitually vermin-free."

He opened his mouth to say something, then closed it. Pursing his lips, he ran his gaze over her. "Why did you refuse the maid?"

"Because I'm tired and I have no patience to deal with a

frightened and likely drunken girl. You saw how that maid reacted earlier."

He bit back a grin. "Oh, hell. You've likely frightened them into a tizzy down there. They are probably all shaking in their shoes." He considered. "Or they may be plotting against you. They are a disreputable lot."

She stared. "That's how you regard your staff? The people who share your home? Care for your things? Prepare your food? A disreputable lot?"

"They don't prepare my food. And some of them are disreputable. Some are perfectly safe, though, I'm sure."

She shook her head, suddenly certain this was all going to be far messier than she'd already expected. "Well, the hall boy seemed fine, at least."

"Is that who that was?" Whiddon sounded as if she'd solved a puzzle he'd been worrying at. "The hall boy? I think he's new. On second thought, he might be the only one sober. If you send for a maid, he might be the one to respond."

She folded her arms and gave him a mulish look. "It was your oversight that put us in this situation. You didn't tell me of the conditions here and I did not come prepared. I will see what is to be done tomorrow, but tonight, you can help me undress."

He frowned and looked as if he might object, but she forestalled him. "I'm sure it is not your first time undressing a lady."

He, very wisely, did not answer. They stood, braced like a pair of combatants. Her heart began to pound. He stood tall, broad and implacably remote. She stifled the urge to throw herself at him, to burrow into his embrace and reach for his kiss. With another man, it might have worked. It might have breached his walls and thawed his demeanor and led to the wedding night she wished for.

But this was Whiddon, and she knew better. His fingers

were already beating his unhappiness against his leg. He would only retreat further and grow more defensive.

Strategy.

The door opened again, and the valet came in with her luggage. "Here you are, my lady. Are you sure you don't require anything else?"

"No, thank you, Chapman." She turned away as he nodded and left. Shrugging out of her pelisse, she folded it carefully and draped it over a stuffed chair near the cold hearth. She fetched a nightshift from her portmanteau. A new one, lacy and made of fine lawn. She took it with her, returned to the chair and placed her hands on the back of it. "Would you mind helping with my buttons?"

Whiddon nodded rigidly and she turned away, bending her head forward.

His steps came slowly, but she felt him come close behind her. The rasp of his breath sounded loud, and her skin tingled with the feel of him, so near, so large and powerful, looming behind her.

His warm finger traced a faint caress on her nape, then he was unbuttoning her. Her dress sagged forward as he finished. "Now, just the laces of my corset, please? After that, I should be able to manage the rest."

He finished quickly and she breathed a long sigh of relief as the corset loosened. Holding everything against her, she turned and glanced up. "Thank you. It won't take me a minute to change."

His chestnut hair had fallen forward onto his brow. His expression was shuttered. She thought for a moment that he meant to stay where he was, but he gave a sharp nod and moved away to look out of the window.

Moving quickly, she changed into the nightshift, folding each piece of her clothing over the chair. When she finished, she went to him and stood by his side. After a moment, she sighed and leaned against him.

His arm automatically moved around her, but he scowled. "Charlotte," he said in warning.

"I'm sorry. I know. I promised separate lives. But this is only for one night." With her head tucked against his muscled arm, she tilted her face up and smiled at him.

His expression came alive with shifting emotions. Exasperation fought with irritation and gave way to a deep hunger that roiled behind his eyes. He gave a growl that she was sure she could feel starting in his chest and he bent down and kissed her.

His arm snaked around her waist. He hauled her around and pressed her tight against him. Angling his head, he kissed her deeper, harder.

Oh. Good heavens. Yes. This was different from the kiss at the altar. More. Shockingly demanding and blatantly hotter. Beneath the fine lawn of her nightgown, her skin was ablaze. She'd gone molten and melted up against his broad, powerful form.

He made another noise, deep and rending, and pushed her against the wall next to the window. He kissed her like he was starving for her. She raised her arms, wound them around his neck and kissed him back, fiercely. His tongue plunged into her mouth, battling with hers. She gave him kiss for kiss and threaded her fingers in his hair.

He moaned. She felt his manhood, a hard spike pulsing between them. He cupped her breast, kneading it with one hand while the other drifted up to pinch her nipple. Sensation shot through her, from peak to peak and deep into her womb. Her breath was coming fast. She was nothing but sensation and raw, wild *want*.

Suddenly, he stilled. His hands dropped away, and he

turned his face from hers. She could feel the heated air against her skin as he panted and reached for control.

He began to pull away and she watched his mouth as he went. That beautiful, sensuous, commanding mouth.

"No," it said. "This is not what we agreed to."

She raised her eyes to his angry, hungry glare and he took another step back. His gaze raked over her, lingering, then he turned to go. He stopped at the bed, grabbed a pillow and turned away.

"Where are you going?" she whispered.

"Somewhere else. Anywhere else."

He stalked out. The door slammed behind him.

She lifted her fingers to her lips, then tilted her head back and grinned at the ceiling.

Reliving every moment of that embrace, she let down her hair before climbing into the bed. Curled amongst the blankets and pillows that carried his scent, she smiled and fell into a deep and dreamless sleep.

CHAPTER 9

Whiddon sneaked out of the mews just as dawn began to send pink streaks through the sky. The grooms had not yet begun to stir, thank goodness. The house staff certainly was not up and moving, not after last night's debauch. He did see the hall boy in the kitchens when he entered through the back. The wretch smirked at him as he went by, raising his hand in salute and biting off a huge piece of toast at the same time. Whiddon just rolled his eyes and continued on.

He hesitated outside the door to his rooms. His tired brain stirred up an image of Charlotte inside, in his bed, sleepy and warm. With a curse, he kept going and entered Chapman's rooms instead.

The valet had gone already. To fetch breakfast? Whiddon sank into a chair and hung his head in his hands. He'd known he was going to be terrible at marriage, but he hadn't expected to make a mess of it so quickly.

Getting back to his feet, he started to pace. How could he have forgotten to make arrangements for his new wife? His shoulders sagged. It was probably for the best. Now Charlotte would see that she shouldn't count on him. She wouldn't get her hopes up and she wouldn't be disappointed.

Better for everyone, all around.

He threw himself back into the chair. For several moments he watched the brightening sky. Where was Chapman?

The long, uncomfortable and mostly sleepless night began to catch up with him. Laying his head back, he closed his eyes.

He awoke with a start. The room was full of morning light. He heard voices. They came from *his* room.

He flew out into the corridor and flung open his door. Charlotte sat there, in his sitting room, at the table where he habitually took breakfast. She was fully dressed in a gown of sprigged muslin in light blue. It looked worn and she looked achingly young, but her expression was all business as she perused a stack of papers before her. Chapman stood at the hearth, placing crumpets onto a toasting stick.

His crumpets.

"Good morning, Gabriel," Charlotte said brightly. "Sit down, won't you? Chapman and I have already done a thorough inspection of the countess's rooms. Getting them in shape will be my first priority, along with finding a suitable lady's maid." She smiled. "Luckily, things in there are not as bad as I feared. The mattress must go. There's an entire village of mice living in it. The bed hangings and window curtains have played host to rival colonies of moths, I believe, and the chimney is blocked. But the rest of it just needs a thorough scrubbing." She consulted her list and took up a pencil. "Would you care to let me know what the budget should be?"

"Budget?"

"I believe you understand the concept. A limit to the

amount of money you would like me to spend on the project?"

"No. No." He waved a hand, but still did not join her at the table. "Spend what you will. Send the bills to me. Just get it all done quickly."

"That's very generous. Thank you." She was fidgeting with the pencil and all he could think of was the feel of those fingers on his shoulders last night and the shiver of pleasure that had gone down his spine when she buried them in his hair.

"But what of the rest of the house?" she asked.

"What of it?"

"Is there a limit to what you'd like me to spend as I restore the rest of the house?"

"Restore? There's no need for such a bother. Just have your rooms done and stick to them." He gestured. "It works for me."

Her lips pursed and she glanced over at his valet. "When was the last time that the Marquess of Broadham was in this house?"

Chapman shot him a look.

"Chapman?" she demanded.

"He's never been here, madam, not in the six years that I've been here with his lordship."

Her brows raised as she stared at him again. "You've been letting a Mayfair townhouse slide into a molding heap of dust and filth to spite a man who has never been here to discover it?"

"Oh, he knows," Whiddon told her.

"How? You've told him?"

He made a face and shook his head. "No. I don't correspond with my father."

"Then how?"

"He has informants among the servants here."

"Does he? Truly?"

He nodded.

"Well, then we will take care of that. Add it to the list." She narrowed her eyes at him. "Whiddon, you don't mean to send me off to the family estate in Devonshire, do you?"

That startled him from contemplation of her creamy skin against the sky blue of her gown. "God's teeth, no. I wouldn't rescue you from one pit of despair just to consign you to another."

"Well, I must thank you for that. But may I ask, what do you do when you wish to invite your friends over?"

"I don't. I meet them elsewhere."

"I see. Where?"

"At the club. At a chophouse. At an event. At their homes. Just, elsewhere."

She scowled. "Several of those options are not open to me. And I am sorry, but I will not be content to keep just to a couple of rooms." She folded her arms, pushing her bosom higher. "Unless you intend to change your mind about our arrangement—"

"No," he interrupted harshly. Glancing at Chapman he jerked his head. "Please give me a moment alone with the countess."

The valet fled, looking relieved.

Whiddon retreated to a safe spot behind a sofa. "There is no need for the servants to know of our private agreements."

"Servants always know," she told him. "Especially when there are disagreements."

"We are not having a disagreement."

"I am." She lifted her chin. "You don't wish for me to interfere with your lifestyle. Fine. I have agreed to it. But I must be free to make some sort of life for myself. That means I will need the trappings of a lady. It means making calls and receiving them. *Here*. Luncheons. Teas. Committee meetings, perhaps. Not to mention the fact that you have promised me that I may have my siblings to visit."

He groaned, knowing he could not deny it.

"This house will be cleaned, organized and restored from the attics to the basements," she said firmly.

"Oh, hell," he moaned. "There will be noise. Workmen. Upheaval."

"Better than filth, mold and decay," she said, unrelenting.

"Damn it, Charlotte." This was exactly what he did not want. Interference. Change.

"I will do my best to keep the commotion to a minimum," she vowed. Her gaze softened. "I am sorry to remove the anticipation of your father's ire, but you can take comfort in knowing you will not be living like him. It will not be about the appearances. I will be sure this house is in perfectly good repair, comfort and taste."

Damn it all to hell. He didn't want to be understood. He didn't want flashing eyes or a generous, blue-clad bosom tempting him before he'd had coffee. Or crumpets.

Crumpets.

He crossed to the fire and pulled out the toasting sticks. Nothing but charred lumps were left at the ends. He tossed them down and turned to leave.

"Where are you going?" she asked.

"To have breakfast at the club. And to find a modicum of peace!"

He stalked to Chapman's room and entered without knocking. "Give me any information you've got on the Comte de Perette."

Silently, the valet retrieved a file from a small escritoire.

Whiddon snatched it and turned to go. At the door, he hesitated. "One of my bed pillows is in the traveling coach. Fetch it before someone finds it."

He managed not to slam the door as he left.

Barely.

～

"The staff are assembled and ready, my lady."

"Thank you, Chapman." She beckoned the valet to take a seat across from her. "Before we go down, may I have a quick word?"

"Of course, madam."

She regarded him with approval. "It looks as if you've done a most impressive job under strange and difficult circumstances. I need to hire a lady's maid and it seems to me that she'll require the same sort of *extra* skills that you possess. I thought perhaps that you might know someone suitable."

"What qualities are you looking for, my lady?"

"Well, she must be experienced. Someone who understands social intricacies and knows how to outfit a countess for whatever I might encounter. Goodness knows we'll need someone around here with that sort of knowledge. She'll need all the usual skills—repair and sewing and caring for a wardrobe and my rooms. In addition, though, I think I shall require someone with . . . backbone."

"I see."

"You do, I'm sure. I would guess that you exercise confidence and a certain savviness to be able to do your job and also interact with the staff, here."

"True."

"I will require the same in my maid. And loyalty. To me. I suspect I will need her to advocate for me here as well as to make me presentable for the outside."

He gave her a shrewd look. "You are about to stir things up about here, aren't you, ma'am?"

"Oh, yes. I believe I am."

"Good. It's time someone did."

"So, do you think you might know someone who would be interested in the job?"

"Possibly." He cleared his throat. "As you noted, I do attend to duties that are outside a valet's usual purview. I am also very well compensated for doing so."

"Oh, well, that should present no problem. You heard his lordship." She waved a hand. "Apparently, money is no object. The right maid will, of course, be compensated for her extra qualities."

"Very good. I believe I might know someone to ask. She is indeed experienced, but she is not best pleased with the situation she has now. She also has the . . . strength of character that you require."

"Excellent. Will you set up a meeting?" She grimaced. "At a tea shop, perhaps. She must be warned before she shows up here."

"Very wise. I will make the arrangements."

"Thank you. Now, let's see to the staff, shall we?"

They awaited her in the entry hall at the bottom of the stairs and a motley crew they were, too. She gazed intently at each of them, more than a little thrilled at the idea of using her abilities to figure them out.

A youngish man, perhaps in his mid-twenties, stood at the head of the line. He stepped forward and Chapman introduced him as Hurley.

"I am the house steward, ma'am. It is a pleasure to meet you."

It was not a sentiment he professed with any level of sincerity, but Charlotte smiled warmly at him. "Goodness, you scarcely seem old enough to hold such a position of responsibility. You must be skilled indeed to have achieved such a post at so young an age."

He smiled. "I do like to think so, ma'am," he said

smoothly. "My family has been connected with the earl's for years. I am happy to serve in such a capacity."

And happy to spy for the marquess? She recalled Gabriel's words and looked him over carefully. He was quite smartly dressed and sported a waistcoat of silver grey, lavishly embroidered with a floral design in rose and white. "That is quite a beautiful waistcoat, Hurley."

He preened the smallest bit. "Thank you, my lady. I enjoy a bit of fashion here and there." He rolled his eyes. "I am not one of Brummel's followers. Too plain for me. I do like a bit of color."

"I agree with you there. I like a gentleman who can wear colors."

He nodded. "This waistcoat was done by Mr. Timms, of Bond Street. He's doing another for me, of cream silk and embroidery of teal and the palest pink. I came up with the design myself."

"I look forward to seeing it, then."

"It will be a while yet, madam. But in a little over a month's time, I'll have a fine, new piece to include in my wardrobe. As I'm sure you know, quality work is worth waiting for."

"Well, I'm glad enough to hear you think so, for quality work is exactly what I shall be looking for."

He looked surprised but bowed. That one would bear watching. He tried to appear at ease, but there were tell-tale signs of tension in him. The only thing that did feel sincere about him, in fact, was the hint of malice in his eyes as he straightened. Nodding, she moved on to meet the cook, Mrs. Prigg. The woman wore a wary expression and an unsightly, soiled apron.

Charlotte's fingers twitched. Oh, this was going to be a challenge. She wanted suddenly, to sketch each of them. To observe and study.

Margie was next. She was the maid who had been so inebriated and embarrassed last night. Old Alf was the footman who had been stretched out on the floor. He still looked cupshot, to be honest. After that, there were two more housemaids, two kitchen maids and the hall boy, who lurked in the back.

"Is there no housekeeper?" she asked in surprise as the introductions were finished.

"Can't keep one," Margie volunteered.

"We do well enough without one," Hurley said, shooting the maid a silencing look.

Charlotte ran a dubious gaze around and then nodded and smiled. "Then it will fall to you to give me a tour, Hurley." She held out a hand to Chapman, who handed her a notebook.

"Of course." Hurley gave her a condescending smile and gestured toward the room behind her. "The main rooms begin here, at the front parlor."

"Not just the main rooms. I want to see everything," Charlotte clarified.

"Everything?"

"All of it. Every nook and cranny," she confirmed. "I gather it will take some time. Let's begin." She looked to the maids. "Margie, I will put you in charge of starting on my rooms while I am busy with the tour. Take the other girls with you. I want the mattress taken out, as well as the bed hangings and the curtains. After they are gone, you can start cleaning and polishing everything, from ceiling to floor."

Margie's eyes widened. "Yes, my lady."

Charlotte spent the rest of the morning and the early afternoon forcing Hurley to take her all over the house. He tried to skip several spots, but she insisted on seeing it all, from the attics, to the servants' quarters, family and formal rooms, to the kitchens, pantries, wine cellar and storage cellars. She made intricate notes in each room and when they were done, she sat down in Gabriel's sitting room to a late luncheon of lukewarm soup and coarse bread, going over everything and prioritizing tasks.

With a sigh, she pushed away the unappetizing food and drew out another notebook. She summoned Chapman, determined to begin on the second prong of her plan.

"I need a few more moments of your time," she told the valet when he answered. "Come and sit. You've been with Lord Whiddon long enough to thoroughly know his tastes . . ."

CHAPTER 10

Whiddon was mourning the lack of crumpets with his breakfast when Tensford and Sterne showed up. They took seats at his table and called for a porter to bring another.

"Chester will be here directly," Tensford told him. "But why in three hells are you here? Shouldn't you still be abed with your bride?"

"She's cleaning the house," he replied sullenly.

His friends exchanged glances. "Ah, we thought that might happen," Sterne said. "Truly, though, it's a good thing."

"You didn't honestly expect her to live like that, did you?" Tensford's brows were raised. "It's time. If your father hasn't shown up by now . . ."

"Yes, but he might still come thundering in when he hears of the marriage—and now I will have lost my chance."

"Lost your chance to do what?" Chester had arrived. He took a seat and inserted himself into the conversation at the same time.

"To give my father fits when he sees the townhouse,"

Whiddon said, swatting his friend's fingers away from his bacon.

"Charlotte is cleaning," Sterne told Chester.

"Already?" Chester shrugged. "You have to admit, it will be nice to be able to visit him at home."

"Not any time soon," Whiddon grumbled. "It will be nothing but chaos for weeks."

"You'll survive," Tensford soothed. "And in the meantime, just enjoy the compensations of married life."

"Compensations? It's been naught but complications, rather, from beginning to end."

The other three stared at each other, then at him.

"He's not sleeping with her!" Chester blurted.

"Why aren't you sleeping with her?" Sterne asked.

"Hell and damnation," Tensford swore. "Whiddon, what is wrong?"

"Nothing is wrong."

"Don't you want to sleep with her?" asked Chester, incredulous.

"Of course I do! I don't need to, though."

"You don't want to need to," Tensford said, wisely. Damn him.

"I just think it will be for the best if we wait."

"Wait for what?" Chester looked truly puzzled.

"For things to settle down. For us to grow . . . used to each other." For him to gain some distance and get his volatile emotions under control.

Glances flew between the others again.

"Two days," Chester declared. "Three, tops."

"I give it a week," Sterne countered.

Tensford merely watched Whiddon closely.

Whiddon threw down his napkin. "If I hear of this hitting a betting book, I'll string each one of you up by your balls, and then *none* of us will be sleeping with our wives."

"You should know better," Tensford reproached.

"What I know is that it is time for me to seek out my next refugee. I promised not to pursue another without telling all of you, so let this serve as your notice." He stood.

Chester did as well. "I'll go with you. You were not to go alone, that was the bargain. You need one of us with you, at least until you discover if the latest one is dangerous."

"Fine." Whiddon moved his gaze around the table. "None of your wives needs to know any of this. *Any* of it."

"Oh, we won't say a word." Sterne's eyes were alight with laughter.

"We won't have to, I'll wager," Tensford told him. "Be careful, both of you."

∽

HOLDING the paper up into the afternoon light, Whiddon looked over Chapman's list. A stray wind ruffled his hair and brought with it the scent of the river. He frowned as it triggered a sudden memory.

"Chester, do you recall me telling you about the last refugee? The one I found in a warehouse down at the docks?"

"The one who beat you about? No, I'd forgotten," his friend said sarcastically. "Of course, I remember."

"I just remembered something. Something odd. I'd forgotten, because I was focused on the drubbing they gave me."

"What is it?"

"Yet. He said yet. Did I have his mother's pearls, *yet*? I meant to ask him what he meant."

"But you were too busy getting beaten black and blue?"

"Well, yes. What could he have meant by that?"

"I don't know, but I think we should concentrate on one at a time. What does Chapman say about this one?"

The valet had listed three possible contacts, and so far, two had proved to be a waste of time. Both swore they knew nothing of the Comte de Perette. Both insisted they had heard nothing of the man since they'd fled the Terror in France, years ago.

Now, he stood with Chester outside the last address. "Not much. The man is an artist of some sort. Let's go."

The door was located in a cramped, cobbled courtyard not far from Leadenhall Market. Several worn stairs led down to what promised to be a dark, dank hovel of a place, but fortunately, they did not have to go in. The door stood open and the occupant sat outside, bent over a small easel.

"Monsieur Laspar?"

The grizzled man scowled as Chester moved closer. "Stay out of the light, will you?" He squinted down at the illustration he was working on.

"You've got the King's nose all wrong," Chester pointed out.

"You knew who he was, did you not?" the man snarled back. He looked up and his eyes widened. "Ah, but you're..." He fixed his gaze on Whiddon. "And you are..."

"We are looking for someone," Whiddon said. "We heard you could help."

A crafty look stole across the man's face and Whiddon wondered how much this was going to cost him. "Who is it you seek?"

"The Comte de Perette."

The man's expression closed. He turned back to his illustration. "No. Very sorry. I'm not familiar with that name."

Whiddon reached for calm. Chapman's work was always thorough, and his information was usually flawless. Today they were being put off. But why? He looked over the man's project. "You create caricatures for the print shops and broad sheets?"

"When I can find a subject amusing enough," the man muttered.

Whiddon was more than familiar with the satirical prints. He and the rest of his friends had been the subject of them more than once. He studied the image more closely. "I recognize your style, I believe. Didn't you draw the one of me and Keswick racing ponies across Hampstead Heath?"

The man's face lit up. "Yes, indeed, I did. Although that one nearly drew itself, so amusing it was to see the pair of you, feet dragging on the ground while the ponies trotted on and you sang so loudly—and so badly." He shook his head. "Ah, that one sold so many copies," he said with fond remembrance. "I also did the one of you last summer, with your friend Sterne, chasing a stone crocodile across London."

"Oh. I must have missed that one." He folded his arms. "Perhaps we might work out a bargain."

"Would that we could," the man said mournfully.

"We know you have information on Perette."

Laspar shook his head. "I don't."

Chester moved closer, his large form further blocking the light.

"I cannot," the man whispered.

"No one would know we heard anything from you," Whiddon assured him. "You have our word on it, as gentlemen."

"It's not that I don't trust you, sir."

"We would make it worth your while." He held up a gold guinea.

Laspar thought about it. "Would you give me exclusive access to the next prank the pair of you put together?"

"No." Whiddon nodded his head toward the man's rooms. "But if you have copies of the broadsheets you've done of me, I will sign them. They will fetch a decent price from certain collectors."

The man looked tempted.

"You won't even need to do anything with them, straightaway. Save them. Put them back against a time when your sales run dry. Or when I make a bigger fool of myself," he said wryly.

Laspar narrowed his eyes. "And you will not say you heard anything from me?"

"We will not."

The artist scrambled from his seat. "Wait here. I'll find the copies."

Whiddon shared a glance with Chester as the man disappeared. Chester leaned in to examine the illustration on the easel. "He's not that good, is he?"

"He's no Cruikshank, but that one has pledged not to mock the King, further." He shrugged. "If he knows something..."

Laspar emerged with a fistful of papers and a well of black ink.

"I'll sign two each," Whiddon told him. "The scarcer they are, the more valuable they will be."

Laspar nodded and watched avidly while Whiddon affixed his signature. He looked nervous gain, though, when Whiddon held the papers up. "Tell us," he reminded the man.

The older man looked around furtively. "Look to Perry Brothers Printing and Engraving," he said, his voice low. "Ask for Perry. Go early, while he is in a good mood. And remember—you heard nothing from me."

Whiddon gave him the papers and a nod of thanks. The man stood and watched them go. He raised a hand as they passed back out onto the street.

"This one sounds as if he might be a challenge," Chester ventured as they made their way to where the carriage waited.

"Go early," Whiddon mused. "That's what he said. I suppose we'd be foolish not to listen."

"Yes. It's growing late. I should get home, in any case. I told Julia I would be home for dinner."

"I'll drop you off, then."

"And we'll meet for breakfast, tomorrow, and head out together?"

Whiddon agreed. He scowled once his friend climbed out in front of his home. In the old days they would have gone to a chop house for a meal before heading out to make a night of it. He thought about searching out Tensford, but he likely had plans, too, and he would question him about why he wasn't at home with his new wife.

He was in a mood by the time he reached home. His disposition was not improved when he entered and heard a loud banging from above. Old Alf was nowhere to be seen, but a movement caught Whiddon's eye up on the stair landing. It was the hall boy. The slight figure slipped away and in a moment the pounding above stopped.

Whiddon continued on to his rooms and heaved a sigh of relief when he entered. It was brightly lit, warm—and empty. Slumping into a chair before the fire, he let himself slip into a good brood.

It was interrupted within minutes when a knock sounded. Old Alf came in with a tray. Whiddon stared. The footman had never been in his rooms, in his memory.

"Compliments of the countess," the old man wheezed. He set the tray down on the table, bowed and withdrew.

Whiddon was too curious to ignore it. His stomach growled when he lifted the lid and warm, comforting aromas wafted out. There was a cooled bottle of ale and a crusty pie, leaking brown gravy at one seam. He sniffed appreciatively. Steak and kidney. There was a note, too. He sat, took a large bite of the pie and unfolded the paper.

DEB MARLOWE

. . .

Gabriel,
 I refused to eat the slab of sauce-covered raw meat your cook tried to pass off as dinner. I ordered a lovely pie from my favorite cook shop and thought you might like one, too.
 Charlotte

There was a second page, too. It was a sheet of paper, covered with sketches, all of the same woman. She wore a cap and looked bright and animated in one. In another she concentrated fiercely on something she stirred in a bowl. A third showed her shaking out a length of fabric. He frowned at the images as he ate and finally decided she was one of his maids. The one that had met them in the entry hall last night, wasn't it? God's teeth—had that only been last night?

Sated, he sat back and stared at the page again. Charlotte was talented, no doubt. She'd caught the girl exactly and portrayed her with a tender and respectful dose of humor. He could nearly feel the girl's eagerness. But why had Charlotte sent it to him?

Only one way to find out.

He was on his feet and knocking on their connecting door before he could think better of it. He went on through before she could think better of it.

Caught by surprise, he halted on the other side. The room was bright with the light of several lamps and a multitude of candles. It was scrupulously clean, though somewhat bare. The bed was made up, though it still lacked hangings. The dressing room door stood open, and he could see a bath inside, still full. All of this he caught in a swift glance, before his gaze locked on the figure of his wife, sitting before the fire with a book in her lap. Her long hair was combed to one side, a waterfall of gold, drying in the heat of the flames.

Seeing him enter, she closed her book, straightened and smiled. Gesturing, she bade him to take the chair across from her.

He wanted to move, but his traitorous brain was locked on the sight of her, curled up so comfortably and beckoning him to come and share. It focused on the curling ends of her hair, draped over her shoulder and caressing her breast. It lay right where he'd touched her when he'd kissed her. He could feel the warm weight of her flesh in his hand, still.

"You see?" She smiled and waved a hand to encompass the room. "We managed it. Got enough done for me to sleep here, in any case. Your rooms are your own, again."

There they were, the silver flecks in her blue eyes. They shone like stars in the fire light. "Oh, yes. Thank you."

"Come and sit. Did you want something?"

God's teeth. Yes, he wanted something. He wanted to kiss her again, her mouth on his, her body beneath him. He wanted her . . . everything.

He cleared his throat and suddenly recalled the paper in his hand. He held it up. "Yes. I wanted to know why you are drawing sketches of the maid."

She beckoned again and he—finally—moved forward and sat across from her. If, for a moment, he might have harbored the fear that she might try to seduce him, it was put to rest by the sight of her. She was scrubbed clean and fresh and wrapped up tightly in an old flannel robe that was too large and cinched up to her chin.

"Oh, that." She looked slightly uncomfortable. "It's what I do, when I'm trying to . . . learn someone. I watch and listen and draw and think."

"You're trying to learn the maid?"

"Yes, and I think I like her."

"I could tell."

She looked surprised. "You can?"

He handed over the page. "From the way you drew her. I could see that you liked her."

"Could you?" She blinked down at the images she'd created as if she'd never realized she was revealing things about herself as she studied others. She didn't look entirely happy about it, either. He didn't blame her. If it were him, he'd toss away his charcoal and never pick it up again.

"Well." She nodded. "I do like her. She's quite willing, almost relieved, to be tackling the house. She knows what she's about, too." She lifted her head and breathed in. "Do you smell that?"

"What?"

"Just smell," she ordered.

Dutifully, he leaned forward and sniffed. "I smell rose water."

Unexpectedly, she flushed, a deep pink that spread up from the closely drawn collar of her robe. "That's just my bath water." She pointed. "Go stand over there and try again."

He did, eager to get away from the image that overtook him—laying her on the bed, peeling away her nightclothes and exploring to find that heady scent in her every nook and cranny.

Damnation, now he was flushing. He moved behind the bed and sniffed. "Lemon? Beeswax?"

"Yes. Exactly. Margie possessed a lovely receipt for a polish that cleans and shines and leaves behind such a fresh scent. She wanted to mix it up, but the household didn't contain the supplies for the making of it."

"Margie is the maid?"

She nodded.

"Well, I suppose it makes sense," he pointed out as he

returned. "They wouldn't have had use for such things before."

"Yes, but it was the strangest thing. She did not wish to ask the cook to put the ingredients on her market list. She wouldn't say why, she just asked permission to go herself."

"Perhaps she has a beau in one of the market stalls."

"I accompanied her. She didn't even attempt to linger, but hurried right back to mix up her concoction."

"All right, then." He waited. "From your manner, I assume there is some other significance I'm missing?"

"I believe someone in your household is cheating you, Gabriel, and Margie knows it."

"Oh, well, yes. It's very likely."

"*You* knew?"

"Well, I didn't *know*. Not for sure. But I did tell you they are a disreputable lot."

She heaved and exasperated sigh. "I take it, then, that you will not mind if I . . . dispose . . . of a few of them?"

His gaze sharpened.

"I'm in no hurry," she assured him. "I want to see how things go as I put them all to work, as in any other Mayfair home."

He raised his brow. "Are you going to fill a sketch book with images of *all* of the staff?"

Her chin lifted. "I very likely will. I will also be going through the household accounts. I believe I shall go back to the market and compare the prices charged and those entered in the books. If the cook is cheating you, then she will be dismissed. Frankly, I should send her packing based on this day's offering of meals, alone."

"Handle it as you will. But find someone who can make a pie like the one you sent me, will you?" His gaze softened as he glanced at her. "Thank you, by the way."

"They are delicious, aren't they?" She hesitated. "Unless

you object, I also mean to make some changes in the furnishings in the rest of the house. Will you mind?"

"No." He sighed. "If you insist on cleaning the mess, then you might as well have it all the way you want it."

She looked gratified. "Thank you."

"I have thought about it and I imagine that discovering that I married you hastily, in the midst of scandal and without telling him, will send my father into a rage. That will have to do."

"Yes, well. So glad I could provide a rage-inducing substitute," she said wryly.

"As am I." He straightened suddenly. "I will make sure that my man of business knows to deliver the quarterly household monies to you from now on. But, Charlotte, I do have to warn you. Don't fire Hurley unless you have good cause."

She frowned. "I wouldn't." He could nearly see the gears turning in her head. "But why do you say so?" Her eyes narrowed. "Is he the one spying on you and sending word of you to your father?"

He only shrugged.

"I don't like the idea," she declared. "In fact, I severely dislike it. It's disloyal. I don't want him watching us and sending gossip to a man I don't know, and you despise."

"Nonetheless, you will heed me. Hurley is well connected back in Devon. We cannot dismiss him without an ironclad reason. It will kick up a fuss that you won't understand. Exactly the sort of large and complicated mess I don't wish to deal with."

"Very well."

Now she was brooding and staring into the fire. He sat back, drowsy, full and content, and watched her.

Don't you want to sleep with her? Chester's incredulous question drifted into his head. Of course, he wanted to. He was a man, and she was a beauty. More than that, she was talented and funny and thoughtful and interesting in a way that other women never had been. But she was a woman and likely to attribute more along with a physical relationship. To tangle it up with feelings and expectations he was in no position to return or fill.

He would stick to the plan, despite the fine sight of her profile against the flames. In spite of the warmth and humor that showed so often behind her blue eyes. Despite the shining river of gold her hair became when it hung down over her shoulders and curled into beckoning tendrils and despite the stirring of his cock, eager to answer.

She looked over at him, suddenly, and seemed surprised to find him staring at her.

"Well, then," she said, standing and moving away from the fire. "I think Margie has forgotten to come back and empty the tub."

More likely the maid knew he was in here and thought they were . . . otherwise engaged. His groin tightened further at the thought.

"It's late," she said on a yawn. "You must be tired. I know I am and tomorrow promises to be an even busier day."

Oh. She was waiting for him to leave.

"Yes, well." Reluctantly, he stood. "I'll bid you goodnight."

"Thank you, Gabriel. For everything." She smiled sleepily. "Goodnight."

He went back to his rooms, closing the door behind him. He stood there for a long moment, lost in thought.

He started when Chapman entered. "There you are, my lord." He paused and stared at his hand. "Why is the door latch sticky?" Shaking his head, he asked, "Shall I ring for a bath?"

Suddenly Whiddon felt cold and . . . bereft. "No. I'm tired. I just need to sleep." That was all that was awry, surely.

"Of course, sir." The valet puttered about, turning down

the bed and the lamps. He reached to help Whiddon from his coat, and began to fold it to put away, but suddenly, he couldn't stand the fussing.

"Just leave it for now, Chapman. I'll be fine. I'll see you in the morning."

His valet nodded and left him. Whiddon slowly peeled off his clothes and blew out the remaining candles. The dark enfolded him. He was exhausted. Not surprising, after a restless night and a long day. Still, he stared at the ceiling for a good while before, at last, he rolled over and drifted to sleep.

CHAPTER 11

Charlotte woke early the next morning. Dawn was only a low shimmer in the eastern sky and the house lay quiet. Too quiet.

Pulling on a light gown with simple buttons, she wrapped herself in a shawl and ventured out into the house. She'd thought there would be a bustle in the kitchens, but all lay dark and quiet, there, too. With a sigh, she went to the front door, unlocked it and stepped out onto the front stoop.

Ah. There. She drew a deep breath. That was better. The garden in the middle of the square was coming awake and alive with the first sleepy chirps of birdsong. From beyond the square came the sound of rumbling carts and the start of early morning traffic. She closed her eyes and let the sounds soothe her.

She jumped, though, when the door behind her suddenly swung open. Whiddon stepped out, his jaw dropping in surprise. "Charlotte? What are you doing out here?"

Her heart twisted a little. He looked better this morning. Rested. Not so . . . haunted. She wished she'd had a hand in the improvement.

"Listening to the world wake up," she answered with a shrug. "The house is too quiet."

His brow lowered. "Is there such a thing as too quiet?"

"Yes." She pulled the shawl tighter around her shoulders. "There is."

She wanted him to ask, to inquire about the dark thoughts that drove her to fill the silence—all the silences. But he didn't wish to. She could see it in his face. The need to move on, to escape.

And she wouldn't force it. Not yet. She would stick to her plan. So, she smiled and nodded. "You must have important business, to get you up so early."

"Yes." He took a step down, eager to move on.

"Have a good day, Gabriel."

He turned back. Paused.

Their gazes met. His eyes looked very green against the brightening background of the lush garden square.

"What is wrong with the quiet, Charlotte?"

She hadn't been expecting it. Triumph and pleasure leaped sharply inside of her, but she took care not to show it.

"It reminds me too much of my father."

He frowned. "Not good memories, then."

"No. Though I do have good recollections of him, to be sure. There was a time when he was carefree and full of songs and smiles and bracing, warm hugs. But he came back at the end of the war . . . changed."

Understanding shone in his expression. "Many men did."

"There were still bright spots, but he grew increasingly broody. Querulous. Distant. It was as if he'd retreated far away, or deep inside himself. Those were the times when he could not bear any noise. None at all." She sighed. "Not so easy, with small children in the house."

"No. It wouldn't be." His head turned and he looked out over the garden. "At least you have the good memories. If our father was quiet, he was likely plotting something. If he was loud, then one of us was being railed at for not portraying the perfect image." He shrugged. "But at least we had each other. Until my mother died, in any case."

"How old were you when your sister was born?" she asked quietly.

He had to think. "Seven, perhaps. I think William was four."

"I was eight when George was born. I was in love."

His expression lightened a bit. "Yes," he said vaguely. "There is little better than a baby's laughter, is there?"

He snapped back to himself and cut her a look—and she mortified herself by blushing furiously.

"I must be going." He paused and she flushed again as he met her gaze directly. "Good day to you, Charlotte."

She nodded and watched as he walked away. When his powerful form disappeared into London's streets, she turned to go and see if the household had begun to awaken.

CHARLOTTE DID NOT SEE her husband at all for the rest of the day and he was gone by the time she arose the next morning. After she dressed, she stared at the breakfast tray she'd requested from the kitchen. She'd perched upon her bed to eat, but she meant to copy Gabriel's idea and have a table and chairs in here—perhaps by the window.

Or perhaps somewhere else. Staring, she remembered how he'd kissed her next to the window in his room. Propped her up against the wall and kissed her so soundly and touched her so urgently. Perhaps she could tempt him into doing it again, here, by her window.

She would place the table elsewhere—and make sure to have two chairs.

The breakfast tray distracted her from such pleasant musings. She'd asked for a boiled egg and toast. She knew a little about cooking. Enough to understand a boiled egg needed to be actually immersed in boiling water. This one might have been passed over a flame. Once. Perhaps. The toast, however, more closely resembled flat slabs of coal.

She'd be more distraught over the situation if she hadn't had the foresight to order a few pastries along with last evening's pie—and charged Margie with finding a metal-lined box to keep them in, and the rodents out. She kept the tea pot and sent the rest of the tray back and enjoyed her impromptu breakfast while she went over her lists.

She couldn't quite understand what Mrs. Prigg was trying to accomplish, sending up such terrible fare. Was it a message? Did everyone in this house want to warn her not to expect anything of them? Well, they would see. All of the staff and their master, too.

Charlotte wasn't too upset over the latest culinary offense. She had two main projects in play now. The house needed attention, but Whiddon was her real focus. Both schemes required a decent, if not sublime, cook. And that meant Mrs. Prigg must go.

She resolved to take care of it, first thing. However, she found Margie lurking just outside her door when she emerged.

"Good morning, my lady!" The maid poked her head in the door. "Shall we finish washing down the walls of your sitting room?"

Here, at least, was someone willing to work with her. "Yes, please, Margie. Let's finish in here. And will you send Alfred and the hall boy up to the attics to bring down that drum table of elm and yew? Scrub it down well and we'll find a place for it in here."

"Yes, ma'am. We'll have all that done in two shakes of a lamb's tail."

That gave her pause. She didn't know how difficult her confrontation with the cook would be. She'd rather the three young maids were well occupied upstairs for a while. "I do want to get started on the entry hall and the parlor downstairs, but I had a thought this morning. Step across here with me? I want to see the light in these rooms." She led the way to another set of connected bedrooms further down the passage. She went in, pulling the curtains wide and passing into the connected room, as well.

"Yes. This will do. I had the idea to bring in a group of seamstresses. They can live in while we go through the house. Most of the hangings, bedding and some of the linens will all need replacing. The light is good in here and—"

"Ahem."

She turned to find old Alf in the doorway. "Excuse me, my lady. Mr. Cheltan is downstairs. He has requested an audience with you."

"Oh? Who is Mr. Cheltan?"

"He is Lord Whiddon's man of business."

"Very well." She paused. "Where does Lord Whiddon usually meet him?"

"In his offices."

She sighed. "Where do they meet when Mr. Cheltan comes here?"

"Oh. In his sitting room, ma'am."

"Show him in there, please, then, Alfred. Thank you. Tell him I'll be there directly."

"But . . . ma'am!" Old Alf looked aghast. "No one but Chapman, his lordship and his invited guests are allowed in those rooms."

Charlotte looked to Margie. "Is there anywhere else decent enough to put him?"

The girl reddened. "No, ma'am."

"Alfred, do you expect that Lord Whiddon has barred me from his rooms?"

"Well, you were in an all-fired hurry to get yours in order," he answered.

She raised a brow at him.

"Ma'am," he added.

"Put him in his lordship's sitting room, as I said, Alfred. Thank you."

The footman, obviously disapproving, bowed and left. On a hunch, Charlotte crossed to the door and bent to inspect the latch. As she'd thought. Sticky.

Sighing, she gave Margie a list of things to check in the rooms and went out to meet Mr. Cheltan.

WHIDDON WAS HAVING A LESS productive time of it. He and Chester had finally tracked down the location of Perry Brothers Printing and Engraving. They arrived early, but the place was open. The small front room, though, held only a counter, behind which sat stacks of assorted paper, newspapers, books and chap books and stacked printing trays filled with type. The walls were covered with notices, tracts, pamphlets, broadsheets and satirical prints. A door back there led to the printing rooms, if the ruckus coming from behind it was to be believed.

"Good morning, gentlemen."

A girl stood behind the counter. On guard—that was the impression she gave. She had dark hair and slanted, knowing eyes and a wide mouth that smiled in welcome. The smile was patently false.

"Good morning." Whiddon stepped up to the counter. "We should like to see Mr. Perry."

The deceitful smile held fast. "I'm sorry. Mr. Perry isn't in today. But if you tell me the sort of project you are interested in, I can match you with someone who can help you."

Chester was examining a satirical print showcasing a dandy on parade in the park, his pantaloons filled with a breeze that threatened to lift him off the ground. "How much does Mr. Perry pay for an original print like this?" he asked.

"I believe it varies, depending on the quality, and also on the subject," the girl answered. "Are you an artist, yourself, sir?"

"No. I am not, but I do know a fair few."

"We're here on a personal matter, not business," Whiddon told the girl. "When might we return and expect to find Mr. Perry available?"

"I couldn't say, sir. His schedule is erratic. Why don't you leave your card and I'll give it to him when next I see him?"

"Please just tell him that Whiddon would like to meet with him."

"Of course, sir." She smiled and nodded, and he turned to go.

Just as he and Chester reached the door, a great crash sounded in the printing room beyond the counter. The racket stopped. A man cried out. "I'm sorry, *monsieur*! A mistake! Forgive me."

There came a crack and then another cry. "Yes, Mr. Perry. Of course, I meant Perry, sir."

Ominous silence sounded for a moment, but it was broken by a barrage of low, vicious-sounding French and, after a moment, a shout of pain.

Whiddon turned back.

"No, my lord." The girl had both hands braced on the counter, as if she meant to block his way. She shook her head. "Go, now," she whispered.

Another anguished cry.

Whiddon didn't move.

"You'll only make things worse."

Chester tugged his arm. With a last look back, Whiddon followed him outside. They walked past several other store fronts before Chester rubbed his hands and grinned. "Well. Now it's getting interesting. Perry must be your elusive refugee, yes?"

"Perhaps."

"Well, that girl *my lorded* you quick enough. She knew who you were, the whole time."

He nodded grimly. "We need more information. Come on." Whiddon nodded toward an alley. "Let's go around to the back and see if there is a spot where we can keep an eye on the comings and goings of the place."

∾

"Oh, Charlotte, do come and see this one." Penelope Sterne's eyes were bright as she bent over a set of chairs. "It's a library chair, and it also converts to library stairs, so that you may reach the high shelves!"

"It's ingenious to be sure, but I haven't even begun on the library yet." Charlotte shuddered. "I suspect I'll have to throw out half the books and furnishings and scrub the place several times over, but I must have a couple of living spaces completed before I tackle such a task." She moved on, her critical eye moving over the selection of furniture Mr. Morgan and Mr. Sanders offered in their extensive shop.

"I'm impressed with how much you've accomplished in such a short time," Julia, Lady Chester, told her with a grin of approval.

"Most of the staff is willing, thank goodness. I do wish to get everything in order quickly so that I might send for my brother and sister. I miss them dreadfully. Thankfully, the new cook handled the cleaning of the kitchens. He refused to cook so much as a loaf until they had gone over the place from ceiling to floor and every shelf, pot, pan and implement in between."

"Hunger is a great motivator," Julia said wryly.

"Yes, and he won their devotion with the first meal he served them." She sighed. "He won mine too, with the most flavorful roast I've ever tasted. He is a great believer in culinary seduction, too, and will prove to be very useful to me, I'm sure." She was distracted, suddenly, by a set of chairs in a corner. "Oh, yes. These are perfect. The elm wood will match the table perfectly and I can have cushions sewn for the seats, perhaps in a sage colored green that will go with the new hangings."

"Sounds like we need a trip to the linen drapers. What a trial," Penelope teased.

"I do love a good house project," Julia said. "But Charlotte, tell us what we truly wish to know. How goes it with Whiddon?"

"I haven't actually seen him at all over the last two days," she admitted.

"I've scarcely seen Chester either." Julia stuck out her lip in a mock pout. "Whatever the two of them are up to, it's keeping them busy at all hours."

Charlotte grinned. "I have continued to implement my strategies. How effective have they been?" She shrugged. "I suppose I will learn that when next I see him."

"I have the utmost respect for your restraint," Penelope said in earnest. "Whiddon is stubborn and likely to shy like a nervous and irritable stallion if he gets even a hint of your goals."

"Yes, and run as far and fast as possible, too—if you don't mind if I continue your analogy. I must be careful. But it is time to take things a step further—and I meant to ask your help."

"Do tell!" Julia urged.

"Well, I am excited at the idea of attending Lady Carston's musicale this evening."

"Are you?" Penelope made a face. "I confess, I am nervous about it. The viscountess is a tad too fond of asking personal questions, in my view. I am glad that we may attend together."

"Well, I am a little anxious too. But it's my first society event since we were married, and the invitation gives me hope. More importantly, it gives the three of us the opportunity to gather at our house afterward. If you would care to come? To relax and discuss the evening, perhaps?"

"And to show Whiddon that you are holding to his bargain and making a life for yourself?" Penelope asked shrewdly. "Very wise, to give him exactly what he asked for."

"Only if he finds it is not as satisfying as he thought it would be," Charlotte sighed.

Her friends exchanged glances. "Oh, he will come around, dear. We have no doubt."

"So, you will both come?"

"Certainly! As long as we don't have to take tea in the library," Julia said with a grin.

"No worries! The front parlor is now perfectly respectable. I don't even need to shop for furniture for that room, as I found the entire set that was meant to be in there in another part of the house."

"Excellent. That will leave us more time for the linen drapers."

Charlotte placed her order for the chairs, and they all left the shop together. They were walking toward Julia's carriage and debating which fabric shop to start with when she heard her name called.

"Here you are!" It was her cousin, moving toward her with a tight smile on her face.

"Harriett," she answered flatly.

"I called at your new home. A very brash young man told me you were furniture shopping here in Catherine Street. I thought it worth the chance to venture over and see if I could spot you."

"Why?"

"Why? To speak to you, of course."

"Very well, then. Speak."

Harriett smiled and nodded to the other ladies, then pulled Charlotte away a few steps. "I heard you were invited to Lady Carston's musicale this evening."

"Yes."

"Do you mean to go?"

"Yes. Will you be attending?"

"I will."

Charlotte waited.

"I just . . . I thought it prudent that we speak first, privately. Before we see each other socially, I mean."

"Was there something you wanted to say, Harriett?"

"No. Yes. I just . . . I thought it would be best . . ." She sighed in exasperation. "You see? This is why! I knew you would make things difficult!"

"And that's why you wanted to speak to me privately? Because you don't want *me* to make things difficult for *you*?"

Her cousin lifted a shoulder. She didn't even have the grace to look embarrassed.

Charlotte huffed out a breath and turned to go.

Harriett grabbed her arm to stop her.

She pulled away and rounded on her cousin. "I don't know whether it is hubris, stupidity or just sheer, unmitigated gall that makes you think you can ask such a thing of me. I suspect it's an unfortunate mix of all three."

"Oooh!" Harriett snarled and now, at last, she let loose her true emotions. "I don't care what my father says," she sneered. "I don't care what you think you know. Because I have information of my own. Say a word against me and I'll add my own bit of grist to the rumor mill. Do you truly wish your marriage to be the object of gossip again? So soon?"

"Your bluff is even worse than your pitiful attempts at civility."

"Oh, it's no bluff. I don't know who that girl is, hanging and gazing pitifully at your home, but I've got a good look at her, more than once. All it will take is a mention of her. A good description, a few questions and whispers, and suddenly everyone will be speculating about which of your husband's past indiscretions is taking his marriage badly."

Charlotte lifted her chin. "Go to the devil, Harriett."

She went back to her friends and dismissed her cousin's poor manners and even managed to enjoy herself a bit while they shopped for the rest of the morning. But when Julia's carriage dropped her off, she waved her friends on, then paused on the step outside the door.

There she was. Harriett hadn't been inventing tales. A dark-haired girl with pale skin and a curious, calculating gleam in her eye stared back at her. She sat on a bench in the park in the middle of the square, turned sideways at the end so that she could easily watch the house—and meet Charlotte's gaze.

Charlotte held it for a long moment before she turned and went in, contemplating this new complication. As she entered, she caught a glimpse of the hall boy slinking away from the parlor window.

"Hold a moment," she called. The boy had been avoiding her. "What is your name again?"

"E—" He paused, his shoulders hunched and his hands clasped. "Eli. Ma'am."

"Good morning, Eli. I've been wanting to ask you . . ."

"Yes, ma'am?"

"How long have you been employed here?"

The boy shifted his stance. "Oh, just a few weeks, my lady."

"And where were you before that?"

"I were in another nobleman's house before, ma'am." His fingers moved rhythmically against the back of his other hand. "I weren't happy there."

Her heart softened. "And are you happy here, Eli?"

The boy looked quickly up into her face and back down again. "I don't know yet, my lady."

"An honest answer." She held out her parcel of fabric. "Please take this up to the seamstresses. And Eli, if I can help you make up your mind about this house, please let me know."

Another quick glance as he took the fabric and he nodded. "I will. Thank ye, ma'am."

Charlotte watched him go and then she glanced out to where the girl still waited in the square.

There were so many dilemmas piling up, she could scarcely see over them.

CHAPTER 12

"I'm telling you, they are all gone." Before Chester could argue, Whiddon stood up from the spot where they sat concealed behind a stack of casks. He slipped down the alley to the corner of the building that housed the print shop. Holding onto a thick drainpipe with one hand and the rough corner stones with the other, he shimmied up to peer into the high windows.

"Dark as my father's soul," he said as he descended. Chester had moved to await him at the bottom. "We should have split up. He must have gone out the front."

"Two days and we still don't know which one is Perry," Chester said on a sigh.

"We do. It's the man in black. It must be him. Those two louts always emerge before him. They linger and then follow him out of the alley when he leaves. They must be his guards, watching for trouble. But what sort? Who might accost him? Why?"

"None of those bully boys came out this way today, either. Perhaps you are right." Chester shook his head. "How are we supposed to speak with him, then? The man clearly has no interest in meeting with you. The chit at the counter has turned you away three times. Sterne couldn't find anything from the building's lease. We cannot just barge in the back, not with his guards and a room full of tools and large equipment at the ready."

"I suppose we'll have to wait until Tensford hears back from Stoneacre."

"What if he knows nothing about what Perry is up to? Perhaps you should just leave this one be. Move on to the next French refugee on your list."

Whiddon shook his head. "I can't. Especially if he is dangerous."

"He is dangerous. Every sign is there. There's something going on with this one, Whiddon. We need to proceed carefully."

"I know. But all the more reason why I must see him and settle with him. I can't have that sort of debt, from this sort of man, hanging over my head."

Chester sighed. "Oh, hell. You are right, at that. Perhaps we should follow him tomorrow, when he leaves. See what he gets up to. But we'll have to be on our toes."

"You don't have to get entangled in this, Chester. I would prefer if you would not." He couldn't bear it if his friend was harmed because of this business.

"I would prefer that you don't talk stuff and nonsense. You are not facing this alone." Chester yawned. "But let's go and hail a hack now, eh? I want to go home to my wife."

Whiddon supposed he would go home, too. He'd managed to stay away until late hours, the last two nights. He'd spent the first catching up with Tensford and the next hiding in a private room at the club.

Now, they took a hack to Chester's and Whiddon climbed out with him, thinking he would walk home. He set off on foot and found himself making an unplanned detour and a purchase he'd been thinking about during those long hours of watching and waiting at the printshop. Heading home, he found his step quickening, the closer he got.

He let himself in the back and paused to breathe in. The house smelled different now. Better. Not stale, but fresh and comforting with the scents of herbs and starch and soap and baking.

He hurried up to his rooms. Two nights ago, he'd returned late and found a box with a bow upon his bed. Inside, he'd found the soft, worn robe he'd seen Charlotte wearing before her fire. It had been freshly laundered, scented with her rose water scent and was accompanied by a note.

Gabriel,

This robe is one of the few things I have left of my father. I have worn it often, as it reminds me of his better days and makes me feel safe and cared for. Now, you make me feel those things. I don't have much to give, but I wanted to show my gratitude. I'd like for you to have this. I think he would be happy, knowing you wear it now.

Yours,
Charlotte

Such a simple thing, to inspire such a flood of conflicting emotions. He'd been touched, he admitted it. But as he stared at the garment, waiting in its box, his brain had dredged up an old, buried image of a little girl, extending a wilted posy with a smile. He'd seen his brother, wan and pale, pressing a shining medal into his hand, asking him to take it away and keep it.

He'd lifted the robe and pressed his face into it. The

flannel felt soft against him, and he'd thought of her tender skin, touching it, being enveloped by it, in the same way.

He had not slept much afterwards.

Last night, he'd entered to find a covered tray upon his small table. Another note had been propped against it.

GABRIEL,

We have a new cook. Remind me, sometime, to tell you the story of Mrs. Prigg's firing. What a dust up! Tonight, I asked Mr. Flemming to make an apple cake, in the way they prepare it in Devonshire. I hope it lives up to your memories. If you wish, there is a lovely custard sauce in the kitchens. Send for it, if you would like to have it poured over the cake.

C—

HE HAD NOT SENT for the sauce. He'd marveled at the thought that she'd remembered his brief mention of apple cake, then he'd sat right down and moaned in delight at the first bite. He'd polished off the rest, forthwith. It had tasted like home and transported him back to the coast, teasing him with the taste of cinnamon and the memory of sea air. It made him recall the indulgent cook who had pretended to look the other way when he came down to sneak an extra serving.

The thought sobered him as he approached his rooms now. It was a sad fact that a tolerant glance in the other direction was one of the few kindnesses that stood out in his childhood. He wasn't accustomed to thoughtful gestures, kind notes or small gifts. He'd always been the one to shield, to protect, to provide refuge. Never had someone listened to him so closely or showed such thoughtful kindness.

Until now.

Perversely, it made him uncomfortable. It hadn't ended

well when he'd tried to look out for others. Nor would it do to become used to such things. Like the wooing his father had used to trick his mother, or like the romance that once consumed his brother—it wouldn't last.

He reminded himself of that truth as he approached his door—and he was both vindicated and disappointed to be right. The room was dark and empty. Devoid of any notes or tokens. Crossing to the connecting door, he eased it open and peeked through. Charlotte's room also sat dark and empty. Devoid of life and wife.

He set the package he'd bought on her bed. He must proceed carefully, if he meant to avoid the pitfalls and failures he'd encountered before. Forcing himself to leave it, he turned his back and returned to his own room.

Chapman must have heard his step in the corridor, for he came bustling in, talking of a bath and supper. Whiddon allowed him to fuss and told himself that he'd always been content with his valet's brand of caretaking. And so he would remain. He was just finishing up a meal of cold chicken and crusty bread when something caught his attention.

Laughter?

Straightening, he looked to Chapman.

"I believe that the countess meant to return early from her evening out. She asked that a tea tray be ready for her and her friends."

Before he could formulate a conscious thought, Whiddon was on his feet and heading for the door, drawn by the lilting sound of happy chatter.

He noted the changes as he went down. The passageway was well lit, and the floors gleamed with polish. The rich wood of the stairs shone.

The parlor was alive with light and laughter. Whiddon paused on the threshold, caught by the sight of his wife. She was smiling—and she was stunning.

Was he a genius or a fool? Likely both. But he could only marvel that the men of the ton had failed to truly see her.

She sat between her friends, a wash of pink excitement in her face and a gleam of happiness emanating from her whole person. She wore a simple, sky blue gown with a band of dark blue beneath her curvaceous bosom and patterned dark trim at the neck and sleeves.

His gaze was drawn to her glowing curls, drawn high to the back of her head. He'd seen her hair curling down the front of her, caressing her breast. Now he suffered the sudden fantasy of pulling out one pin after another, until that golden river flowed over her bare shoulders. Down her naked back.

"Oh! Good evening, Gabriel." Catching sight of him in the doorway, she sparkled and beckoned him in.

Nodding, he stepped in and responded to the chorus of greetings directed his way.

"Won't you join us?" Charlotte gestured at the furniture in the room. "There is plenty of seating now. I found the entire set upstairs. It matched the color on the walls so well that I could only suspect it was meant to be in here."

He looked around. "It wasn't here all along?"

All three ladies tittered.

"No, there were several mismatched pieces in here, but I took them out and had these moved in."

"You must be right, Charlotte." Penelope was looking around the room. "The light and blue stripes in the furniture exactly match the colors in the wallpaper."

"And the shades on the lamps," Julia added.

"Do come in, Gabriel," his wife urged. "I promise we will speak no more of furniture. I will tell you, though, that my siblings have sent you a letter and a couple of simple gifts to welcome you to the family."

He blinked. "Have they?"

"How sweet," Penelope said. He felt the weight of her gaze upon him. He ignored her. She saw too much. "What did they send?"

"Oh, nothing earth shattering," Charlotte said, coloring a little as she met his gaze. "Anne has sent you a poem she's translated from the original German, and George has written to say he heard you are a great gun and thought you might like the sketch he has made of the squire's prized hunting hound."

The thought dazed him a little. "How thoughtful of them." A trait they'd learned from their elder sister, no doubt.

"It's good to know that they are happy about your marriage," Julia said thoughtfully. "I don't think we can say the same about your cousin, Charlotte."

His wife shook her head. "Oh, pay no attention to that one. She's never happy unless all the attention is on her."

"Harriet was rude to you?" he asked sharply.

"No more than usual. Now, will you come and sit? Take a dish of tea?"

He hesitated. She had looked so content before he entered. "I thought I might go down to the kitchens and see if there is any apple cake left."

"Oh, yes. Mr. Flemming will be happy to meet you, I know."

He ran a glance over her as his throat tightened and an odd ache uncoiled in his chest. "Goodnight, ladies."

He moved blindly, making his way to the kitchens. The cook was hanging up his apron when he stepped in, but he donned it again, welcoming Whiddon in and serving him cake with the custard sauce, this time. Praise and appreciation were easy to offer, and they talked for a while and parted on good terms. Whiddon headed back to his rooms, taking the servants' stairs this time.

Charlotte had been right about the cook. Her changes were not so intrusive, so far.

She'd looked happy tonight. Lovely. At ease and settling into her new role.

He was happy, as well. She would adjust and arrange her new life and leave him to his.

Exactly what he'd wanted.

This empty, dissatisfied feeling was only temporary, surely.

He'd tarried long enough downstairs, so that it wasn't long before he heard movement from her rooms. Tensing a little, he waited. It took only a few moments before he heard the quiet knock on the connecting door.

He called admittance and she came in carrying the box he'd left on her bed, opened now.

"Did you leave these for me?" Somehow, she managed to wear an expression that was both soft and wary. Her fingers caressed the line of colored pastel sticks.

"I did. I thought you might like to add a little color to your sketches of the staff. I made sure the selection included a red stick, as I thought you might need it to illustrate the firing of Mrs. Prigg."

She shuddered. "No. I've no inclination to dwell on that scene. She's gone and that's the end of it."

"That bad, was it?"

"And worse." She set the box down on his table and looked up at him, assessing. "Whiddon, what is Monkford?"

He flinched. "Why? Who told you about it?"

"Chester's grandmother was at the musicale this evening. She asked if you'd told me about Monkford yet. When I said you had not, she said I must ask you."

He cursed inwardly. He adored that old woman, but she was a champion meddler. He gave a nonchalant shrug. "She must mean Monkford Park. It's one of the estates. It's in Wiltshire."

"Is there something I should know about it?"

He made a face. "Not unless you are fond of sheep. That's the main enterprise there. I've hired a man who is developing a breed known for its size, it's longer wool and decent meat."

"Hmm. I wonder why Lady Chester brought it up?"

"I'm not sure, but I'd much rather hear about Prigg and how you sent her packing."

She laughed a little. "Oh, my timing was atrocious. I walked in while she was in a rage."

"Over what?"

"Over your man of business meeting with me. She was slamming pots and flinging spoons and furiously ranting over this being the last of their easy take and how were they going to get their cut off the top and next I'd be asking to see the books!"

"God's teeth." His eyes widened. "You didn't even have to examine them. She just said it all right out loud."

"They didn't notice me in the doorway, so caught up were they. Mrs. Prigg was ladling soup into a bowl and barked at Old Alf to get it up to me quick, or I'd be moaning about a cold meal again." She made a face. "He promptly stuck his finger in the bowl and pronounced it warm enough."

Whiddon choked back a laugh. "I thought I noticed he was wearing gloves when I came in, last night. That explains it."

"I hope it eliminates the sticky railings and door latches, too," she said on a sigh.

"So, Mrs. Prigg eventually noticed you, I presume."

"Yes, thanks to Hurley. He entered through the other door and saw me right away. He asked me what I wanted, coming downstairs, and the scene changed. They all froze. The cook turned eight shades of red and started to bluster, but I just informed her she was neither honest nor skilled enough to continue working here. She tried to justify herself, and grew angry again, but in the end, she tore off her apron and flung it on the table and stalked off. I sent Eli after her, to be sure she didn't steal the silver on her way out, but she was gone within the hour."

"Eli?"

"The hall boy."

"That stripling?" he scoffed. "Mrs. Prigg could have cold cocked him, had she been of a mind."

She frowned. "Gabriel, does Eli come from Broadscombe? Like Hurley?"

"Not that I know of. I thought he was a London guttersnipe. Why do you ask?"

She shook her head. "There's just something about him . . ."

But her frown had sent Gabriel's thoughts off in another direction. "Hurley isn't giving you trouble, is he?"

"No. That's not quite it. It's more that I'm troubled about him."

"Why?"

She shrugged. "Well, for one thing, I've had two perfectly good candidates for lady's maid refuse to come work here when they found he's still in charge of the house."

"They knew him by name?"

"Yes. I know servants do gossip, but what sort of reputation must he have fostered? But mainly, I object over his manner here. He's the house steward. He is paid to see that the house is run smoothly. Clearly, he does nothing toward that end. You might also expect him to look after the staff, but he speaks callously and treats them harshly. All this dereliction of his duty, and yet he remains strangely confident. He is utterly lacking in respect for me or my orders—which, in my mind, translates into a lack of respect for you."

"Oh, he has no regard for me." Whiddon lifted a shoulder. "He never has. He respects only my father, who holds all of the power in the family, on the estate and in the village." He frowned, not liking the idea of her facing off against the man. She was too damned innocent. She had no idea what a man like Hurley might do, if thwarted. "Listen, Charlotte. There are two things that make Hurley a dangerous opponent. First is his ambition. It is boundless. Second is the fact that my father returns his regard."

"I don't like it. I don't like him. Did you know that he sleeps in the guest wing? That parlor furniture that I found above stairs? It was set up in the room next to his. He's fashioned himself a private sitting room."

"It's cheeky," he admitted. "But honestly, I didn't know or care. If he makes the mistake to try and switch it back, then you'll have cause to confront him. But he won't. He's not stupid." He stepped closer to her, wanting her to take heed of his words. "Be careful of him. It would be best if you could find a way to rub along with him."

The mulish look on her face frustrated him. He had to make her understand. With a sigh of resignation, he began to peel off his coat. "Help me with this, will you?"

"Certainly." Her eyes had gone wide. "But . . . why?"

"Because I'm going to convince you, one way or another. And it begins with a story."

She paused in the act of folding his coat over the nearby chair. "Is it a story about you?"

"Well, partly. Yes."

"That will be a refreshing change."

He could not deny she had a point, but he wouldn't be sharing even this much if he did not have one to make, too. "Every summer, in the village at Broadscombe, there is a fishing competition amongst the young lads. It's unofficial. There is no prize, save for a year's worth of bragging rights, but they pick a day, and any number of young men go out and spend the day trying to pull in and bring back the largest fish. Hurley won the prize for several years in a row. His father and mine are thick as thieves, and the elder Mr. Hurley is quite the force in the village. Young Hurley always strutted about like a young cock amongst the hens, and he relished his victories."

Whiddon paused in the act of unbuttoning his waistcoat, recalling the charged atmosphere of those days. "Unfortunately, my brother William and he were about the same age, and they often butted heads. Hurley resented sharing the spotlight with anyone, but especially with William. This particular year, my brother was determined to oust him as winner in the fishing contest."

"Did he?" She looked fascinated with the story, or perhaps with the sight of his fingers undoing his buttons.

"He did. Hurley got a bull huss nearly three feet long and was assured of the victory, until William returned just before dusk, with a polluck well over three feet. He was named the winner and Hurley was furious. He raged and accused William of cheating. It was ridiculous, of course. Hurley is just an extraordinarily bad loser. He's just like a banty rooster, all strut and flashy feathers, and he hates to be thwarted. He pushed the issue until a fight broke out between them." He tossed his waistcoat on the bed and untucked his linen shirt.

Her focus centered squarely on his chest. He hoped to God she couldn't see the sudden pounding of his heart.

"What happened?" she asked.

"It was a fierce battle. Tensions had been brewing and I believe they both relished the chance to vent them. They were relentless, each in his own way, but Hurley began to tire first. I think he saw both victories slipping away from him. He grabbed a fishing gaff and tried to gut my brother."

Her gaze flew up to his face. "You intervened?"

"Of course I did. I had to." He tugged his shirt off over his head.

She went pink and made a sound of surprise. Almost, he could feel the weight of her gaze roaming over him.

"So, it's a habit." She flushed a little as her voice squeaked.

"Excuse me?"

"Your habit—of rushing in. To the rescue."

He scowled. "It's not a habit."

She made a noncommittal, completely dubious sound. "Go on."

He held up his arm. "Look. This is what I am trying to say. Hurley has a sharp temper and a short fuse. This is what you get when you stand in his way."

She gasped when she saw the thick, jagged scar on his upper arm. Stepping closer, she grasped his arm and peered closely at it. "He did this with a fishing gaff?" she asked, horrified.

"It sunk in here." He pointed to the spot. "And then he ripped it out."

"Good heavens. You were lucky you didn't lose your arm."

"I nearly lost the use of it, but I'm stubborn. I wasn't having it. I worked ceaselessly to build the muscle back, after it healed. Even so, I still sometimes drop things, if I am tired."

"Why?" she demanded. "Why have such a man in your house?"

"Because he did apologize, long ago. And I accepted. But it left him with a sort of debt to me—and he hates that. And so, I keep him close, as you should, with your enemies."

"It didn't work with Harriett," she said wryly.

"Well, Hurley is living here, happily pocketing my household money each month and reporting on me to my father. It's a minor sort of trouble, but it keeps him from causing worse. And I can keep an eye on him."

Her hands were still wrapped around his arm. Moving closer, she laid her cheek against the old wound, looking up at him with concern in her blue eyes. "I'm sorry such a horrid thing happened to you."

Her skin felt soft and silky smooth against his. The rhythm of her breathing had slowed. He could feel each breath pressing her curves against his bare chest. He waited, agonizing, for each one.

"You did the same for me. You came to my rescue. I'm so grateful."

Were those tears in her eyes?

"I would console myself with the thought that at least you didn't come away with a scar, except I know the sacrifice you made for me was much greater."

He hadn't. Not really. Not yet.

And therein lay the danger. Hunger surged inside of him. It came from the places she'd touched with her small gestures and large smiles.

"I never want to be a burden to you," she whispered. Letting go, she started to move away.

Instinctively, he reached out to stop her. He had to forcefully remind himself not to tighten his hold on her soft flesh.

She tried to move away again. He should let her.

Her mouth opened.

She was going to be wise. He didn't want to hear it. Instead, he pulled her closer still. "You should come with a warning sign," he rasped. He took her mouth with his.

Gods, her lips were soft. She felt fragile and slight in his embrace, and yet her warmth heated the empty spaces inside of him.

Danger ahead. That's what her sign should say. It lay in each curve, each shift of her mouth as she moved with his, kissing him back and taking his tongue deep, thrusting back with her own. Most of all, jeopardy lay in the yearning that swamped him. He ached with it, with the need for her care and concern. For *more, deeper* and *further*—echoes of the longings she'd dredged up in that kiss during their wedding.

His hands were roaming over her bosom, along the sweet curve of her waist, around to the buttons on the back of her gown. Her bodice sagged, but his nimble fingers pulled at the ties of her stays and in a moment, all the fabric covering her dropped away to her waist and she was bare before him.

Growling, he filled his hands with her.

Damnation, what she did to him. The sight of her struck him hard, like flint, making him flare to life, shooting light and heat and savage lust all through him.

Her breasts were plump and round, the nipples erect and inviting. He answered their call, thumbing roughly, then savoring with gentle kisses. He took his time, sucking softly and running his tongue over the peaks until she moaned with incoherent pleasure.

His cock throbbed with unruly, nearly painful need. Her breath came faster now, the cadence urging him on. Her hands roamed over his shoulders, burrowed into his hair.

He shivered. He was on fire.

Too much. She made him feel too much. She was so giving and sensual. She offered things he'd never known he wanted. Warmth. Support. Closeness.

He was not used to this yearning. To wanting so much.

Danger.

With a groan, he pulled away. Straightening, he pulled her into a tight embrace. For one breath. Two. Three.

She stood, gone stiff in his embrace. "Whiddon, I can't trap you. You are already caught. We both are."

"I know."

"Then why don't we . . . continue?"

Because she was instinctively generous. Passionate. Kind.

And he was swaying back and forth between the need to clutch her to him and the urge to toss her away.

He compromised, letting her go and spinning on his heel. He took several steps to the hearth, fighting to get himself—and his erection—under control.

"How long?" she asked softly. He glanced back to see her holding her bodice up and watching him. "How long do you mean to wait?"

He didn't know the answer.

She waited a moment. When he had no answer beyond the shake of his head, she held her clothing against her and quietly returned to her own room.

Cursing, he laid his head on the mantel. He'd spent his life carefully *not* wanting too much. Not expecting his father's approval or his mother's notice. He'd often sacrificed his own such needs to shield William from disdain or disapproval. In the end, he'd found it wiser and safer to cease wanting, yearning or craving for anything.

And yet, that's all Charlotte made him do.

CHAPTER 13

When the faint light of dawn broke over the city, Charlotte gave up tossing and turning, fled the silence and climbed out of bed. She dressed in a simple round gown and bundled her hair into a knot at her nape. She knew that this time the kitchens would be awake and bustling, so she took her box of pastel sticks and went down. Mr. Flemming tucked her into a corner with a cup of chocolate and bade her wait for the breakfast pastries to be done.

She happily sipped and sketched, capturing the cook in several images, all showing him intent and focused on his creative process. Tearing out the page, she folded it and gave it to a kitchen maid, with instructions to include it on the tray that went up to his lordship. When breakfast was ready, she left the staff in peace so they might enjoy their meal and took hers alone, upstairs. It left her thinking that she really should get the staff moving on the dining room next. She went down to give it a look and Margie found her there not long after.

"Here's the basket you asked for, my lady."

"Thank you. Any sign of our mysterious watcher this morning?"

"Not yet, and that's a break in her pattern. She's been there at this time, both the past mornings. P'raps she won't come back again."

"You might be right." Charlotte gestured to the room. "I'd like for you and the girls to tackle this today. The furniture needs a thorough dusting. Those chairs have a fair few tricky twists and turns that will need attention. Have Eli help polish the chandelier. He has long, clever fingers. And be sure to have one of the girls dust the parlor before she begins in here, just in case we have callers."

"Yes, ma'am."

Charlotte left her happily organizing. She took up the basket and went out to the garden in the center of the square. The bench across from the house was indeed empty. There were a few hidden spots amongst the trees and shrubberies, and though she searched them out, she didn't find the girl. She stood a moment at the empty bench, thinking, then she left the basket in the girl's usual spot and started back home.

She'd just reached the pavement when she heard her name called.

"Mr. Rostham," she said, stopping to let the gentleman approach.

"Lady Whiddon. I am so glad I caught you."

"How nice to see you." She eyed the basket he carried, and her eyes widened in surprise. "Oh! Have you been successful so soon?"

"Indeed, although when I offered you help, I never imagined it taking such a turn as this." He lifted the lid.

She bent over to peer inside. "How charming," she sighed.

"My watering eyes prevented me from delaying the delivery." Closing the lid again, his smile faded. "Are you well, Charlotte? Truly?"

She gave him a nod and a smile. "I am, sir. Thank you for your concern."

"I haven't forgotten our archery contest, you know. My cousin loved the idea. Look for an invitation before too long."

"Oh, how lovely! What fun we will have. Thank you for remembering."

"You must bring Lord Whiddon along, as well."

She laughed. "Oh, I will insist upon it!"

"Very well, then." He gave over the basket. "Enjoy your wedding present."

"Thank you, Mr. Rostham. I will. We all will."

Bowing, he took his leave and Charlotte carried the basket inside. Striding into the dining room, she set it on the table.

"My lady, that ain't the basket ye left with," Margie told her.

"I am aware of that. Will you call all the staff in here, please? And have the seamstresses bring down my special request."

"Aye, my lady." Mystified, the maid made the rounds of the house. Everyone gathered in the dining room except for Mr. Flemming who could not leave off kneading his bread, and Chapman, who was waiting on his lordship.

"Where is Alfred?"

As someone was reportedly at the door, she nodded. "Very well. Someone may fill him in later and make the introductions."

"Introductions?" asked Eli.

"Indeed. We have two new members of the staff." Charlotte pulled back the lid of the basket to show the two sleeping kittens inside. A collective sigh went around the room.

"Aww."

"How sweet."

"Little darlin's."

"They are indeed sweet. And unlike the previous, unfortunate feline that lived in this house, these two are to be treated like kings."

"Kings?" Hurley repeated, incredulous.

"Kings. Princes in this house." She speared each servant with a piercing gaze. "Do you understand? These cats are yours to mind and I will have them treated like royalty. You will name them. You will find them a cozy, warm corner downstairs where they will sleep. They have their bed." She indicated the large, quilted cushion the seamstresses had brought down. "You will procure them a box of earth for their needs. You will cuddle and comfort them, train them and feed them. Not overfeed, mind you, for I want them sleek and in hunting shape. You will praise them when they are successful and even when they fall short. In short, you will spoil them rotten. In part, to make up for the past, shameful neglect done here. And also, to help you remember that we are all working together in this house, each of us doing our best to help each other."

She looked around. Hurley looked contemptuous. A few looked doubtful. But most appeared intrigued by the idea.

"Am I understood?"

"Yes, my lady." The chorus echoed around her.

"Very well. You must all decide on names, first. Be sure to tell me what you choose."

Debate broke out immediately.

"Excuse me, my lady?"

She turned. "Yes, Alfred?" The footman hovered in the doorway.

"Where would you like the workmen, Lady Whiddon?"

"Workmen?"

WHY DO EARLS FALL IN LOVE?

Several minutes later, she burst into Whiddon's rooms. "Was it you? Did you hire workmen to adjust the windows on the third floor?"

Looking up from his breakfast, her husband pointed his knife toward the sketches of the cook. "I doubt Mr. Flemming would approve of the one with his tongue out."

"He makes the most fascinating faces when he's concentrating," she said absently. "Well? Was it you?"

He lifted a shoulder. "If we are to be explicit, it was Chapman, but he acted at my request." He paused in buttering his toast. "Why? Have I intruded upon your decorating territory?"

"Of course not." She flushed. "It's just . . . if you wished for something in particular to be done, I could have handled it for you."

"Yes." He took a bite. "But that would have ruined the surprise."

She stilled. Her heartbeat stumbled and her skin tingled with anticipation. "Surprise?"

He stood. "I can see my breakfast is going to get cold." He took a couple of quick bites and swallowed. She watched while pleasure and hope began to blossom inside of her. He took a long swallow of tea, then set his cup down and headed for the door. "Come on, then."

He took her to a large room on the north side of the third floor. The workmen were already there, carrying out a bookcase and taking measurements of the windows.

"The nursery is next door. I believe this was meant to be a schoolroom, but we never spent much time in this house as children."

"How do you mean to use it?"

"I don't." He gave her a look that raised the hairs on the

back of her neck. "I asked them to expand the windows and look into the possibility of a skylight. You'll need plenty of good light in a studio."

"Studio?" Her pulse began to pound, a mad, frantic pounding in her ears.

He took her hand and held it lightly. "I saw the longing in you, that day when you spoke of art and your painting. When I stopped to get the pastel sticks, I ordered a quantity of paint supplies and canvas and brushes and primer ingredients, as well as a great many other things the shop owner insisted an artist must have."

She made a strange gasp of a sound that even she didn't recognize.

"There's no hindrance to your pursuit of painting any longer. In fact, it would be a shame if you did not proceed. You see people, and the world, in a different way. A better way, I think, with more clarity and compassion. I can't wait to see what you bring to life in here."

The workmen had opened the windows, but still, there was not enough air. The pounding in her ears, the pressure in her chest . . . it was all too much.

His mouth twisted into a half smile. "Flummoxed you. That's one for me. Have I pulled ahead? I've lost count."

She wrenched her hand from his and fled.

He caught her at the bottom of the stairs, on the second floor. Shaking her head frantically, she backed into the wall, next to a curved niche. Days ago, it had been festooned with cobwebs. Today it was immaculate and the nymph standing on the pedestal inside watched them coyly over her shoulder.

"Is it all just a game to you?" she whispered. "No more?"

"Of course it isn't a game." He sounded indignant. "I just wanted . . ."

His words trailed away. Why wouldn't they? He couldn't admit to any feelings for or about her. He didn't want them.

"I don't know what to do with you," she moaned.

"Why must you do anything?" His tone was rough, but his touch, when he took her shoulders, was gentle. "Why not just say your thanks and leave it at that? What's wrong with the way this is, right now?"

"Nothing! There's nothing wrong with it. It's all perfectly *right*." She stepped forward, into his embrace. Bending her head, she leaned it against his chest. "Don't you feel it?"

He did. She could feel his heartbeat, as wild as her own. She wanted him to admit it. Craved the words like her father had craved silence.

"You don't understand." She tipped her head back again, to look up at him. His hands on her back warmed her. Made her brave. "I thought when I came to London, it would be different. Everyone would be new. They would meet me without bias, without the patina of my father's death clouding their vision, without the certain knowledge of my humble cottage and threadbare pocketbook." She gave a bitter laugh. "I thought I could come to Town, possessed of a decent bloodline and the right wardrobe, and I could at last be seen for myself. I could be judged by my wit, by knowledge and humor and the ability to bring laughter or a smile."

He sighed. "You were doomed to disappointment, thinking such a thing."

"So I was. It was just the same. Worse, perhaps. Nobody wanted me. People looked past me. Through me. No one saw me at all. Until you did."

His eyes closed.

"You made them look, too, with your rescue and your dance. I was so grateful. You'd given me my chance at last."

His grip tightened. "Until your nasty cousin stole it away."

"Yes. But still, there was you. You look at me and you *see*. You listen and you *hear*." She pressed closer still, pressing her bosom against his chest and letting her hands move up across his back. "You know me like no one else does, Gabriel. And yet..."

He didn't want her, either. Not really.

The awful truth hung between them. The silence stretched out, dissolving all the hopeful longing in her heart.

"My lord!"

Rapid footsteps sounded on the stairs. "Lord Whiddon!"

He stepped away, taking the reassuring warmth of his touch with him. Her hands fell to her sides.

Margie, breathing hard, reached the second floor. "My lord, there is a messenger boy downstairs. He brung you this, from Lord Stoneacre." She held out the missive and stood, catching her breath.

Whiddon read it quickly, his eyes darting over the words. Looking up, he met her gaze. "I'm sorry." He was, but she could see relief in his face, as well. "I have to go."

He took a step, stopped, reached back and squeezed her hand.

And he was gone.

CHAPTER 14

T he Hen's Tooth, the coffee shop in the Strand where Stoneacre had summoned him, sat not far from Half Moon House, where the earl's wife held sway. All the staff in the shop were female, and Whiddon wondered if they were beneficiaries of Hestia's famous vow to help any woman who asked.

Perhaps. Perhaps not. But they all paid attention when Chester entered right behind him, his big form blocking the light from the doorway. Stoneacre looked up too, from where he sat with coffee and a pile of newspapers. He indicated they should sit with him and he wasted no time once they were settled.

"Whatever, however you are messing about with Perry, stop it at once." It came out an order.

"Why?" Whiddon asked bluntly.

"I could give you a hundred reasons. Officially, he's a printer and publisher, connected to every radical and revolutionary group in England and across Europe. He will print anything, even the most vile and vicious calls to arms. It's said he funds some of them, as well." He leaned in. "Unofficially, he runs one of the most particularly violent criminal gangs in London. The government is watching him from several different directions. And he's watching back. He has eyes and ears everywhere."

"In the Privy Council?" Whiddon asked, surprised.

"Lord, no. Thank goodness. But in the Home Office. And elsewhere." Stoneacre raised a brow at him. "He's one of your refugees, isn't he?"

Whiddon glared at Chester.

"Don't look at me like that," his friend protested. "I didn't tell him."

"Nobody told me." Stoneacre sat back and folded his arms. "Did your father think no one would ever speak of his . . . treachery? There are several old reports and complaints filed against him." He shrugged. "As far as I can tell, nobody was ever able to produce any proof, so he was left alone."

A serving girl brought two more cups and fresh coffee. Stoneacre waited until she had finished and gone, then he met Whiddon's gaze directly. "The Home Office knows what you have been up to, as well."

Whiddon bristled. "Do they think they can tell me to stop altogether?"

"Only with regard to Perry. I haven't heard any other orders, or even any suggestion of it. A few who know your purpose think you daft, but most find the notion honorable." He frowned. "If you think Perry is—"

"We think he's the Comte de Perette," Whiddon interrupted. "Is he?"

Meeting his gaze, Stoneacre gave a slow nod. "If Perry is on your list . . ."

"Of course, he is," Chester huffed. "Why else would we be mucking about with such a man?"

"Well, the worry did cross a few minds that you might be revolutionaries yourselves, but I disabused them of the notion. But in the case of this particular refugee, you should stand down."

"Good luck getting him to listen to sound advice," Chester muttered.

"Actually, you might be right. Both of you." Whiddon gave Chester a look. "This time."

"Quick. Write it down." Chester searched frantically among Stoneacre's papers. "Have you a quill? Note the day! Whiddon is taking advice."

"Very funny." Whiddon sighed. "But if you are right, Stoneacre, and if Perry is so well connected, then he also must have heard what I am up to. I've approached him. He's not interested. Perhaps it should stay that way."

"I am relieved to hear you say so. You do have more than yourself to worry for, now, do you not?" Stoneacre raised his cup. "To leaving this alone."

Chester echoed him enthusiastically.

Whiddon made the toast, but the brew went down bitterly.

AFTER WHIDDON DISAPPEARED, Charlotte went to her room to press a cold cloth to her eyes and to struggle for a bit of composure. *It was just a setback.* She told her reflection so, sternly. A setback. That's all. She was playing the long game and she would not give up now.

She could not take the silence and inactivity for long, however. With a sigh, she went to check on the progress with the dining room.

She met Hurley on the landing. He was dressed like a lord, in buff and blue. "How very smart you look, Hurley." She eyed the hat in his hand. "Going out?"

"I am. I have an appointment with a brewer. I'm searching for a new contract for the house."

With someone who will pay you a handsome fee for the chance, she thought uncharitably. "Perhaps you might consult with Mr. Flemming as well," she suggested. "He seems to have a varied palate and might have some valuable opinions."

The steward's expression chilled as he gestured for her to precede him. "I shall consider your suggestion, my lady."

"Thank you, Hurley." She left him at the bottom and headed for the dining room while he moved toward the front door. "See that you do."

She found the dining room much improved, but the chandelier was not even half cleaned. "Where is Eli?"

Margie pointed with her chin as she polished the elaborate back of a chair. "He said he had an errand upstairs."

Charlotte had been wanting to sketch the boy. He always seemed to be slipping away. Focusing on him might distract her from her own thoughts. With a word of praise for the progress so far, she went back upstairs. Fetching her book and her pastel sticks, she thought perhaps that the boy had been drawn by the workmen, up to the third floor.

He wasn't there, though, and she couldn't bear to linger. Wandering the third floor, she didn't find him. Struck by a sudden notion, she hurried down to the second floor and straight to the rooms that Hurley had taken for himself.

Eli was there. He didn't hear her approach and she stood in the doorway, watching him rifle through the drawers of a small writing desk.

"What are you doing?"

He froze, then slowly stood tall. "Just straightening up, ma'am."

She moved into the room. "Did Hurley ask you to clean his rooms while he was out?"

"Not exactly." The boy moved away from the desk as she drew nearer.

"By *not exactly*, do you mean that he forbade you to come in here?" She let a wry tone color the question.

The boy grinned, then looked quickly down at his feet. He continued to edge away.

"You do seem uncommonly watchful in general, Eli," she remarked.

He'd made it to the window, where he leaned on the ledge and looked out. Abruptly, Charlotte stilled. That profile, edged in sunlight—

"Aye. A good thing I'm watchful, ma'am."

"Why?"

He nodded toward the street. "Because I can see Hurley coming back this way. But also—that girl that's been watching the house? She's back." He turned toward her with a grim expression. "She's looking like thunder and heading for the front door."

They exchanged a look, then headed together for the stairs. By the time they reached the floor below, the girl had already pushed her way past a protesting Alfred.

"There she is." The dark-haired girl flourished a slip of paper in her hand, her eyes flashing. "What is the meaning of this? I demand to know it!"

Charlotte recognized the note she'd left in the basket on the bench. "I believe it means what it says. I would be happy to speak to you, if you wish."

"Ah, but speak with *who*? That is the question." She pointed to the signature. "*Lady Whiddon*? Absurd!" She ran a derogatory gaze over Charlotte's form. "He has not gone and married *you*!"

"I'm afraid he has," she answered gently.

The other girl's expression darkened. Turning away, she muttered a few truly vile curses in French before she looked at Charlotte again. "What of the papers? Where are the announcements? The parties? When a man such as this one marries, the world knows, celebrates, gossips endlessly! Why does no one talk about this sham of a union, then?" Her gaze brightened. "Is that it? Has he lied to you? Tricked you? And why not?" she scoffed. "I thought you to be the housekeeper!"

Charlotte bristled. "Well, to tell the truth, I feel like the twice-blessed housekeeper! But the house needed attention and it is a lady's duty to see to such work. I am doing it, because I *am* Lady Whiddon. Believe what you must, but we married in a quiet ceremony attended by family and friends, not in a splashy Society event." She crossed her arms and scowled. "And it suited us both very well indeed!"

More French cursing ensued. Good heavens, the chit was going to make Charlotte blush. But then the girl narrowed her eyes. "Fine, then. Married." She said it with disgust. "Then you will tell your *husband* that I want the brooch. The one from the Royal collection. Blue enamel with rose diamonds."

Charlotte blinked. "I don't know what you are talking about."

"Did he save it for you? A bridal gift?" she spat. "Just tell him. The brooch was meant to be mine. *My* birthright! His lackey said it was long gone, but I saw it in his eyes. I did not believe him. I think Whiddon has it still. I want it. Tell him to deliver it to me at the shop. Discreetly. And after that, you tell him to keep himself away. He is not to tell my father I came here, do you understand? He was lucky to get a payment last time instead of a garrote. If he keeps hanging about, my father *will* kill him."

Charlotte blanched, but the girl wadded the note into a ball, tossed it at her feet, and whirled away. In a moment, she was gone.

CHESTER AND STONEACRE showed every inclination to linger over their coffee, but Whiddon felt the need to move. He made his farewells and headed out.

Traffic ran briskly in the Strand, as it always did. He set out on foot for home. He would need to consult William's list and set Chapman to searching out information on the next refugee. God's teeth, but it felt wrong leaving the Comte de Perette unresolved, but he—

A step sounded too close behind him. Turning, he ducked a little, reaching for the knife in his boot, but something flared bright . . . and the world went dark.

He came back to himself gradually. He was bent over, his face pressed into stiff brocade. He was moving, his head rocking and aching anew with each jolt of the . . . carriage? He fought to get his eyes open. He'd been reaching for his belt knife. He tried again, but found his hands were tied behind his back.

"Ye got a fine, thick skull, yer lordship."

He was hauled upright. Blinking, he tried to clear his vision. A carriage, yes. Finely appointed. The opposite bench was filled with the bulk of the two big men he'd noted leaving the printshop with Perry.

One of them leaned over and poked his temple with the butt of a knife. "Time to get Perry's message through that rock atop yer shoulders, my lord. He's already dealt with yer lacky, and in good faith, too."

"Lackey?" The word came out as a croak as he tried desperately not to vomit.

The man across from him sighed. "'Tis time for ye to listen, not to talk. Perry's already paid once for what was already his. Ye were lucky he decided to go along. He respects yer head fer business, but he's had enough."

Whiddon struggled to listen past the painful pounding in his head, to make sense of the words the man spoke. "But we haven't spoken yet, or even met. I don't have a lackey. There's been no business."

"Now, now. We are all men here, with an understanding of the world. Ye made yer play. Now the business is finished. Perry's not wanting more. He don't want to see or hear from you again."

"But—" He stopped at the cold press of steel against his throat.

"Enough, now. Take the message, yer lordship. Leave Perry alone."

The other man thumped on the ceiling. His assailant withdrew the knife from his neck.

The carriage slowed. The door opened. The big man leaned close again. "Next time, I'll just cut yer throat."

He pushed and Whiddon tumbled out of the carriage, hitting the pavement hard.

CHARLOTTE STALKED to the front door and stood a moment, watching the impudent girl stalk away. She was fuming. Consumed with a raging fury. No wonder Whiddon wished to be left to his own devices. He was carrying on with some sort of secret life. One that involved jewels and women and lackeys and garottes.

She spun around, but the hall had emptied out. Everyone had scattered. Drawing a deep breath, she slammed the door. That had been an actual threat of death. Why? What was going on? There were too many damned secrets in this house.

On that thought, she went looking for Eli.

It took her a while to find him. At last, she spotted him in the long corridor below stairs. It was often busy here, as the passage held the laundry and boot rooms and the butler's cupboard. It also held the steward's office—and Eli stood outside Hurley's open door, in an otherwise empty passage. He stood straight as a pin, his chin high and his hands straight down at his sides. Charlotte's eyes narrowed when she saw his fingers tap a rhythm against his thigh.

"The brewer said he left a message about changing our appointment today. A message he left with a boy in the kitchens." Even from down the corridor, she could hear the note of anger in Hurley's voice. "Did you take it?"

"I did, sir."

"Why did you not deliver it?"

"I must have forgotten. Sorry, sir."

Charlotte heard the man's exasperated exhalation. "You are walking a thin line, boy. There is also the matter of your . . . donation. You are lucky I'm not charging you interest, as you've yet to turn over even a penny."

"I won't be making a donation."

Charlotte couldn't see Hurley's face, but she could hear the hardening of his tone. "You agreed to the arrangement when you hired on, boy, just as everyone else did."

"Things changed, though, didn't they?" The boy's eyes blazed. "There's a new mistress now. What do you think she'd say if I told her yer takin' a skim off the top of our wages?"

"She won't do or say a thing."

Eli scoffed. "If that's what ye think, ye haven't been payin' attention."

Charlotte was heartened by the boy's belief in her, but it only made the steward angrier.

"She won't say a thing because you won't be telling her, you guttersnipe."

Charlotte jumped as a hand shot out and grabbed the boy

by the shirt. It gave a hard yank and he disappeared into the room.

She dashed to the doorway. Hurley had his hand fisted in the boy's shirt. His temper shone clear in his high color, but it looked more like shock than anger on his face. He frowned, looking puzzled, as he stared down at his fist and then into the boy's face. "Who the hell are you?" he snarled.

Charlotte knew then that her half-formed suspicions had been right. And that she would have to get rid of this man. Right now.

"Unhand the boy," she ordered sharply.

It was a battle of wills as they glared at each other over a head of unruly curls.

"Let him go. Now, Hurley."

With a snarl and a curse, he pushed the boy away.

"I've had enough of you," she told the steward. "You are done, here."

"No!" Eli gasped.

"Yes. Eli, run to the kitchens and bring back Mr. Flemming and his largest kitchen knife."

The boy hesitated. "I don't think . . ."

"Now!"

He went, brushing past her, then racing down the corridor.

Hurley's lip lifted. "You don't know what a storm you will kick up, firing me."

She snorted. "I think I can withstand it, thank you. Now, you will pack your things. Only your things, mind you. And you will go."

The man moved to pick up the ledger on the desk.

"Not the books. Your things only, I said."

Mr. Flemming arrived, with a shining butcher knife and the news that he'd sent Eli to fetch some lads from the stables. If Hurley thought they might back him, he was quickly disabused of the notion. Staff gathered and watched from a distance and each and every one seemed pleased or relieved at the turn of events.

They escorted the steward to his rooms and supervised as he packed his belongings. He grew surlier and more contentious as Charlotte stopped him from taking several ornamental figures and bottles of wine and liquor. He snarled and fussed, but at last he was done, and the men escorted him out. Charlotte watched from a window as they walked him out the back, through the garden and into the alley before the mews. Hurley tried to talk to them, but he met only shaking heads and pointing fingers. A stable hand spat after him when he finally turned to go.

She sank into a chair. "What a day."

Margie nodded sympathetically. "It was nicely done, ma'am. We are all well rid of him."

Eli came to the doorway. "The day ain't done with you yet. You'd better come downstairs. His lordship is back."

CHAPTER 15

When Whiddon recovered enough to roll over and take stock, he was both mortified and relieved to find he'd been dumped onto the pavement before his own house. Scrambling to his feet, he stumbled to the door and kicked it repeatedly.

It took several long, agonizing moments before Old Alf answered. "Your lordship!" He blinked in shock as Whiddon pushed past him.

"My hands! Set me free, quickly!"

"Yes, my lord." Alf hesitated, shifting back and forth, clearly at a loss, before departing in the direction of the dining room. He came back with a small, sharp fruit knife.

Whiddon spun around. "Quickly, man." His mind whirled as the footman sawed at the ropes binding him, trying to think past the pain in his head. He'd just worked his hands free when Charlotte came rushing down the stairs, the hall boy in her wake.

"Gabriel! What is it?" She paused, aghast, then surged toward him. "You are bleeding! Have you other injuries? What's happened?"

"No, no. I'm fine. It's just a bump on the head." He moved past her toward the stairs. "Where is Chapman? Send him to me. Tell him I need him at once."

He had to pause on the landing and clutch his head. God's teeth, the pain felt like a knife stabbing into his skull. Sucking in a breath, he hurried on. Someone else had the list. It was the only explanation. Someone had the list and was contacting the people on it.

Charlotte followed him into his room. "We must talk. And sit down. That wound is still bleeding. It needs seen to."

"Not now, Charlotte."

"Now," she said firmly. "The time for secrets is over."

He groaned. "I don't have time for this."

"You'd better make time, for I've had enough. Oh, and I have a message for you."

He stilled. "From whom?"

"A young woman. Dark hair, dark eyes. Pale skin and a particularly filthy grasp of French vernacular."

He did sink into a chair, then. "Here? She came here?"

"Yes. I'm to tell you that she wants her brooch. Blue enamel and rose diamonds. Your representative told her you don't have it, but she doesn't believe him. She thinks you kept it, to give to me."

He cursed under his breath. "This is bad. Very bad."

"It is," she agreed. "She also said her father intends to kill you, should you keep hanging around."

He started to rise, but the room began to spin.

Making a noise of alarm, she pushed him back down. "Enough. We are going to take care of this first." She opened the door, called for Margie and ordered hot water, clean linen and hot, sugared tea.

"Where's Chapman?" He closed his eyes against the streak of pain behind his eyes.

"I believe he went out soon after you did."

He began to rise again. "There's something I must find."

She put her hands on his shoulders to keep him in place, then sat on his lap for good measure. "In a moment." Carefully, she began to brush the hair away from the wound on his head. "You've got a knot growing here." Her fingers extended the careful strokes into a caress. Each one seemed to draw away a bit more of the pain.

He didn't want to relax beneath her soothing touch, but it felt so good, and her face was so determined and full of concern. When was the last time anyone had comforted him like this? Never. He was used to dealing with his own pain, to solving his own problems, and others' besides. He sighed. It was better that way, in any case. Safer. He didn't want to come to depend on something or someone who wouldn't be there the next time.

But she smelled so damned good. And her bosom was right there before him. Longing flooded him, as fierce and painful as the throbbing in his skull. He eased it by leaning forward, pressing his face into her soft curves and inhaling deeply.

Her fingers stilled. Rose water. Chalk. Lemon. And just . . . fresh, sweet Charlotte. His hands rose up to skim her waist and explore those curves.

The door banged open, and Margie came in, her hands full, trailing maids. Charlotte started to rise from his lap, but he tightened his grip on her.

Their eyes met.

Don't go. He said it with look and touch. Never out loud.

She seemed to hear it, nonetheless. She stayed where she was, her bottom nestled into his lap and she gave orders for the table to be moved next to them, and the supplies laid out.

With quiet competency, she bathed his wound, cleaned and plastered it. Gently, she cleaned the blood from his hair and neck, and removed his stained cravat. Her touch was soft, full of its own tender healing. She bade him drink the hot, sweet tea. She directed the cleaning up, dismissed the servants, and only then did she start to rise again, from his lap.

He had serious complications to attend to. A potentially large and dangerous mess to sort out. But she was here. Supporting him. Tending him. Staying, even though she had questions and suspicions. And she was doing it again, making him crave *more*. More tenderness. More of the care she offered so easily, as if it wasn't a strange and irregular occurrence in his life. As if it didn't feel miraculous. Sacred. Irresistible.

He didn't resist.

He cast aside the fear that tried to rise in him, along with the desire and need. He pushed back the urgency that hovered, calling him to investigate the things those ruffians had said, that Perry's girl had unwittingly confirmed.

He gave in to need. To the scent of rose water and the soothing sound of her voice and the bosom that tantalized him. He cupped her breasts and pulled her down for his kiss.

He kissed her with all the feelings he'd been keeping in a stranglehold. They rose in a flood. He must find a release for them—so he gave them all to her, sent in this kiss. In searing heat and sweeping tongues and the caresses he ran over her.

She heard it. Felt it. Answered. She kissed him back, holding nothing in reserve. Giving. Always giving. And for once, he allowed himself to take. To feel.

He buried his hands in her golden hair. He trailed kisses along her jaw and down the slender curve of her neck. He teased her with lips and tongue, and then he moved his hands down to feel, through her shift and stays, the peaks of her nipples. He pinched them while running his tongue along the neckline of her gown and reveling in the delicate heat and sweetness of her skin.

"Gabriel." She leaned back and his cock stirred further at the movement. He reached to bring her back.

"Gabriel." She framed his face with her soft hands. "This is a lovely, maddening distraction—but we have serious matters to address."

He breathed deeply, pulling in more of her scent. He clutched her tightly for just a moment more, sighed . . .and let her go.

She climbed to her feet, backed away a little. "Tell me, please."

He groaned. "It's so complicated—and it started long ago."

"I want to hear it. All of it. I want to help, Gabriel, but you must stop shutting me out."

She didn't know what she asked. Could he do it? Air all of the dirty family laundry? But that wasn't truly the problem. He would have to confess his worst failings. She would be repulsed. He would have to tell her about the list and his increasingly dangerous attempts to make amends. She would be frightened.

But what was the alternative? To turn her away? To dismiss her, lock her out of the most important parts of his life? Weeks ago, he would have swiftly answered in the affirmative. But now, he was tempted to trust her. Closing his eyes, he saw flashes. Her wicked grin when she proposed he invade London's drawing rooms dressed as a cherub. The way she'd teased him during their marriage ceremony. She'd told him about her siblings and her father and she'd shared the secret longing she had to paint. She'd made him sketches and apple cake. She'd been telling him every day, in small ways, that she cared. That she was there, listening and waiting.

Waiting for him to show up.

Finally.

He drew a deep breath. "It all started with my father.

Before I was born. Before he married, even. When he inherited the marquessate as a young man."

Her eyes closed. In relief? When they opened, she gave him a smile of such joy and gratitude . . . and the words suddenly came easier.

"I told you he fashioned himself king of his domain? I meant it. He holds complete sway over the estate and the village. As magistrate, he's the arbiter of justice, too. When he was young, after he inherited, he also moved to take over the local smuggling ring."

"Smuggling?" She pulled a chair closer to his and sat.

"Well, it *is* coastal Devonshire. The local gang has been in operation since the beginning of the last century. Many of the village families have come to depend on the extra income it provides. But my father didn't want such a lucrative scheme going on unless he had a hand in it. He couldn't openly run the gang, though, so he arranged a proxy. John Hurley."

She paled.

"Yes. Father to our Hurley. The pair of them, our fathers, are thick as thieves. Together, they set about reorganizing the operation. There was a bit of grumbling, at first. But they arranged for safer, steadier transport and set up safe houses along routes to the larger towns, where the tub carriers would transport the goods. There is a quarry on our estate, and my father built a secret room off one of the tunnels to hold incoming shipments. There are also several chambers built into the cliffs below our home of Broadscove. The smugglers stopped complaining about his interference when the jobs became easier, and they began to make significantly more money."

"Speaking as the daughter of a man who fought the French, it doesn't seem quite . . . honorable," she objected. "Your father is, after all, a peer of the realm."

"And a richer one, now," Whiddon said on a sigh. "Do you think I didn't try to dissuade him? Both my brother William and I objected, as soon as we grew old enough to understand." He shuddered. "More than just his honor, it goes against his duty to protect the realm, to be a caretaker of the people. His greed always wins out, though. He hungers for both money and power and ignores all else." He hung his head. "It's shameful. A blight on my family. But not only did my father refuse to listen, he did worse."

She pressed her lips together, obviously bracing herself.

"Eventually, the Customs office began to notice that the Broadscombe gang had increased their activity, and their profit. Once they realized, they sent a new officer to look into it. My father first tried to warn him off, then to pass it off as an insignificant local tradition. The officer didn't fall for it. My father even offered a bribe, but the man was resolute. One night he was lured out to investigate a fire, supposedly set atop the cliffs as a signal. I don't know what happened or who was involved, but the customs man was found broken at the bottom in the morning."

"Good heavens," she breathed.

"William and I desperately tried to talk Father into breaking it up, after that. William especially, hated the whole idea of our family involvement. He argued constantly that it was un-English, as well as immoral. He'd always been mad for the sea and enamored of the navy. He pored over the naval dispatches and the descriptions of the battles. He longed to apprentice to a captain and go to sea, but our father would not hear of it. William wouldn't give up, though. He got himself accepted to the Royal Naval Academy."

"Your father let him go?"

"It was a near thing. Heaven knows, I argued hard and long for it. Father was mean and volatile. I did my best to stand between them, but it grew so much worse once I went to school. I wanted William out from under Father's rule. In the end, he finally agreed. I had to help support William for the two years he served onboard before he could become a Midshipman, but it was well worth it. He did exceedingly well. He'd taken his exam to rise to lieutenant and was waiting for the results when the patrol ship he served on tangled with a French smuggler off the coast of Jersey."

"Oh, no."

Whiddon breathed deeply. "He was injured. He lost a leg and was shipped home." He looked at her with bleak despair. "His life, his future was ruined. By smugglers."

"I can only imagine the anger he must have felt," she whispered.

"He lashed between fury and despair. His sweetheart, the girl he'd pledged to marry, once he'd gained a rank of good salary, declined to wed a cripple. She abandoned him for a banker in Dartmouth."

Her eyes filled. "He lost everything."

"I feared for him. He was so low. He blamed Father for everything. He became obsessed with finding a way to punish him, to take away something that meant something to him. He settled upon the smuggling ring."

"Oh, dear."

"William wanted to destroy it all, but he felt he had to do it from the inside. He started with the lower tier men, befriending them and listening to their advice, their stories and thoughts and grievances. I think he meant to stir them up, and stage a coup, taking over the gang from both Hurley and Father, but something stopped him. He discovered something."

"Something worse than murdering a Customs official?"

"As bad, at the least. More far reaching, in any case."

"I'm almost afraid to hear it."

"I am afraid for you to hear it," he admitted. "God knows, I've been sick over it."

"Just say it," she whispered.

He looked away from her. "William, in spending time with the villagers who were involved with the smuggling, heard their stories, old and new. And some of the older tales . . ." He shook his head.

"How old?" she asked.

"It began with the Terror in France." He lowered his head onto his hand. "It was before you and I were born, but surely you've heard the stories."

"We all have. Torture. Betrayal. Murder. Old and young. Women and children." She shivered. "*Madame la Guillotine.*"

"Most of England was horrified at the stories coming out of France at the time, but my father and Hurley had apparently seen a chance to line their pockets. They set up a network. From the coast, through the countryside, even into Paris, itself."

"They smuggled aristocrats out?" She straightened. "But surely, that was using their operation for good?"

"It might have been, had they not charged exorbitant prices."

"Oh."

"And it wasn't enough that they charged those refugees a fortune to save their lives and get them out of France. Once they had them away, they robbed them blind. Men, women, families. Those people lost nearly everything. They brought what few valuables they could carry, to help them survive, to allow for a chance at a new life. Jewels, art, coin. My father stole it away. Their very futures."

She drew a shuddering breath.

"Yes. I should have told you before I married you. Now you are stained with our shame."

"Your father's sins are not yours," she countered. "Or mine."

"Of course, they are mine. I've lived off of their misfortune my entire life."

"You didn't even know of it!"

"It doesn't change anything." He rubbed his head where the ache had started to return. "William was shocked when he learned of it. The smuggling men described a great many of the things stolen. They whispered that Father still had a cache of the best pieces."

"Oh. What better way to jab at your father?" she whispered.

"Yes. William started to search. He was methodical about it. It took him some time, but he found several new rooms we had not known about, in the cliffs below the house. It was tucked away in one of them. A great chest full of coins and jewels. With it, he found a list of what Father had taken and from whom."

"Why? Why would he keep track?"

"Hubris, likely." Whiddon snorted. "It's the sort of thing he would be proud of. But perhaps he meant to sell them back, later? Or perhaps he wanted to be able to give details of their history when he went to auction them off? I don't know. William made a copy. He brought it to me, here in London. He said there were more, treasures that Hurley and the men had kept. He wanted to keep listening, discover as many as he could. He wanted to complete the list and start to return all the pieces we could."

"Restitution. It would have driven your father mad?"

"God's teeth, yes. But I told him to wait. I had pledged to bring Tensford along to a house party. He was having trouble with his reputation at the time. But I promised I would return home straight after. We would work on it together." He stopped.

"He didn't wait?" she asked quietly.

"No. I should have known he wouldn't. He had the bit in his teeth. He needed something to keep him from feeling useless. He needed a purpose and he wanted to get back at Father. He went back home and kept asking questions, I suppose. Only days later, I received the news. He'd been killed in a tavern fight in the village."

"I'm so sorry." Leaning forward, she reached for his hands and gripped them both tight.

"The worst part . . ." He stopped, swallowed. It was done. William was dead. "I don't know that my father didn't have a part in it."

"What?" All of her color drained away. "Surely not?"

"I am not sure. That is just it. William apparently stole the chest of jewels. I arrived home for the funeral to discover my father furious and convinced that William had taken them and brought them here, to me, in London."

"He hadn't?"

"No. We had agreed to wait until we knew more about the people on the list before we disturbed the jewels and risked alerting Father. But sometime after William's death and before my arrival at Broadscove, Father discovered the treasure was gone."

"Good heavens."

"I did find the list. We had a private spot, in a crumbling wall in the woods, the two of us. It was where we kept our small, private letters, our treasures and small things away from Father's prying eyes. The original list was there, along with the second one that William had started, detailing the jewels that hadn't gone to Father, the ones the men in the gang had kept or sold."

"The jewels weren't there? None of them?"

"No. Only the two lists."

"You never found the jewels?"

"No. I thought them lost, still. I didn't think anyone had found them."

She frowned at him for a moment, then understanding dawned in those blue eyes. "Until today?" She gestured toward his head. "What changed today? What happened?"

He sighed. "Since William's death, I've been going down the list, finding the refugees. I couldn't return their treasures, but I've tried to do as he wished and restore the value of them."

She blinked. Her face softened. She looked down at their clasped hands, then back up at him. The silver in her eyes shone bright as her gaze met his.

He couldn't help it. He reared back. She looked touched. By his actions. She looked . . . proud. Of him.

His pulse pounded. His heart swelled.

It was, perhaps, the most wonderful rush of emotion he'd ever felt.

It was terrifying.

He pulled his hands away.

She didn't say anything. She just waited, giving him time.

He exhaled slowly.

"What happened?" she asked again.

"The latest refugee is a violent man. He had his brutes pick me up. They said he'd already paid my lackey for what belonged to him. And that he was not interested in any further business."

"*Further* business? What belonged to him . . ." She looked shocked. "Oh, good heavens. He'd bought back what was stolen from him? Then someone *has* found the jewels!"

"And William's copy of the list, as well, it would seem. He must have been selling the jewels back to them, the bastard." Fury shot down his spine. "Whoever it is, he's thieving from them again."

"But who? Who would do such a thing?"

The suspicion hit them at the same time. They looked at each other in stunned dismay.

The door connecting Charlotte's room crashed open. The hall boy came in. "It's Hurley," he said, his tone ringing. "It's Hurley doing it!" He pointed an accusing finger at Charlotte. "And she sent him packing!"

Appalled, Whiddon looked to his wife. "Hurley's gone?"

Anger visibly moved over her like a storm taking over the sky. She vaulted to her feet. She glared at the boy, then at him. "Yes, he is gone. There was nothing else to be done."

Whiddon started to speak, but she raised a finger and pointed it at him. "Don't say a word. Either of you. That is enough. That is the outside of enough!" Her bosom heaved enticingly as she drew in a great breath. "This household is far past due for a few fundamental truths." She grabbed the boy by the wrist. "Isn't that true, *Elizabeth?*"

The boy—wait, no. Elizabeth?

The realization hit him, blazing bright as lightning. Elizabeth! His sister? Whiddon stared. Was it true? Judging by the sheer panic crossing the urchin's face, he judged it must be.

She tried to wrench free, but Charlotte held on to her. "He grabbed you by your shirtfront," she said fiercely. "I saw his face! He'd realized you were a woman. He would have figured out who you were, soon enough. And what do you think he would have done with that knowledge? He was already skimming your wages when he thought you were the hall boy! What would he have done to the daughter of the house, in his power? Caught in disguise, with no one else knowing it was you? He could have done anything. Blackmail. Rape. Kidnapping. He is above none of it! I had to get him away from you."

Elizabeth stopped struggling. Elizabeth. His baby sister. When was the last time he'd seen her? She'd been ten, perhaps eleven. She would be just past fifteen, now. He narrowed his gaze, trying to see past the cropped hair and the smudged face. "God's teeth, how did I miss it? You look like William did, as a boy." He frowned, suddenly. "Wait. Why are you not in Hertfordshire?"

She glared back at him, the minx. "Because I'm tired of being stuck in the back of beyond. Tired of being pushed out of this family!"

"But there's been no word. You've been here. . . how long? There's been not a whisper that you've gone missing."

"You don't even know how long I've been here," she sneered. Tossing her head back, she slung her explanation at him, "Aunt Emily thinks I am touring the Lake District with a friend."

"Elizabeth." He took a step toward her and her color blazed. She stepped back against Charlotte. "Don't come near me," she cried. "I hate you! You left me in Hertfordshire. You stopped visiting." Tears began to flow down her face. "They wouldn't let me go to William when he was wounded. They wouldn't let me go to his funeral! I never got to say goodbye!" Turning, she began to sob into Charlotte's shoulder.

Whiddon stared at his wife, stunned. "I only just figured it out, today," she said quietly.

They both stilled as the door opened and Chapman rushed in. Whiddon sighed as he caught a glimpse of Old Alf lingering in the passage outside.

"Sir! I've only just heard you were injured?" The valet stared in horror at the discarded neckcloth and the blood stains on his shirt. Whiddon started to answer, but Charlotte beat him to it.

"His lordship is fine, Chapman. He'll need new linen. Please help him dress." His wife turned to him, her expression fierce. "We need further discussion. Now. And we need to do it where we won't be overheard. E—" She swallowed.

"Eli and I will be in the garden in the square. Meet us out there as soon as you are able."

Taking a hold of Elizabeth's arm, she pulled his sister out into the corridor. He could hear her admonishing Old Alf for loitering about as they moved away.

"What on earth has happened, my lord?" Chapman's worry was clear as he came close enough to inspect his wounded skull.

"Help me change and I'll fill you in."

By the time his clothes were restored, Chapman had a grasp of the situation.

"There might be reason to take heart, sir," the valet mused. "If it is Hurley and he only has the list of names, then it's possible he has not been able to reach very many of them. Not to give myself airs, sir, but some of those men have tried hard to reinvent themselves. Most were not at all easy to find."

"It's slim comfort, but I'll take it. Get out your notes, man, and when I come back inside, we'll figure out who Hurley might have been able to track down. We know of one for sure and I suspect at least one other—that last refugee's *yet* has lingered in my head longer than the drubbing he gave me. Now I know why."

"I'll have them ready."

"We'll have to double our efforts," he told the valet as he set out. "We have to reach as many as we can before Hurley does."

CHAPTER 16

Elizabeth did not resist as Charlotte towed her downstairs and toward the front door. Old Alf followed them, watching avidly, and Charlotte spotted at least one maid peeking around a corner downstairs.

"I have several questions for you, Eli," she declared firmly. "The Earl has his own issues to discuss with you, as well. Come along, we'll have a stroll and a chat."

Fortunately, Elizabeth caught on. "Questions, ma'am?" she asked uncertainly.

"Yes. I want to understand the extent of the education you've had so far and make plans to fill in any gaps." She gave the girl a stern look. "If you want to continue to work in service at this house, I insist you must be able to read and write, at the very least."

The girl bowed her head. "Yes, ma'am."

Charlotte paused to let Old Alf scurry past to open the door. The footman smirked as they left, but Elizabeth kept her head down as they went through the gate into the garden square. Charlotte kept her hold on the girl as they walked all the way around several groupings of young elms and mature shrubs. There was no one about, so she led the way to a bench tucked amongst them, where they would be hidden from view.

Elizabeth rose a teary gaze to her. She collapsed against her suddenly, sobbing into her shoulder again. Charlotte held her tight and let her cry it all out. Such tension the girl must have endured. Playing her role. Seeing her brother. Dealing with villains like Hurley and Mrs. Prigg.

Gradually, the girl's shoulders stopped shaking and her wracking sobs quieted. Heaving a sigh, Elizabeth straightened. "How did you know?"

"You have your brother's nose," she answered wryly. "And you share his habit of tapping your fingers when you are anxious."

The girl nodded. "Thank you," she said, wiping her eyes. "I couldn't see it at first, but you are right. You were right to send Hurley away."

"I'm happy to have the excuse to get him out of the household," Charlotte confessed. "But I do wish you'd been able to trust me, to confide in me, sooner. It must have been dreadful for you."

"Honestly, it wasn't so bad." The girl sank down onto the bench. "I've never known such freedom. Once I managed to get a bedroom to myself in the servant's quarters, it was quite liberating. When I first hired on, they meant to put me in the stables with the other lads." She shivered. "I told them that hay made me snuffle and sneeze and that fixed that. I've learned ever so many new things! Did you know you can pick a lock with just a couple of small, metal tools? And I'm learning my way around London. You wouldn't believe, though, how easily I've got around town. It was like I was invisible and could go and do whatever I wanted."

"I'm afraid I'll have to curtail your freedoms now. You must stick close to the house. If Hurley suspects your true identity, he will likely send back to Broadscombe, asking about you. In the meantime, he'll be watching for every opportunity to snatch you up." She looked the girl over appraisingly. "The seamstresses are here. We could have them make you some simple gowns—"

"No," Elizabeth interrupted with a shake of her head. "I can't become *me* again. Not yet. Don't you see? We must think of my friend Celia, too. She's the one touring the lakes. My aunt thinks I am with her. Celia is posting letters home from me, as she travels. I can't suddenly turn up in London. Questions will be asked. Celia will get in trouble and I'll be found out."

And Elizabeth would be ruined, before her life had truly begun. Charlotte would not let that happen. "You are right, I suppose." She gave the girl a warning look. "Still, I mean to keep you close. We can tell the household that I'm teaching Eli to read." Squeezing the girl's hands, she gave her a grin. "You still must have a bath, though. And everything will be easier if we have at least one person here in our confidence. Margie, perhaps?"

Elizabeth considered. "Yes," she said slowly. "Margie is trustworthy. And she is devoted to you. She will do whatever you ask."

"Good, then. I'll tell her all, later." She paused, listening. "In the meantime, prepare yourself. I hear your brother coming."

Whiddon appeared a moment later, coming around a grouping of trees. He stopped a moment, then came forward and took his sister in his arms.

Charlotte went to scout around once more, to be sure no one lurked nearby, and to give her husband and his sister a moment of privacy.

"I am sorry," Whiddon said softly. "I didn't think. I was so distraught after William died. I knew Father didn't send for you, and I didn't question him. I suppose it comforted me, somehow, to think of you safe and far away, but I should have known you wouldn't be untouched."

She'd gone stiff when his arms went around her, but at his words she relaxed into his embrace. "I felt so alone. Abandoned," she said thickly.

Pulling away, he framed her face with his hands. "Listen, very carefully, for I want you to understand something. After Mother died, Aunt Emily began to ask questions, very quietly. She spoke to the house staff, to the local vicar, to Mother's friends, who had kept up a correspondence with her. She even questioned William and me. I was only just old enough to understand what she was doing. She did not like what she heard. And she was brave enough to confront Father with it."

Elizabeth's gaze widened.

"She wanted to take us all away with her to Hertfordshire." His eyes closed. "Oh, I wanted to go, but she couldn't take us without Father's permission, and he refused. She was persistent, though, and she argued that you, at the very least, needed a mother's care.

"And he relented," his sister said bitterly. "As it didn't matter, as I am just a girl, in any case."

"I thanked God every day that he did," he said solemnly. "We did miss you. You were so sweet, full of sunshine and laughter. You used to pick flowers and give them to me, and I would tuck them in my buttonhole."

"I remember," she whispered. "And you would pick me up and swing with me on your lap. On the old tree swing at the edge of the woods."

"Yes. You would insist we go higher and higher and then you would laugh and laugh. God's teeth, but I loved that sound." He rubbed his aching temple. "And yes, I missed it. Missed you. But I was happy that you were gone, because it meant you stood a chance at keeping that sunshine and laughter."

She stared into his face. "Was it so bad, then?"

He nodded but paused as Charlotte came back. He knew what he had to say to them, and he knew they were not going to like it. "Come and sit." He gestured toward the bench and beckoned his sister, as well, after Charlotte took her seat. She refused, though, and sank down into the grass before the bench.

With a sigh, Whiddon sat beside his wife. "I feel like I've awakened into the middle of a play on Drury Lane."

"Well, I feel as if I've become a heroine in a Gothic novel," Elizabeth countered. She frowned. "I need to know the truth. Was it so awful, living with Father?"

"Living under this thumb, you should say." He nodded. "You are safer and happier in Hertfordshire, believe me."

"Well, that is just it. Your long absence hurt and William's death broke my heart. But they were not all that made me concoct this scheme." She clasped her hands together in her lap. "After the funeral was over and the guests departed, Father wrote then, to summon me home." She cast a look at Charlotte. "He didn't want me about all of those years, didn't want to let me mourn my brother, but now he wants to evaluate my education and make sure I am prepared for my debut, next year."

"No," Whiddon said flatly.

"I could see how it upset and unnerved my aunt, but she wouldn't confide in me." She tossed him an exasperated look. "No one tells me anything! I had to come up with a way to find out for myself."

"It was extremely foolhardy of you to do it this way." Whiddon softened his tone. "But I am forced to admit, it was very brave of you." He sighed. "We can't let Father dictate the terms of your debut." A chill ran down his spine, thinking of the sort of match his father would deem appropriate. His requirements would have nothing to do with Elizabeth and everything to do with his own stature—and pocketbook. "Aunt Emily can supervise your come out."

"Father wrote to her, too. He doesn't think she has enough social consequence."

"It doesn't matter if she doesn't," Charlotte said easily. "Your brother is married to me now, and I have useful social contacts, or I will by the time you are ready for a debut. I can supervise. With your aunt's help, of course."

"Yes. Thank you," Whiddon said with relief. Here she was again, supporting him. And this time, it didn't come with a jolt of panic. He wished he could pull her close. He wished he could settle the remainder of his alarm so easily. Sighing, he pointed a finger at his sister. "We have plenty to worry about before we worry about your debut. We've got to get you—and all of the rest of us—through this mess unscathed." He leaned forward. "But right now, I wish to know how you came to know about Hurley and the jewels."

She ducked her head. "I didn't know about the refugees and the jewels until today—when I listened at the door."

"God's teeth," he muttered.

"But I did suspect Hurley." She fixed him with an earnest gaze. "I think he killed William. Or, arranged his death, rather."

Whiddon covered his eyes for a moment. "Start from the beginning," he ordered.

Elizabeth grimaced. "Well, I didn't come straight to London when I left Hertfordshire. I went to Broadscombe first."

He straightened. "In that get up?"

She nodded.

"Hell and damnation. It's a miracle you weren't found out." He could not bear to think what might have followed.

"Well, I wasn't," she said indignantly. "And you didn't see through my disguise, either."

To his everlasting shame, she was right. He reached for calm. "Why go to the village?"

"To discover the truth. I wanted to hear what the villagers thought of Father. And I heard something at home that made me want to know more about William's death."

"What did you hear?" Charlotte asked gently.

"My aunt and uncle were talking together one evening. He had heard gossip about William's death even so far away as our own county. People said that William and Father were fighting terribly, nearly every minute since he got sent home." She pressed her lips together. "Aunt Emily said no one could blame William for his fury, having lost his leg to a smuggler, and she said . . . she said she wouldn't be surprised to find that Father had him killed."

Whiddon reached down and gripped her shoulder.

She gathered herself and continued. "People in Broadscombe had plenty to say about Father, and they still gossip about William's death. That's how I heard that the day that William died, it wasn't Father, but Hurley he fought with. They had a loud and public confrontation in the village. I heard about it from several different people."

"Hurley the younger?" Charlotte asked. "But wouldn't he have been here, in London?"

"No. Father didn't send him here until after William's funeral." Whiddon lifted a shoulder. "But there would have been nothing unusual about the two of them arguing. They fought every time they came within several feet of each other."

"Yes, I heard that too." Elizabeth nodded. "But this time, it nearly came to blows."

"Hurley would fight a man with one leg?" Charlotte sounded indignant.

"I suppose not, but they came close. And then, after they were broken apart, one of the smuggling men took William to the Sunken Anchor."

"The tavern where he died," Whiddon said quietly to Charlotte.

"He was there for quite a while, sitting in a corner and drinking with Reeves all afternoon."

"Wait?" That didn't sound right. "William was drinking with Reeves? But he is one of Hurley's cronies. He has been since we were young."

"The villagers seemed to think William had decided to reconcile with the idea of the smuggling. He'd become friendly with a good many of the smuggling men, asking questions, listening to their ideas and grievances. There were whispers that William meant to wrest control of the gang away from the Hurleys."

"Away from Father," Whiddon corrected. "So he could shut it down."

"The villagers thought not. They all expected William and Father to cut out the Hurleys and run the gang without giving away a headman's portion."

Whiddon snorted.

"You might have known different, but that's what all of the Broadscombe gossips believed. That's what Hurley confronted William about. And later, after William was good and foxed, Hurley came into the tavern, too. He sat down and stayed, with William boxed between him and Reeves, while they leaned close and questioned him."

"No matter how drunk he got, William would never confide anything in Hurley." He shook his head. "They were mortal enemies."

Elizabeth looked solemn. "The tavern keeper tells folks he

thinks there was more going on than everyone else could see. He said William didn't order so many drinks as to grow so drunk and slurred as he was that day. Now they all whisper that Reeves slipped something in his ale. Something to loosen his tongue."

"Good heavens," Charlotte whispered.

"Hurley slipped away after a while, leaving William passed out over the table and Reeves drinking with the men at the bar. He was gone for a good while, the tavern keeper said, then he stepped back in, gave Reeves a nod and left again."

Whiddon's pulse quickened. He tensed as she went on.

"When it grew late, Reeves went back to William at the table. To wake him, he told the other men. He sat close to William again and spoke low, nudging him to wake and talking in his ear. William did come awake, roaring mad. He went for Reeves' throat. The men say that William was in a frenzy, shouting about thievery and dishonor . . . and Abigail."

"His betrothed?" Charlotte asked, low.

"His sweetheart," Whiddon spat out. "The girl he loved from the moment he first glimpsed her. They were inseparable from the start. Everyone knew they had an understanding, that they meant to marry just as soon as William reached a salaried rank." He could not hide the bitterness he felt. "Until William was crippled. Her mind changed quickly enough, then. She deserted him."

"Poor William."

Sorrow swathed Charlotte's expression, but there was something else there, too. Whiddon didn't like the way she looked at him, as if she'd just found an anchoring piece of a puzzle.

Elizabeth blinked back tears. "The tavern keeper said they tried to calm William, but he wasn't rational. Gone out of his head, is how he described it. William stumbled about and tried to rush anyone who approached him. He kept lunging for Reeves. He broke loose of the tavern owner's hold and went for him again. Reeves sidestepped and William went down, cracking his head on the bar."

"Father said they carried him home unconscious. He never woke up and died the next day." Bleak horror and grief swamped him once again, as it always did when he thought of his brother fighting, dying alone.

"You see?" Elizabeth was on her feet again. "Now it all makes sense. Hurley must have baited William. He drugged and questioned him. William must have let some bit of information slip. Something Hurley used to go and find the jewels. And then he came back to give the signal that he'd been successful. They would have wanted William out of the way, then. Reeves must have agitated him, hoping he'd have some sort of fit or accident while he was still muddled and drugged."

Whiddon exchanged glances with Charlotte. "We can't know for sure. It all sounds plausible, knowing the personalities involved."

"Your Father could not have known of Hurley's involvement," Charlotte said. "He would not have sent Hurley here to watch you and look for the jewels."

"No, he didn't know Hurley had them already. And he sent the man to the place where it would be easiest to dispose of the goods." He shook his head. "I'm tempted to just tell Father the whole story and allow him to take care of it. That justice would be brutal."

"Well, we cannot wait that long," Charlotte said firmly. "Hurley is a danger to Elizabeth, now. And what if he hears of that young girl that was at the house today? He'll worry that you will begin to figure out what he's been up to—and he'll likely come after you."

Whiddon bristled. "He wouldn't dare."

"He would dare anything if he felt endangered. Look what he's done just in the name of greed. It would serve his purpose to harm you. He could lay the blame for his malign activities on you and tell your father that one of the refugees took their revenge."

Whiddon raised a brow at her. "You have quite a diabolical mind, yourself, Charlotte."

"Yes. You may be grateful it is on your side."

He braced himself. "Yes, and I will ask you to use it to protect Elizabeth. I think it would be best if the two of you left town. I thought perhaps to Monkford, but Hurley will likely know about the estate, so perhaps your home in Dorsetshire—"

"No!"

The refusal came simultaneously from both women.

Charlotte looked grim. "This will not be the excuse you need to push me—us—away, Gabriel."

Frowning, he opened his mouth to answer, but she held up a hand. "Do you think Hurley won't think of that, as well? And my devious mind will be of no use keeping him out of our small cottage, nor will my aunt or younger brother."

"I don't want you at risk, Charlotte."

"It's too late for that. And we will discuss this further, but we've been out here too long." Sighing, she stood next to Elizabeth. "You were right about keeping on with your role as Eli. You'll be safer that way, from Hurley and from scandal. But that means you are going to have to go back and finish cleaning that chandelier."

Elizabeth shrugged. "I don't mind. And Mr. Flemming has promised the staff a plum duff for our pudding tonight."

"Go on up to my room afterwards, and I'll have Margie draw you a bath." She wrinkled her nose at his sister. "And we'll find you a new set of clothes. You've been wearing that set since I arrived."

Charlotte turned all of that determination and imperious manner on him. "As for you, I know you are dying to summon your friends for a war council, but it will have to wait."

"We can't wait—"

"We can. You haven't eaten properly or rested in days. Mr. Flemming has acted a hero today, and he's also fixed a fine dinner in anticipation of really feeding you, at last. You can wait that long. We'll dine together in your sitting room, since the dining room is still not finished."

With bad grace, he nodded. He was anxious to start after Hurley, but Chapman was out searching already, and he could send for Chester and Tensford and Sterne after they'd eaten.

They all started back, Elizabeth moving ahead, and Charlotte edged close and tucked her arm in his. He had to admit, he didn't mind the thought of sitting quietly alone with her a moment. He would store up her smiles, her calm assurance and her warm beauty against the dark whirlwind that was sure to follow.

CHARLOTTE WENT STRAIGHT to her room and collapsed at her vanity table. She'd called for Margie to attend her as she came in, and the maid soon knocked at the door.

"Close the door behind you, please, Margie." Charlotte sat with her before the fire and told her all.

Margie was horrified.

"Oh, Miss!" She stared in horror. "When I think of some of the things I said to the boy, the orders I gave." She gaped. "I told him ever so many times to look smart and get to work!" Her hands rose to cover her mouth.

"And so you are going to have to continue," Charlotte told her. "We must hide Lady Elizabeth's identity until we can sort all of this out. We cannot have Hurley knowing who she is. And I was nearly ruined just because I fell in the Thames." In her head, she asked forgiveness for leaving out mention of that *kiss*. "Imagine what the scandalmongers will do if they hear of this."

Charlotte bit her lip, thinking. Perhaps it was time to flesh out some of the ideas she'd been mulling. "I've been thinking of asking you something, Margie, and now might be the perfect time."

"Yes, ma'am?"

"As you know, I've had difficulty engaging a lady's maid. The prospects might improve now that Hurley is gone, but I've been wondering if perhaps you might wish to train to take the position?"

"*Me*, ma'am?" The maid looked utterly flabbergasted.

"Yes. You've already proved your loyalty and shown your willingness to work. That is what I need in a lady's maid. The rest you can learn. In fact, perhaps Lady Elizabeth can begin your training. She'll need to keep closeted as much as possible. We'll let it out that she is learning to read, but she might wish to be well and truly occupied."

"Oh, your ladyship, I would be honored!"

"Good. You can at least learn the basics of fashion and hair. We can arrange for some more advanced learning once you have mastered the fundamentals."

And that stood a chance of keeping them both busy and away from prying eyes for long stretches of each day.

"As for tonight, I promised you would help the girl get a bath in here, hidden away. Will you have the maids bring up hot water for me, as well? And put the curling tongs on to heat, will you please?" She stood. "I want to look my best tonight."

Margie bustled off, smiling, and Charlotte went back to her dressing table. She sat a moment, examining her reflection, but not really seeing it. Whiddon had opened up to her today. He'd let her catch a glimpse of the real man inside the frivolous shell he used to distract the rest of the world. That was the man his friends knew. Honorable. Fearless. Fair. Willing to make real sacrifices in the name of justice.

Hope sprouted inside of her and she longed to feed it, to let it grow wide and tall and lush. It was possible. A true marriage of minds and bodies, of purpose and true, honest emotion.

Of love.

They could find their way to it. Staring at herself in the mirror, she knew it. Because she'd spoken true this morning, when he'd given her a studio and hope and despair all at once. When Whiddon looked at her, he saw her like no one else.

To her uncle, she'd only been a nuisance.

To her siblings, she always been a comfort, provider, protector.

To her aunt, at first, she'd been an obligation. But that had softened and changed until they were friends and companions at arms in the struggle to survive and thrive.

But Whiddon? Only he looked closely and saw *her*. All the myriad pieces of her. Sometimes sarcastic and occasionally still innocent of worldly concerns. A bit bossy. Not afraid to want good things for herself and those she loved. Artistic. Observant. Always fascinated by people and inordinately interested in what lay beneath their facades. Whiddon had mined all of those qualities in her and not only did he see them, but he seemed to actually like them, too.

It felt ... miraculous.

But she knew what he was going to do. She'd put him off for now, but he was going to try to push her away. Keep her out of this business with Hurley and the French refugees, from the smugglers and the jewels.

But that was not what she wanted.

She wanted to do the same for him. She knew his funny and generous sides. She knew that he was also observant. She knew the part that was never hesitant to rush in to rescue the underdog. She loved all of that about him. How could she not? But she wanted more. She wanted to share their lives. She longed for the chance to love all of him, in the way it seemed no one else ever had.

He was going to use their agreement against her. She knew it. Well, she wasn't going to go along with it. In fact, she was more than willing to turn it all up and over, for a chance at happiness.

With grim determination, she reached for her sketch pad and her pastel sticks. She went to work, sketching furiously until the door opened behind her and a maid came in with hot water. She set aside her work then and stood to fetch her scented soap.

Strategy.

Her plan was entering a new phase and she wanted to use every weapon at her disposal.

CHAPTER 17

Whiddon paced while the dinner service was set up in his sitting room. He rehearsed his arguments and bolstered his resolve.

She was going to put up a fight.

But he would stand firm. Gird his loins. Hold the line.

He was running out of masculine phrases for stubbornness. It all went out of his head, in any case, when she came through the connecting door.

She wore a frock of pale yellow and white, with a dangerously low scooped neckline, a shallow bodice and tiny, frivolous sleeves of sheer lace. Her hair had been caught up high on the back of her head and left to fall in a shower of golden ringlets.

She smiled at him—and she glowed like the sun.

Something inside him stretched toward her, reaching for the warmth she gave.

Oh, no. No, no, no.

A knock sounded, the door opened, and Old Alf came in, carrying the first course.

"Why don't we just enjoy our dinner before we talk?"

Charlotte suggested. "I did ask Mr. Flemming to keep it simple."

Simple turned out to be a clear soup with mushrooms, a filet of perch, thick with herbs, and beefsteaks prepared with butter and shallots. It was delicious. Charlotte was at ease and charming. Even Old Alf waited on the table as if he'd done it every night for years.

Whiddon barely noticed any of it. He needed to rally, to gather his thoughts. But all of his attention was focused on his wife and the connection he felt sizzling between them.

It had been there from the first and somehow, she had been making him feel more every day since. Sympathy. Admiration. Amusement. Tenderness. And just now, hot, soul-blistering desire.

He'd never had such a reaction to a woman. One so multi-faceted and complex. One that made him want to explore all the layers between them as well as each soft, intoxicating inch of her.

"Charlotte, we have to discuss the risks we're taking," he said at last, pushing his plate away.

"We do." She set down her cutlery. "But my thoughts on the matter are complicated."

"Mine are simple. I do not want you in danger. Nor Elizabeth."

"It's not so simple for me to decide who poses the bigger risk—Hurley or you."

His jaw dropped in shock and horror. "Excuse me?"

She stood and left the table. "Consider it from my point of view for a moment. Hurley may indeed wish to grab me or Elizabeth, presumably to use as leverage against you. If he did, wouldn't he be foolish to harm us?"

"Harm you?" He stood and paced after her. "He *killed* my brother!"

"Perhaps," she said, raising a brow. "We do not truly know."

"Oh?" He stopped when he grew close enough to catch her scent. She'd disordered his senses enough already. "Tell me, then. Honestly, for we've always been honest with each other. Do you think he did it?"

She drew a deep breath. "Yes." She released it slowly. "Listening to the information Elizabeth gathered, and judging Hurley by what I've seen of him these last weeks? Yes, I think she's likely right."

"Then I tell you, honestly, that if he gets a hold of you, he will harm you."

"He might," she conceded.

"You see why I must get you safely away."

"No." She pursed her lips. "I see that sending us away only leaves open unknown opportunity for anyone who might wish us ill. If we stay here, we are surrounded by a houseful of staff who already hold a grudge against Hurley and can be put on the watch for him. We'll have you to protect us, and your friends as well. Elizabeth has already pledged to stay close. I vow to be careful. Given all of that, I feel like the chance that Hurley could get near us is small." She paused and breathed deeply once more. "On the other hand, if you seize this opportunity to send me away, I feel like it will be only the beginning."

"The beginning of what?" he asked hoarsely. He was afraid he knew the answer.

"Of the physical and emotional distance you will place between us. And I tell you here and now, Gabriel, that it will mean a one hundred percent chance of you breaking my heart."

He reared back, physically taking a step away from her. "I —" He stopped and walked away to the other side of the room.

"It's hard for me to measure," she said, unrelenting. "What is worse? The chance of a quick end or the certainty of a lifetime of yearning?"

Arguments and denials tumbled in his head. "We spoke of this before. We had an agreement—"

"Yes. We did." She straightened her shoulders and faced him. "But I do not believe that you, in good conscience, can expect me to hold to that agreement."

"Of course I can," he retorted, indignant. "Why wouldn't I?"

"Because you were not honest with me. It was entered into under false circumstances."

"In what way was it false?"

She held up a finger. "First, you agreed we would live together." She broke off his attempt to protest. "Yes, I know. Separate, but together, under one roof. Yet here you are trying to remove me."

She ticked off a second finger. "Secondly, you allowed me to believe that your separate life would be one that I might expect of any gentleman. I imagined clubs, estate business, friends, social events. Perhaps racing, gambling or a mistress, at the worst. There was no mention of filthy houses, villainous stewards, smuggling, jewels or murder."

"I didn't—"

He stopped when she moved in close. The scent of her drifted on the air, the same ever-shrinking expanse of charged air that moved between them. His nostrils flared and he fixed his attention on the pale, slender column of her neck and down to her bosom, where her breasts swelled over the embroidered edge of her bodice.

She didn't object. Instead, she moved closer still. He raised his gaze to her expression, which for once mixed a bit of bashfulness in with her usual determination.

"Also," she said huskily. "I believe you agreed that we

would address the matter of . . . heirs."

Hell and damnation.

"I want to renegotiate our agreement," she declared.

He should be annoyed. Instead, he was only hotly, torturously aroused. "I'm fine with the way it stands." Damn, but it was his cock that was standing, swift and full and urging him to get on with it and give his wife what she wanted.

"I'm not," she countered. "Just as I worried would happen, I want more. I think you want more, too."

He couldn't even deny it.

"I can read the signs you don't know you are showing, remember? I know you do." Her tone softened. "And I know you don't want to want it."

He flushed, stuck without a reply. How could he tell her she was right, without insulting her?

"I think if you only clarify a few things, you'll feel better about it." Stepping in, she reached up and tapped his temple. "Understand here." She moved her hand down to let it rest on his chest, over his heart. "And here. Know that it is *me* you would choose to trust. Charlotte. Your wife." She lowered her voice to a whisper. "Gabriel, your mother wasted her chance and never let herself really know you. Your father selfishly demanded perfection without offering even the slightest bit of love or support in exchange. Neither of those things were caused by you."

He shook his head.

"Look at it this way. Your brother's betrothed gave in to fear and grief and pride instead of listening to the love in her heart. Do you blame William for her betrayal?"

"Of course not!"

"Then you cannot blame yourself for the shortcomings in your family. You cannot blame me for them, or expect me to act in the same manner, either. I am not them. Don't punish me, or yourself, for their sins."

It shouldn't be possible for a man to feel so many things simultaneously. He wasn't sure he was going to survive it without exploding like a stuck steam valve. His spine stiffened in defensive denial. He felt mortified, but also incredibly touched.

Because she was right. He should absolutely judge her for herself alone. She was the one who *looked*. Who peered past his shenanigans and saw all the odd, empty places inside of him. And instead of condemning him for them, she promptly set about filling them up. With good food and heartfelt gifts and small, trusting glimpses into her own unique vision of the world. She fussed over him and took care of him and just . . . gave a good tinker's damn about him, in a way that no other woman ever had.

Who could he trust, if not her?

Her hand still rested on his chest. Picking it up, he kissed her fingers, the soft skin on the back, the tender spot inside of her wrist. He raised it to rest on his shoulder, gathered her close and kissed her.

Yes. There. Her. She tasted like coming home. Like safety and comfort tangled with the thrill of a furious gallop. Hungry, relentless, he kissed her, and she sighed and kissed him in return, sliding one hand under his arm and up across his back.

Their tongues danced. He pressed her tight against his bulging erection and covered her breast with one hand. The other grabbed a hold of her skirts and began to inch them higher.

"Gabriel, wait," she gasped. "You need to understand. I'm negotiating for—" She paused and ran a searching gaze over him.

"For what?"

"For everything," she blurted. "I want it all. I want to sleep with you and wake up with you. Stay with you. I want to help with your search for Hurley and the jewels. I've already made some sketches of him you can use," she said hurriedly. "I want to know your sister and I want you to know my siblings, too." Reaching up, she placed a hand on his jaw. "I want to laugh and cry with you. Fight and make up. I want it all. A real family."

He swallowed. It sounded wonderful—and impossible.

"You have to at least try, Gabriel," she whispered.

He knew she was right. She wanted him. All the saints knew, he wanted her. There was nothing blocking them except his own doubts and disbeliefs.

They were a damned poor substitute for the woman before him.

She was right. He had to try.

Nodding, he swept her into his embrace again. Claimed her with his mouth. Stole her breath. Opened wider and demanded more, pushing the kiss deeper.

She gave him everything and made demands of her own. Of course, she did. He should have expected nothing less. Her hands ran over him, and his skin heated in their wake. He touched and stroked her, and she copied his urgency. He was sparking, coming alive under her touch and he could not wait to feel her, skin to skin.

A knock sounded on the door. It started to open. Whiddon pulled away and snarled. "Later!"

Eyes wide, Old Alf snapped the door shut again.

Reaching down, Whiddon lifted Charlotte's skirts and hoisted her to his waist. With a gasp and a laugh, she clutched him tight and wrapped her legs around him. He kissed her again as he carried her across the room. When he reached the door, he pressed her into it and leaned in, holding her there while he turned the latch and buried his face in the curve of her neck.

Their tongues played, crossing like blades as he let her

feet drift to the floor. He busied his fingers with the buttons at the back of her gown. When they were all loose, he gently freed her of those flimsy sleeves and eased her bodice down. He made short work of the tapes of her stays—and her glorious bosom was laid bare before him.

He knelt and it felt only proper as he thumbed one nipple into a taut peak and licked the other with short, stabbing strokes of his tongue.

Her breath hitched and her hips gave a short, jerking thrust.

Grinning, he doubled his efforts, sucking and rolling first one nipple, then the other. Her head tilted back. Goosebumps rippled across her flesh. She began to tremble, just a little. "Gabriel?" she whispered.

He let her nipple slide out of his mouth. "Charlotte?"

"There's another door." She gave an ineffectual wave of her hand toward the door that connected her rooms.

"So there is." Mouth quirking, he stood and hoisted her up again, setting out across the room. Every step was delicious torture as her heated core rubbed against his erection. When they reached the door, he locked it and set her on her feet again before sending his hands delving beneath her skirts. His cock throbbed and she jumped when his fingers traveled past her knee to stroke the soft skin of her inner thigh.

"Gabriel?" There was a wealth of questions buried in the syllables of his name.

"Charlotte." All the answers to every question lived in hers.

"What are you . . ?"

"You asked for everything." What she'd asked for was all of him. She'd asked him to try. It went against his every instinct, to share so much of himself. He'd felt safe for a long time, behind his wall of irreverent humor, nonchalance, and general disdain. If he didn't care, it couldn't hurt. It was the mantra that protected him, made him feel impenetrable and unassailable. And very much alone.

Now she asked him to care. How could he refuse when she did it so easily? So thoroughly? Every time she offered him understanding, or did something thoughtful, he lapped it up and wanted more. She'd pushed and prodded him into a state of craving and the only reason he could even contemplate her request was because she'd always been there, offering what he needed. She'd awakened oceans of hunger in him, undying waves of yearning. But he trusted her. The thought gave him a jolt, but it rang of truth. He wasn't alone. There were two of them, now. Together, they could brave the onslaught, ride out the storm, find the calm.

"I can't give you everything all at once, not in one night. But we can find our way together."

Her gaze softened. She understood all that he meant. "Yes," she breathed.

"I mean to start right here, with your pleasure, and with mine."

RELIEF AND JOY and desire coalesced into a fog that rolled in over her. Her bodice had already dropped down to her waist. Now he was raising her skirts up to meet it. She leaned against the door, her breasts bare and her nipples hard and more of her legs showing every second, while he trailed kisses past her knee and up the length of her thigh.

She'd gone breathless. Wild. Wanton. And incredibly nervous. She hadn't meant to push him so hard, so soon. But circumstances had forced her hand and she would never regret asking for a chance at happiness or encouraging him to reach for his own.

He nudged her legs apart a little and her racing pulse settled into a steady throb, right where his fingers had paused.

"So lovely," he breathed. The feel of his breath on her sent her into a shiver of anticipation.

"Gabriel?" she asked again, low. She had an idea what happened in the marriage bed, though honestly, she'd secretly thought it sounded preposterous. But they were not in bed. She was leaned up against the door and he still had all of his clothes on and she . . . "I don't know what to do," she confessed.

He grinned suddenly. "Have I flustered you? I think that puts me two points ahead." He put a hand on the inside of her leg and lifted it high, opening her most private place to his view in the most disconcerting way. "Hold on," he warned. "I'm about to go for three."

He touched her. Right there. She gasped. He didn't pause. His clever fingers continued exploring. Her hips bucked. She flung one hand out to brace against the door. The other reached down to grip his wrist where he held her leg imprisoned. She was splayed open, balancing on one leg and she didn't care. Her attention was fixed on the wicked path his fingers were walking, on the exquisite ripples of pleasure that spread outward from his touch.

"No," he said suddenly, letting her leg fall. He stood quickly and scooped her into his arms in one fluid motion. "I need both hands for this." Setting her down on the edge of the bed, he leaned in and kissed her, nipping and teasing. "And my tongue."

She blinked, trying to absorb that information, as he leaned her back to lay on the bed. He pushed her skirts up again and placed her feet to the edge of the mattress. "Now. That's better."

She lifted her head to look down at him. "Better than what?"

Leaning in, he licked all the way along the seam of her swollen sex.

Her head fell back. "Oohhh."

She could never have imagined such incredible feelings. A combination of pleasure, distress and a great, aching need. He knew her body better than she did. With fingers and tongue, he stroked and licked until she was writhing. He tasted her everywhere, all along her folds and valleys and on up to the raised bud that awaited him. Using both hands, he spread her wide open and he took his time, breathing, dipping, tasting and circling until her breath came in great, heaving pants and she spread her legs wider still. "Gabriel!"

It was a plea, and with a low, throaty chuckle he answered, pressing harder, flicking his tongue over her again and again.

It broke over her like a wave. Her back arched and she thrust into him, moaning in rapture and disbelief until the spasm had its way with her. It held her in its grip for several long, lovely moments before slowly letting her go.

She lay there, stunned, while he sat back. "Three," he pronounced with smug, masculine triumph.

"Four. Five. *Ten*," she said fervently. "I'll extend you a hundred points, if you only promise to do that again."

"I don't think so." He climbed to his feet and stood over her, grinning wickedly. "We'll get to a hundred, but I'd prefer to do it one point at a time."

She propped herself up on her elbows. "None of that bore any resemblance to the talk poor Aunt Bernadine gave me before our wedding."

"Your spinster aunt?" He sounded fascinated. "What did she tell you?"

"Only the things I thought I already knew." She raised a

brow. "But not even the snickering girls at school mentioned what you just did."

He started to remove his coat. It was fitted tightly, though, so she sat up to help. "And what did you think of what Aunt Bernadine and the snickering girls had to say?"

She lifted a shoulder. "I thought it intriguing." Glancing down at the bulge in his breeches, she made a face. "However, I am beginning to entertain doubts."

"Never fear. It will all work remarkable well and you will enjoy it just as much."

She snorted in disbelief.

"I'll make sure you do." Reaching down, he stroked her cheek. "Don't you trust me?"

She took his hand and kissed the back. "I do. That's what all of this is about, Gabriel. Trusting each other."

His eyes darkened and he reached for her, grasping the bodice of her gown and trying to pull it up and over her head. She wiggled, helping him and he kept going, tossing aside her stays and shift and petticoat. Kneeling once more, he pressed a kiss just above each garter before slowly untying each one and rolling the stocking down with slow, sensuous movements. By the time he was done, her heart pounded again, and she was back on her propped elbows, watching him while hunger grew in her once more.

"You are so lovely," he whispered.

She sat up and began to unbutton his waistcoat. "I want to see you, too."

Together, they worked to shed his clothes. Charlotte's attempts were hampered by his stolen kisses, but at last he stood proud and bare before her.

She feasted her eyes. So much strong, masculine beauty. Long legs, muscular thighs. Slim hips that widened and flared into a powerful chest and broad shoulders. She let her curious gaze linger on his manhood, long and erect, jutting toward her eagerly.

She looked up into his eyes. They were both exposed, poised on the edge of a singular, critical moment—and she rejoiced at how raw and elemental and full of wonder she felt. What they were about to do felt eternal, but it was also unique, and they could only achieve it together.

She held up her arms and he surged into them. Shifting her to the top of the bed, he showered her with fervent kisses, all along her abdomen, her breasts, her neck.

"Gabriel? Am I . . . Can I . . . touch you?"

He promptly rolled over to his side and swept a hand in wordless invitation.

Hesitant, she reached out and ran soft fingertips along the length of him. He felt like satin. She trailed the tip of a finger around the round end, and he sucked in a breath. Experimentally, she did it again, then slid her grip down to explore the curious sac beneath.

With a groan, he caught her hand and trapped it over her head, rolling over onto her. "I need you now, Charlotte."

His manhood pulsed between them, pressing against her thigh. She nodded. "What do I do?"

"Just feel. Enjoy. Let me make it good for you."

Her skin felt hot. Too tight, all over. He eased between her thighs, and she felt the broad tip of him poised at the entrance to her body. He rocked and pushed inside.

She stilled.

"All right?" The words sounded strained.

She nodded cautiously.

His hips rocked again. She felt a sudden, sharp sting of pain. She tensed. He stilled. Her fingers bit into his shoulders at the shock of it, but he kissed her softly. The sting lingered, a strange sort of pain, but it gradually eased. After several long moments, it was gone. He was still there, though, filling and stretching her in a way that felt odd and yet, incredibly right.

He pushed further. Her body still adjusted, bit by bit . . . and suddenly, he was in. She was full. It felt strange. She felt again that glorious anticipation, then he began to move.

Steady motion, plunging in and out again. He loomed over her, so large and powerful, but the look on his face was focused and tender. "Charlotte," he whispered.

He shifted her hips, altered his angle and his pace increased. The blaze of excitement inside of her climbed with him. The intimacy was astounding. They were so very aware of each other, so focused on what they were building between them. His thrusts grew more forceful. Suddenly, he reached between them and touched her swollen bud, rubbing with matching, firm flicks.

Desire flared and now she knew what she was reaching for. It came quicker this time. Fiercer and hotter. She felt her inner muscles pulsing around him and he cried out, filling her with a frenzy of sudden, hard thrusts. His body arched over hers.

Gradually, it was over. She found herself shaking. It was all so much. Emotion and discovery. Intensity and surprise.

Shifting to his side, he gathered her close and held her in his arms. She clutched at him until the tremors subsided. With a sigh, she wished that this moment could last. No past. No future. Just him and her and the unbearable tenderness she felt right now.

She reveled in it. Basked in the moment, sure that at any second, he was going to roll away, move her aside, send for his friends and start to organize the hundreds of tasks that lay ahead of them.

But his breathing deepened, and his arms grew heavy. The warmth between them felt so soothing. Nestling closer, she closed her eyes and followed him into sleep.

CHAPTER 18

Whiddon woke before dawn, feeling lighter and more carefree since... since he could remember. It made not a whit of sense. He carried all the same burdens, in addition to the heavy news about Hurley and jewels.

Easing his arm from around his wife, he moved carefully from the bed. She shifted and sighed in her sleep but didn't wake. He stood at the edge, watching her, feeling the rush of emotion wash over him—and allowing it to come, for once, instead of pushing it away.

She was the reason his burdens felt lighter, why he faced the day with optimism instead of dread. Whatever happened, she would stand at his shoulder. They would face it together. She'd given him his sister. She'd given him her trust.

It was that last thought that made him feel like he could move mountains.

He went next door instead, to ask Chapman to help him dress in the countess's rooms, so that she could sleep on. He went downstairs and consulted with Mr. Flemming, who agreed to his request and started chopping, mixing and calling out orders with a flourish. And he called Old Alf and

Margie to the dining room and set them to work while he went to summon his friends.

A couple of hours passed before he returned to his room. Charlotte still slept. He was incredibly tempted to crawl in with her and give her a thorough . . . waking, but there was no time. Instead, he leaned down and nuzzled her neck. "Wake up, slugabed. Mischief is afoot. You don't want to miss it."

She cringed and lifted her shoulder to protect a ticklish spot. "Mmm." Rolling over, she opened her eyes. They widened instantly and he had to move quickly out of the way as she lurched to sit up.

"Good heavens! You are dressed. It's so light out! Have I slept so late?"

"Indeed, you have." He smirked at her. "I would apologize for waking you in the dark of night for point number six, except—"

"I wouldn't believe you?" she asked wryly.

"Nor should you, as every word would be a lie." He kissed her soundly and moved away from the very real temptation to do more. "But you must rise, now. Margie is waiting. I've sent for Chester, Sterne, Tensford—and even Stoneacre. They will be here within the hour, and you don't wish to miss the war council, as you so aptly named it. We are convening over breakfast."

"Over breakfast?" Her mouth dropped. "Here?"

"Yes. Here. We've been making preparations. Let Margie dress you so that you can inspect our work."

She didn't tally long over her toilette, but she looked beautiful when he met her coming down the stairs. Her hair was gathered loosely at her nape and her day gown was of the lightest blue, sprigged with darker blue blooms. "You look like a perfect summer day."

Laughing, she came close and brushed something from

the side of his mouth. "And you look like you started without us."

He grinned. "It couldn't be helped. Mr. Flemming has made hot, buttered crumpets. Now, come and give us your stamp of approval."

He led her to the dining room, where Margie waited with bated breath and Old Alf was setting up warming platters along the sideboard.

"Oh! The chandelier is hung!" Charlotte smiled warmly at the footman. "Did you do that, Alfred?"

"Just this morning, ma'am."

"It looks wonderful. And so does the rest of the room, Margie. Thank you both, so much."

Both servants looked gratified, but strangely, Whiddon thought they couldn't match the swell in his heart as a parade of kitchen maids filed in with dishes from the kitchen. He spotted an egg pie, rashers of ham and bacon, fruited pastries, and of course, the hot, buttered crumpets. He pulled Charlotte aside. "I cannot tell you of the countless times I have eaten breakfast at Tensford's table, or Sterne's. Even Chester's grandmother has fed me. This is the first time I've been able to return the favor—and I never expected to feel such satisfaction from it." He took her hand and squeezed. "It's another gift you've given me—one I had no idea would mean so much."

She smiled and blinked back tears, but a knock sounded on the front door and they both turned to go and meet their guests—and begin to plan their campaign.

They accomplished a great deal. Whiddon caught everyone up on the latest developments. He put Chapman in charge of looking for Hurley through his contacts in the network of London servants. Sterne mentioned that Derby, his valet, might like a chance at a bit of intrigue.

"Charlotte has made up some sketches of Hurley that

might be of help," Whiddon said. He raised a brow in her direction. "Could you do an extra set for Derby?"

She flushed and assured him she could.

Stoneacre requested the names of the refugees Whiddon had yet to locate. He hoped to use his government contacts to perhaps track them down. The others planned to help search them out as well, as everyone agreed that it would be best for them to find them before Hurley did. Whiddon would make first contact with them once they were found.

"I cannot implicate my father when I speak to them," he said with a sigh. "No matter how much he deserves to be exposed. What I've been saying is that my brother and I recently discovered the truth about the thefts carried out by smugglers that operated from our holdings."

"Which is true," Charlotte said stoutly.

"It's not the whole truth, and some of them must know it." He shrugged. "But I cannot betray my father so completely."

"I have an idea or two about how to handle your father," Stoneacre spoke up. "I think that together, we can manage to convince him to shut down the operation. But let us deal with the situation before us, first."

"Actually, Charlotte," Chester interrupted. "It might not be a bad idea for you to make more sketches of Hurley. Whiddon can leave them with the refugees he contacts, with a warning that he is not and has never worked with the man on this matter. He can also share the true statement that he is the one believed to have possession of the bulk of the stolen items." He gave a bitter laugh. "And if they take care of him for us, so much the better."

A debate erupted then about such a possibility and which outcome would be best. Whiddon didn't care who apprehended Hurley, as long as he got the chance to question him about the whereabouts of the jewels. He noticed, however, that Charlotte didn't offer an opinion. She looked distracted, in fact.

When the discussion wound down, she looked suddenly to Stoneacre. "My lord, in your work with Half Moon House and your wife's crusades, have you met many pawnbrokers? Or better yet, any of the more invisible fences that deal in stolen goods?"

"Indeed," Stoneacre answered with a smile. "In both my public and my private work, I've made a great many questionable acquaintances."

Whiddon immediately saw what she was getting at. "Yes," he said. "Charlotte is right. Hurley might try to sell off the jewelry, if he cannot find the owners."

"It might be a good idea to leave a list of the pieces with those men Lord Stoneacre trusts to report back to us, should they show up, or be whispered about."

"A very good idea, Lady Whiddon." Stoneacre nodded. "I know of a couple of good candidates."

They wound to a close soon after and everyone stood and stretched and talked in low voices as they prepared to tackle their assigned tasks. Whiddon paused to bid Charlotte goodbye before he set off.

"Thank you for including me," she said quietly.

"Thank you for being so helpful."

"I'll start making new sketches right away."

He nodded and kissed her softly. Watching her head lightly up the stairs, listening to the friends behind him, who had all dropped everything at a moment's notice to come at his call, he grew contemplative.

It was the same battle he'd been fighting yesterday. But now he knew his real foe. He had a team behind him, beyond poor, faithful Chester. They had a plan.

But most important of all, now he had something truly worth fighting for.

The following days were busy and tense. Even so, Charlotte felt happier than she ever had before. Whiddon was in and out at all hours, but he kept her updated, shared the group's latest breakthroughs, founderings, thoughts and theories and every night, no matter how late he made it to bed, they came together in glorious passion.

She'd had no idea how much she'd had to learn about marital relations, but Whiddon set about treating her to a sensual buffet and she eagerly followed his lead. Neither of them slept much, but they both bore smiles and light hearts in the mornings.

She finished sketching several more images of Hurley for the searchers to use in their pursuits. She spent a great deal of time with Elizabeth and Margie as the girl began to teach the maid about the basics of fashion and the duties of a lady's maid. They read guides about the removal of stains and the care of difficult fabrics. They asked the seamstresses to teach her about buttons and repairs. They pored over fashion magazines, discussing hems and flounces and trims, and the differences between day gowns, carriage gowns, evening wear and everything in between. They lingered in the windows of Charlotte's room to watch the ladies go by. Long afternoons were spent discussing fashionable hairstyles and how to achieve them, and several times Charlotte found herself seated at the vanity while Margie practiced ringlets and braids and Elizabeth hovered and gave instruction.

"You look undeniably charming with cropped hair," Charlotte told her sister-in-law during one of these sessions. One of the new, household kittens slept in her lap while the other worried the ragged end of a ribbon in the corner. The staff had decided to name them One and The Same, as they were nearly impossible to tell apart. "You will have to grow it out, though, I think. We will want as few similarities as possible between Eli and Elizabeth."

"You are right, I know." Elizabeth toyed with her short curls. "I felt so light and free when first I cut it, but I admit, all of this talk of fashion is making me miss my ribbons, skirts and furbelows."

"It's just as well. As soon as Hurley is found, we'll need to find a way to retire Eli and bring Elizabeth home."

Charlotte also recruited the other two women into helping her set up her studio. The boxes of supplies that Whiddon had ordered arrived and she thoroughly enjoyed unpacking them and exclaiming over each new treasure. She took Elizabeth and Margie up to the attics for a good rummage, where they claimed a long table, several sets of shelves and some comfortably worn but perfectly serviceable chairs.

She was alone in the studio one afternoon, arranging pigments and primer ingredients, and thinking about the portrait of Aunt Bernadine she would like to paint. Charlotte had never seen a portrait of her aunt in her uncle's house. It was high time one was done. She would paint her near the cabinet which housed her collection of ancient coins. She would put her in a blue frock to match her eyes and—

She paused when the door opened and Whiddon poked his head inside. "Charlotte," he said softly. "May I bring someone in to speak with you?"

She turned with a smile. "Of course."

He opened the door and ushered in a frail, older lady. Her hair was white, her clothes scrupulously clean but frayed, and the smile on her face was knowing. "Ah." She breathed in the smell of linseed oil and canvas and smiled up at Whiddon. "You have married a real *artiste*, my lord. Very wise of you."

Mystified, Charlotte set down her jars of pigment and went to meet them.

"Lady Whiddon, may I present Madame Marie Louise Calas?"

"How do you do? Please, come and sit, won't you?" She indicated the corner where she'd set up the comfortably shabby chairs and a small table. "I will send for tea."

"Don't bother with tea for me, my lady." The older woman moved slowly but steadily with Whiddon's support. "We've come up with something else to keep your hands busy."

Whiddon seated their guest. "Madame Calas is one of the refugees who passed through Broadscombe after leaving France. She lost a valuable heirloom on the way. I told her how William discovered the story of the thefts perpetrated on some of those refugees, by the smugglers who were purported to be helping."

"It is a very great shame that your brother lost his life pursuing such old secrets," said Madame Calas with a shake of her head.

"Thank you," Whiddon said gently. "We do not wish his sacrifice to be made in vain." He turned to her. "Charlotte, I asked Madame Calas about the piece that was stolen from her. It sounds very unusual. She began to draw it as she described it to me and I was struck by the idea that you could perhaps sketch a realistic image of it, from her description. We could use the image when we speak to the pawnbrokers and fences who might know something of it."

"Oh, yes. Of course. Let me get my sketch pad." Coming back with it, she settled into her chair and nodded. "Tell me as much as you can remember, Madame, and we will see if I can come up with something close to it."

"It was a necklace. Very old. It had been in my family for

generations. It contained twenty-five amethysts. They were all cut with a beveled edge and set in silver."

"Oh, my goodness." Charlotte pulled out the appropriately colored sticks.

"In the middle hung a pendant, made of four separate stones. A large oval one hung lowest. The others were narrower and arranged on top of the main stone, like this." She used her fingers to illustrate the design.

Charlotte began to draw. She asked questions occasionally, as Madame Calas talked on, painting a picture in words that Charlotte sought to capture. "Is this close?" she asked eventually, turning the sketch for the older lady to see.

"Oh, well done. Very nearly perfect." Madame pointed out a few corrections. She took the sketch and ran a wizened finger over it. "Oh, I forgot, it had a small, round stone at the back, where the catch was located. It lay against your nape and teased the gentlemen with a glimpse now and then," she said with cackling laugh.

Charlotte added it. "How beautiful it must have been."

"Yes. You've captured it." The other woman blinked back tears. "I'm far too old to make use of it now. There's not even a window in my rooms, to catch their sparkle in the sun. But I would dearly love to see my granddaughter have it." Her lip trembled. "She works so hard."

Charlotte laid a hand over hers. "We will do all we can to make that happen."

"It's very good of you," the old woman said faintly. "Both of you."

"Now. Your mission is complete. Would you care for tea?"

"No, thank you, my lady." Madame Calas struggled to her feet. "I should like to go home now. If you would be so kind, my lord?"

"Of course."

Solemn, he met Charlotte's gaze for a long moment

before he took the woman's arm. Charlotte followed them downstairs and bid her farewell at the door.

"Bless you, my dear," the old woman said as she left.

Charlotte eased the door closed behind them, then went to the parlor to peer out the window and watch the carriage pull away. She stayed there, lost in thought.

The idea of the crimes Whiddon's father had perpetrated had always been appalling. Now it felt more . . . concrete. Specific. What had Madame Calas' life been like in France? Certainly, far superior to what it had become in England. What might it have been, had she kept her necklace with twenty-five precious stones?

Charlotte still stood at the window sometime later, when Whiddon returned. He looked tired and careworn. She went to him at once and burrowed into his arms. "That poor woman," she said softly.

"It's a travesty," he said, holding her tight. Letting her go, he began to pace about the parlor. "I want to drag my father here and make him sit in a room with these people, make him listen to what their lives have been." He gripped the mantel with both hands. "God's teeth, but I'd like to kill Hurley, too. We need to find him. And those jewels."

"We will." She went to stand near him. "But listen to me, Gabriel. I saw her face. You've given her hope."

"But what if we fail? Will I have made things worse?"

"We will not fail. We simply will not. But you've helped already. I could see it. You've returned some of her faith, just by trying so hard."

He stilled, clearly thinking about what she'd said. "I hope you are right."

"I am." She frowned. "But you've given me a thought. We cannot force your father to meet these refugees, but what if we told their stories another way?"

"What do you mean?"

WHY DO EARLS FALL IN LOVE?

"Do you remember, the first time we were talking about art—and we both enjoyed *The Costume of Yorkshire*? Each print a dramatization of a different profession and person? What if we created a similar project? An image of each of the refugees, with their stories accompanying the print? We could publish it as a book and donate all the proceeds to them and their families."

He stared at her.

She deflated a little. "You don't like the idea?"

"I . . . I think it's a grand idea." Suddenly he swooped at her and swept her up into his arms. He turned her in circles until she laughed and grew dizzy. "I think *you* are grand."

He plopped down on the settee, carrying her with him. "Every time I start to worry, or to entertain doubts and fears, there you are. Reaching for me, pulling me out, propping me up."

She squirmed until she was straddling him. Taking his face between her hands, she kissed him fiercely. "That is because you are always racing to rescue everyone else. It's my job to rescue you."

He ran a finger over her bottom lip, but it was the vulnerability in his eyes that speared her to the core. "Don't ever stop," he whispered.

Her heart swelled. She kissed him again, slowly this time, trying to convey everything he made her feel. He was so large beneath her, all firm, masculine strength. She felt small and feminine, perched atop him, but also powerful with the knowledge that he felt the same desire and wrenching hunger that wracked her. She sank her fingers into his thick, dark hair and could not suppress a shiver of satisfaction.

His tongue teased hers, deepening the kiss slowly, degree by hot and voluptuous degree. The sweet ache of yearning spooled through her. She pulled away, pressing soft kisses along his jaw. Her position shifted and he groaned as she moved against the hard ridge between her thighs. He buried his face in her bodice and his fingers went to her buttons.

"Take me upstairs," she whispered.

"Shut the door, instead," he retorted. He gave an experimental bounce on the settee. "Are you sure this furniture was here before? I don't recall it being so soft and inviting." His gaze twinkled wickedly. "There is plenty of room here for what I have in mind."

"Gabriel!" She was scandalized.

His teeth grazed her earlobe and her head fell to the side.

"We cannot," she insisted.

He sighed in resignation. "Very well." He shifted her position and stood, cradling her in his arms once more.

She protested as he headed for the door. "Gabriel! Put me down. The servants will see!"

"They will," he agreed. "If I put you down, then one of them will approach, needing something urgently from you, or perhaps from me. But if I carry you up the stairs, intent on having my wicked way with you, none of them will dare to interrupt us."

"Well, then." She tightened her grip around his neck. "If you put it that way."

Still, she buried her face in his neck as they went, to keep from glimpsing any shocked faces, but also to keep him from witnessing all that she was feeling right now.

It seemed a very different view, from his arms. She had worked to bring this about—this intimacy and growing trust. This sharing of sorrow and worry, but also laughter. She breathed in the wonderful scent of him, thinking that there was so much she couldn't have known. It was so much better, so much *more*, than she'd expected. She felt new and raw—and so unutterably grateful for the new life they were building and becoming together.

He carried her to his rooms and locked the doors before

he tossed her on the bed. They quickly undressed each other—they were growing skilled at such things. And then he was stretched out on top of her. She reveled in the excitement of his weight pressing her down, of the feel of his hard body and masculine flesh pressing against her. The hair on his chest felt crisp against her nipples, teasing them and sending jolts of heat and desire shooting to her womb.

His mouth closed over a nipple and his fingers were at his core, stroking and gliding against her, where she was already slick with heat and moisture.

He grinned down at her. "Come now, Charlotte, don't you wish to finish what you started downstairs?"

She gazed blankly up at him.

He rolled over, carrying her with him until she straddled him. She blinked. Her legs were spread wide over his thighs, leaving her open and exposed. Her head fell back as he reached his hand down to touch her. Her breathing quickened. His fingers danced over her, slid inside of her, and withdrew to revolve slowly around her hidden peak.

She sucked in a breath, taut with anticipation. He teased her, stroking and circling, but always gentling or pulling back when her body threatened to tumble over the edge.

"Gabriel, please," she breathed.

He rose to kiss her hard, then lay back and pulled her higher up along his body. "Take what you want, Charlotte. Take me inside of you."

His manhood was hard against her. He moved, angling until the broad head of his erection pressed against her hot, aching entrance.

She was wild with wanting him. Arching her back, she took him in. "Yes," she moaned, easing further and further still, until he was completely seated inside her.

He groaned. Silently, she echoed the sound in her head. She was so full. The pressure felt different this way. Higher.

Deeper. More. She could feel her inner channel stretching and throbbing against the tightness.

Reaching down, he adjusted her again, just the slightest bit. "Now move, Charlotte. See how it feels."

She did as he asked, and her head snapped up. An astonishing ripple of pleasure went through her. Experimentally, she moved again. A little faster. A little more forcefully.

"Yes," he whispered. "Ride me, Charlotte. Take your pleasure."

She did just that, bracing her hands on his chest as she thrust and rolled and ground against him, in all the ways that her body demanded. The beauty of it was that she pleased him even as she pleased herself. He felt huge inside of her and she was tight and hot and wet around him. They rocked together, climbed higher, reaching—and it came. Her inner muscles pulsed, and he thrust high and hard against her. They rode the wave together, on and on, until with a last, helpless shiver, she collapsed against him.

He shifted her and they lay entwined, exhausted and replete. Charlotte thought she might have dozed a little, but she woke with her head on his shoulder and his finger caressing her arm in lazy circles.

"Do you remember when you asked me about Monkford?" he asked softly.

"Hmm?" Her head was still fuzzy with the aftermath of passion. Yawning, she snuggled in closer. "Monkford?" She had to think for a moment. "Your estate?"

"Yes. Leave it to old Lady Chester to figure out what I'm doing there. The sly, old meddler," he said affectionately. "But I'd like to tell you about it."

She was awake now. Leaning back, she looked up into his face.

"About what you are doing there?"

"Yes."

"Well, now I am awake—and curious. Tell me."

He looked up at the ceiling. "It's nothing, really. It started out just a small thing. It's growing now, though. It's almost become an enterprise."

"What is? You are torturing me, Gabriel!"

He grinned, and was that a hint of *bashfulness* on his face?

"It started when Chapman and I found the first refugee."

"Yes?"

"He was not a French aristocrat. He was a farmer, actually, but he had worked on the royal properties. Someone named him a traitor to France, though, and well, that's all it took for a death sentence in those dark days."

"So I've heard."

"Monsieur Montespan did not fare well in England. We found him in a parish workhouse, starving and nearly dead. Chapman and I managed to nurse him back to health, but I didn't know what to do with him. He'd had a gold ring stolen, but returning its value was not enough to accomplish much, and he refused further charity."

"What did you do?"

"I got the idea from Keswick. He had bought an estate for himself and was making a tremendous success of it. I already had Monkford, and it was lying there, doing nothing much, barely making enough to pay for itself. It needed attention. Montespan needed a job. I spoke to him about the work he'd done on the royal farms. He'd helped develop a specific breed of sheep—the Rambouillet. They were developed to be a larger breed, with significantly longer and softer fleece. They are also prized for their meat. We came up with the idea to start a flock at Monkford."

"Oh, well, that makes sense."

"Montespan didn't have a family, but he knew others like him, those who hadn't adapted well to life in England and hadn't been able to go home, after the war. He brought in a few of them. I've added a couple more refugees, as well. Notably, a noblewoman who had run a seamstress shop after she relocated. Her eyes are not good enough for fine needlework anymore, but she's at Monkford now, working on creating a new blend of fabric. Something about a warp of cotton and a weft of wool? Or something similar."

"How wonderful."

"There were always a few people at Broadscombe who were not happy there, those who had run afoul of my father, or tangled with the Hurleys. I sent a few of them to Monkford, too. And now, the herd is growing well. We have a few contracts for mutton and lamb as well as markets for the wool. It's become a busy, happy place."

She beamed at him. "I'm so impressed, Gabriel. You've given people a home and a purpose together. And it sounds as if it has room to welcome all sorts. You must be proud of the work you've done. But I don't understand why you've been secretive about it. Why were you reluctant to tell me before?"

He shifted further onto his side, reached up and began to wind a lock of her hair around his finger. "I don't know. It's just easier to let everyone think ill of me."

She sat up on one elbow. "Gabriel! No one thinks ill of you." She made a face. "Well, perhaps your father, but we know what his opinion is worth. Surely no one else, though."

He snorted. "Just ask anyone in society."

"There might be a few who think you a prankster, but that is not the same."

He shrugged. "A great many of them find me shallow and irreverent. Or distant. I don't discourage it. There are times when I reinforce it. That way they know what to expect. They might whisper and grind their teeth at my reluctance to toe the line, but no one gets frustrated."

She pondered those words. He made it sound as if it was

better that no one expected anything of him. She suspected that the truth was the opposite. He found it easier to expect nothing good of others—because he would not be disappointed. Again.

It made her heart ache. Rolling over onto his chest, she kissed him. He returned the kiss, sweetly, quietly.

Pulling back, she trailed a finger across his cheek. "I don't care what anyone else thinks. I know you are a good, kind and generous man."

He gave her a wicked grin—and a naughtier tweak of her bottom. "How do you know?"

"Because I know *you*, Gabriel."

He raised his head and kissed one of her eyelids, then the other. "Do you see me with your incredible blue eyes and your unique vision, Charlotte?"

"I do. I see the man you won't show the world."

"I don't know why you bothered to look," he whispered. "But I'm glad you did."

She gave him a twist of a grin. "Just another part of the job."

"Is that what this is? Part of the job?" He swept a hand to indicate their nudity, the state of the mussed bed and the clothes strewn across the room.

She waggled her brows at him. "Good heavens, I hope so."

CHAPTER 19

To his gratification, Whiddon found the idea of a book of essays and prints was well received amongst some of the refugees he spoke with, although several refused to expose themselves in such a way. There were significantly more who were interested in sitting with Charlotte in her studio to provide descriptions of their stolen heirlooms.

Baron Noyer had been eager to come. He sat now, sipping tea and eating scones while giving details about the pocket watch he'd lost to the smugglers.

"I commissioned the piece myself," he told them, happily dunking his scone. "I had it carved with the raised likeness of my sainted mother, God rest her soul. It was extremely well done, solid gold and her necklace was a ring of small, dark-toned sapphires. Lighter stones accented the swirling frame around her image."

The man's barony had been minor, but he had cheerfully traded it for marriage to a wealthy merchant's daughter, and he seemed content enough with the outcome. He sighed now, though. "I do hope you find it. It was a lovely piece. I cannot imagine anyone would get as much satisfaction as I would, carrying my dear mama's likeness about, all day."

"We are doing our best to recover the stolen items," Whiddon assured him. "If you do hear from someone claiming to be my representative, though, you must remember to contact me right away."

"I certainly will," he replied, indignant. "I'll do my part to catch the bounder." His expression fell. "I never got to carry that watch for long, at all. We emigrated soon after its completion. It took months to finish, once the design was finalized, you see. But I never complained." He nodded at Charlotte. "Lady Whiddon will understand. You cannot rush an artist. Not if you wish for quality work."

Charlotte smiled at him over her sketch book—but then her face went abruptly blank. Her hand stilled. Eyes wide, she turned to meet Whiddon's gaze directly.

"What is it?" Alarmed, Whiddon half stood.

She stood as well, letting her sketchbook drop. "Excuse me, sir. I shall return in a moment, but I need a word with my husband. Please, enjoy your tea. I shall be right back."

She widened her eyes at him and, mystified, Whiddon followed her to the door. In the corridor, she grabbed his wrist and dragged him into the bedroom across the hall.

"Quality work!" she said, full of excitement. "Quality work!"

"I feel as if I am missing something."

"The first time I met Hurley, I commented on his waistcoat. He said he'd commissioned another but had to wait just over a full month for it to be done, because quality work takes time."

He shook his head, still not understanding.

"Don't you see? He told me the name of the tailor." She frowned, putting a hand to her temple. Mr. . . . . Timms! Yes. That's his name. In Bond Street. Gabriel, I met Hurley the morning after our marriage. And tomorrow, we will have been married a month!"

He finally caught her meaning. "He'll be at the tailor's shop, then. Hurley. Either tomorrow or soon after?"

"I doubt he'll send someone else to fetch it. He's vain enough to want it fitted. He won't expect me to recall such a thing—and so I would not have, had it not been for the baron's comment!"

"Thank goodness, then, for the baron and his pocket watch." He took her hand and pulled her in close for a kiss. "And for you."

His heart raced. Letting her go, he strode for the door. "I'll go today. Talk to the tailor and set a trap. I'll send for Chester, and we'll go, now."

"Gabriel!" She reached for him again, pulling him up short. "Won't you take me, instead?"

"No." His first reaction was violently negative. He winced at the disappointment on her face, though. "I want you here, Charlotte, where you are safe."

"It should be safe as houses. It's too early for Hurley to be there, today. And I shall be with you." Her hand moved to his chest. "Please, Gabriel? I've been confined to the house. And we've never yet gone out together. Anywhere at all. Not once since we married."

She was right—and she didn't even know about the rumors that had begun to circulate. Society had noted her absence. Her wretched cousin had been whispering that he was ashamed of Charlotte and regretted taking her as his bride.

Mentally, he weighed the risks. Honestly, they did seem small. He sighed. "Very well. Go on and finish with the baron and I shall tell Chester what we are up to and order the curricle brought around." He kissed her once more. "But you must promise to stay close."

"I do! Thank you, Gabriel!"

He watched her head back to the studio with a spring in her step and headed downstairs.

CHARLOTTE BREATHED DEEPLY of the fresh air—as fresh as one could get in London, at any rate. She felt invigorated to be out of the house, and better, to be at her husband's side. Not even the groom at their back could dampen her spirits—or keep her from enjoying the silent exchange of touches between them, thigh to thigh and arm to arm. It was a press of warmth with each jolt and bump of the vehicle and Charlotte was thoroughly enjoying them all.

It was still early enough for the ladies to be out on Bond Street, though, so she could give no sign of it. She sat stiff-backed, giving no indication of the grand time her limbs were having, and nodded at those she knew, as they passed.

Someone dropped a barrel from a cart going the other direction, and Gabriel's horse shied. It tossed her against him. She let herself lean against him longer than was strictly necessary and grinned up at him, once he had the horse back under his control.

He smiled down at her. "We must get a thorough idea of the layout of the shop while we are there," he said intently. "They likely have a back area just for fittings. I've been thinking I can hide in there. Chester and Sterne can wait outside the back door and Tensford can move in to cover the front once Hurley enters the shop. Stoneacre too, if he is available."

She sighed. Clearly, they were not focusing on the same things. Still, she nodded stoutly. "There is no way he could escape such a net."

"No, I don't believe so." He drew a deep breath. "I can scarcely believe this might be the end of it."

Neither could she. She could not wait to see some of the burdens lifted off of him. It made her proud to think she might have a hand in bringing it about.

He pulled the curricle to the side of the street and handed off the reins to the groom. They walked the last few feet to the shop and entered casually, as if they were merely out strolling and shopping.

"Good morning, sir. Ma'am." A tall, slim man came from behind a counter lined with bolts of fine fabric. "Welcome. I should be most happy to assist you."

"Good morning." Charlotte stepped forward. "Are you Mr. Timms, by chance?"

He looked startled. "I am."

"I am happy to make your acquaintance. I brought my husband because a man told me how impressed he was with your work. He wore a waistcoat, silvery grey with accents in rose and white."

"Oh, yes. I do know the piece you mean."

"He liked it so well, he ordered another from you."

Mr. Timms brightened. "He did, indeed. But what a happy coincidence. Your friend arrived early to collect his new waistcoat. Fortunately, I had it finished early, as well." He nodded toward the back of the shop. "He is trying the fit right now, as we speak. Perhaps you could help advise—"

He paused as Charlotte stilled. Beside her, Gabriel had frozen, as well. They exchanged stricken glances.

Grim-faced, her husband reached into his coat and pulled out a pistol. "Stay here," he ordered. Moving quickly and quietly, he pushed past the curtain that separated the front and back of the shop.

"What? Was that a—"

A scramble of footsteps and exclamations were clearly

audible. A shout rang out. Gabriel's voice. "Stop right there, Hurley!"

A crash sounded and a muffled curse. Charlotte started for the curtain, but Mr. Timms held on to her arm. "Excuse me, but what is going on? What is this all about?"

"That man is not my friend sir. He is a scoundrel and a dangerous thief. Perhaps a murderer." She wrenched away and threw open the curtain. A couple of long mirrors were lined against the wall, each with a dais before it. Before one of them sprawled a small man, surrounded by pins. Beyond him lay a jumble of patterns and fabrics on the floor and a door, standing open to the alley beyond.

Another, bigger crash echoed from outside. She rushed to the door in time to see Gabriel scaling a barricade of fallen crates and boxes. At the top, he leaped down and disappeared behind them.

Charlotte whirled and ran back through the shop, scooping up a bolt of rolled muslin as she went. She carried it with her as she burst out onto the pavement and turned right, hurrying as fast as she could. That alley must surely let out onto the street around the corner, at the end of the block.

She moved fast. It helped that the morning was fading and so was the midday crowd on the pavement. Rounding the corner, she pelted for the alley and stopped just short of it, struggling to catch her breath.

It took but a moment before Hurley spilled out, right in front of her. He looked wildly left and right, but didn't spot her, against the building. He eyed the traffic, judging the moment he would dart out.

When he made his move, she did as well. She stepped forward and hurled the bolt of fabric, aiming it like a spear. It struck Hurley high on his back, between his shoulders, and sent him sprawling onto the pavement, his head mere inches from the cobblestones of the street.

Cursing, he scrambled back and looked around. He spotted her this time and his face darkened. He took a step toward her.

A shout sounded. Hurley stopped. With a last, threatening look, he turned and darted out into the street, dodging a carriage, and heading for the other side.

Gabriel erupted out of the alley. He paused when he saw her, but she waved him on, pointing toward the spot where Hurley had disappeared. Gabriel nodded. "Be careful!" he shouted as he went after him.

She stood a moment, drawing in one breath after another. At last, she straightened her bonnet and headed back for the tailor's shop.

She found Chester in the doorway, arguing with Mr. Timms. He caught sight of her coming and came running. She explained quickly and sent him off to see if he could help Gabriel, then turned to go and smooth Mr. Timms' ruffled feathers.

"IT'S NOT YOUR FAULT, Whiddon. You've got to pull yourself out of the doldrums. We have work to do."

"Of course it's my fault. We could have had him. I did it all wrong. Everything."

Chester shrugged. "The man is slippery as a fish. We came close. We'll get him next time." His friend took a long swallow of his drink. "He clearly knew the back streets and alleys in that area better than we did. He won't always be so lucky."

Whiddon slid down further in his chair. They were at the club, tucked into a dark corner. He just wanted to drink and brood. And be left alone.

"I likely would have made the same choices. Without

Charlotte, there would have been no chance at the man. She deserved to go with you—and no one would have expected him to be there right at that moment." Chester waved to beckon a porter. "In any case, Charlotte was damned lucky. She was spotted shopping with you on Bond Street, which has put to rest some of the worst rumors about your marriage. And by some miracle, she was *not* spotted pelting down that same street like a mad woman." He chuckled. "That girl is full of pluck, Whiddon."

She was indeed, and worse than the crushing feeling of failure at letting Hurley slip through his fingers was the idea that he'd disappointed his wife. Add the thought that if he hadn't been right behind the man, she might have been in considerable danger . . . He slammed his empty glass down on the table and barked at the porter that had answered Chester's summons. "Just bring the bottle!"

"Enough sulking, man." Chester leaned in. "Listen. I've had an idea—"

Whiddon looked up. The porter was back, without a bottle. The servant bent slightly and spoke low. "There is a message for you, Lord Whiddon."

"Thank you. Bring it here, then."

"The messenger insists he must speak with you."

"Bring *him* here, then."

"I'm sorry, sir. Only members may enter. You will have to meet him in the guest parlor at the front of the house."

"Oh, for—" Whiddon heaved himself out of the chair and stalked the guest parlor, off the entry hall. He pulled up in the doorway. "Chapman!"

His valet looked agitated. "I was at my usual tavern tonight, sir. The one frequented by the higher Mayfair servants? It has proven to be a source of good information in the past."

"Yes, yes. What happened?"

"This arrived with my first pint." He pulled a letter from his coat. "It is addressed to you. The barman could not say who left it, but he knew that I work for you."

Whiddon tore it open.

I GIVE full credit to your bitch of a wife. It took me a while to recall the exchange that included Mr. Timms. You nearly had me there, thanks to her.

But this dance has gone on long enough. I propose we end it now. I have the chest of jewels. You have informed many of the refugees against me, making it near impossible for me to sell them back. I could take them to the pawnbrokers, but even if I break them up into stones and metals, I won't get their full worth.

A trade seems best. You have been prepared to restore the fair worth of the lost items to these pitiful Frenchmen. Pay me the same price and you can return their precious heirlooms.

I will keep the few coins your father did not already spend.

Let us begin with a show of good faith, between us both. I will bring one of the most elaborate pieces of jewelry. You bring fifty pounds. We'll make the trade in Green Park. Tonight. At ten o'clock, at the north end of the reservoir.

ANGER CHURNING IN HIS BELLY, he handed the note to Chester.

Chester blinked when he finished it. "What rubbish. You know this is a trap."

"I know."

"What should we do?" Chester looked thoughtful. "There are so many choices."

"I'll tell you what we are not going to do. We are not going to tell Charlotte."

"Whiddon," Chester chided. "You cannot blame her—"

"I don't blame her. But I saw the look Hurley gave her after she knocked him to the pavement. He's holding a hell of a grudge. For that, for firing him, for disrupting his scheme, all of it. He'll strike back at her if he can."

Whiddon could barely stomach the thought. His mind shied away from even the idea that Charlotte would come to harm, or worse. He could not entertain the smallest notion that she would not be in his life. Oh, how quickly he'd turned so completely about! But she'd crept her way into his very soul and the idea of her not being there, next to him, made him physically ill. He needed her soothing support, her care and concern, and he needed to give the same back to her.

No other option was supportable.

"And since we are not telling my wife, that means you need to keep it from yours." He gave Chester a stern look. "You know Julia and Penelope will tell her, if they catch a hint of this."

Chester's mouth tightened with displeasure. "I hate it, but you are likely right. But I don't even know what I'm hiding. How are we going to go about this?"

"First, let's contact Stoneacre. He said if something else came up to let him know. He can find some experienced men to lend a hand."

"Good. And second?"

Whiddon handed the note back to Chapman. "We spring the trap."

CHAPTER 20

Charlotte passed a tray to Mr. Rostham so he could take another tiny, perfect jewel of a fruit tart. She nodded as he continued talking, but she was only half-listening as he rhapsodized over his newly discovered passion for archery, thanks to her and his cousin.

He was her second caller of the day. Lady Tremaine had called earlier, saying that she couldn't stay long, but that she'd been so relieved to hear of Charlotte's shopping excursion with her new husband. She'd *told* everyone it was a newly married couple's right to have some private time, but she did hope Charlotte would step out a bit in Society now, just to put some of the more bizarre rumors to rest.

Charlotte had agreed and thanked her for her concern, and when Lady Tremaine asked what they had bought on Bond Street, she'd told her they had purchased a waistcoat. She had not told her it had been the one their lying, thief of a former house steward had worn as he ran out of the shop.

Neither did she mention how . . . differently . . . Gabriel had been acting since then.

She'd waited a long time for him in Mr. Timms' shop. At

last, he and Chester had returned, empty handed and despondent. Gabriel had been severely disappointed at Hurley's escape. He'd barely said a word, driving them home. Still not talking, he'd taken her upstairs and made quiet, passionate love to her. They'd fallen asleep entangled with each other, but she'd awakened later to find him standing at the window, staring out at the street. He'd said only that he couldn't sleep, but when she awoke this morning, he'd been gone from the house already.

She didn't think he was angry with her, but she didn't like the fleeting glimpse of desperation she'd seen behind his eyes, or the fact that he was closing himself off again.

She had to suppress a sigh. They had been doing so well. He'd relaxed his guard and allowed himself a bit of light and laughter, the relief of shared burdens and the buoyancy of shared joy. But old habits died hard. She couldn't expect him to change overnight.

This silence worried her though. She'd had a niggling sensation that he was still holding back . . . something. She hadn't a clue what it could be, but she felt it there, hovering just out of reach. Maybe it was just . . . confidence. In her? He'd had only himself and his friends to count on for a very long time. Did he not fully trust her enough to include her in that count, even still?

The thought stung. She didn't know what else to do, how to prove herself.

"In short, I had been feeling quite good about my newfound skills," Mr. Rostham declared.

She thrust aside her worries and focused on her guest again. "Good for you, sir."

"That is, until I went with my sister and her family to an evening at Astley's Amphitheatre. What do you think I saw there?"

"An archery act?"

"Would that it had been so mundane! Yes, but it was more than that. There she was, a slip of a girl, shooting her bow with unerring accuracy—while she stood on a moving horse's back!"

"Oh, dear. How lowering."

"Indeed. It has only strengthened my resolve, however. I shall persevere."

"Until you can shoot from a galloping horse's back?"

He made a face. "No. But perhaps I will keep my mount to a walk. And remain seated in the saddle, of course."

She laughed. "We will be there to cheer you on."

They talked a few minutes more, before he rose to leave. Charlotte walked him to the door, bid him farewell, then turned to find two housemaids industriously polishing nearby door latches and Eli running a cloth along the stair railing.

Hiding a smile, she headed upstairs. "Eli, when you finish with the spindles on the landing, come along to my sitting room." She said, loud enough to be heard. "I have some errands for you to run."

She didn't wait long before Elizabeth darted in and leaned against the door as she closed it behind her. Grinning, she heaved a long sigh.

"Mr. Rostham is handsome, isn't he?" Charlotte asked with a return smile.

"Oh, he is! I'd heard the maids say so, but he quite lives up to all of the gushing." She crossed over and collapsed onto a chair. "Charlotte, is he the sort of man I'll meet when I make my come-out? The sort I'll dance with at a ball, dine with, and take drives in the park with?"

"He is, indeed." Charlotte eyed her askance. "If we can get you back into skirts and teach you to sit properly again."

"Oh, I'll be good, never fear. Especially with such inducements." Her saucy grin faded after a moment. "Was Mr. Rostham one of your suitors?"

She hesitated. "He might have become one, in time."

Elizabeth sighed. "How romantic." She took Charlotte's hand. "But I hope you won't mind me saying that I am glad you did not marry him. You are so good for Gabriel. I've never seen him so happy as he's been with you."

Tears welled, but Charlotte blinked them away. "Thank you for saying so. It is very good to hear."

"Have you been happy, as well?"

"Yes, my dear. Very much so."

"I thought so, but I wanted to make sure." She let her head fall back. "I hope I will find someone to be happy with."

"You will. I'm sure of it."

They were distracted when one of the kittens came prancing from her dressing room, dragging a fur-lined glove between its legs with pride. Serious conversation was lost in the chase, and Charlotte left Elizabeth playing with One and The Same while she went down to see if there had been any word from Gabriel.

There had been no word. Uneasy, Charlotte paced the front of the house, but there was no sign of young Miss Perry, or anyone else, either. With a sigh, she asked Margie to have dinner brought to her room on a tray. "Enough for two," she whispered. "I'll keep Elizabeth with me."

After dinner, Elizabeth went to her room to read. Charlotte was grateful. She was growing more and more worried and finding it more difficult to hide it from the girl.

Once more, she went to check with Alfred, but there was still nothing from Whiddon to indicate his whereabouts or when he would return. She fetched her sketchbook and curled up in the parlor, trying to duplicate some of the images of the lost heirlooms, but she could scarcely concentrate.

Relief flooded her when a knock sounded on the door. She rushed out—to find Julia, Lady Chester striding toward her.

"Do forgive me, Charlotte! I know it is not the time for a social call, but I have been feeling very uneasy this afternoon. I thought I would come and consult with you."

"Not at all. Do come in. I've been restless, as well." She closed the parlor door and clutched Julia's hand. "I don't know why I feel so nervous! Is Whiddon with Chester? Do you know?"

Julia took off her bonnet. "He is. I think they are all together, in fact, but I do not know for sure. I only saw Chester for a short time this afternoon and he was acting so strange! He would tell me nothing, except that if I should need him, I should send a footman to fetch him from Green Park."

"Green Park? What could they be doing there?"

"I was hoping you would know," Julia confessed.

"I haven't seen or heard from Gabriel since last night."

Julia reached out suddenly and gave her a spontaneous embrace. "Could they be more maddening?"

"Yes," Charlotte said thickly. "But they would have to work at it."

They both laughed through burgeoning tears.

"Would you mind if I stayed a while?" Julia asked. "Lady Chester is out and if I must wait, I'd rather do it with you."

"Not at all. I should love the company."

Julia took her arm. "Come, distract me with a tour. Show me all that you've accomplished since last I was here."

They roamed the house and talked and talked. About the house, and society and the possibility of introducing Charlotte's siblings to Chester's young ward. Julia teased her about the library not being done when they went through that part of the house.

"I've not let anyone in there," Charlotte said with a shudder. "It's going to be a large and disruptive job. I can't bear the thought of starting it until we have all the rest of this trouble put to rest."

"I well understand," Julia assured her. "Too much chaos is as bad as too much quiet." She sighed and took Charlotte's hand. "Perhaps I should not say so, but I do think you are getting on splendidly with Whiddon. Chester cannot believe the change you've wrought. I think he feared his friend would never be able to open up to you."

"I'm not sure he has, not completely. Everything had been going so well, but these last days, I can feel the distance growing. And I admit, being left out today has me worried and frustrated."

"Perhaps all he needs is time."

"I hope you are right."

"I think I am. Just hold on a little longer, Charlotte." Squeezing her hand, Julia drew a deep breath. "And on that note, I suppose I should head back. Lady Chester will be returning home soon. I'll see if she's heard anything from any of those rascals of ours. If she has, or if there is any word left for me, I'll be sure to let you know."

"And I will do the same," Charlotte promised.

She bid her friend farewell and saw her out. Once more, she found Elizabeth waiting and watching from the first landing.

"What was that about?" The girl moved quickly in front of her as Charlotte climbed, heading for her rooms. "Is something happening?"

"It appears so. I have no idea what it is, though, only that it appears to be happening in Green Park."

"Green Park? But I visited there one day. It's nothing but fields and trees and cows."

"Apparently Gabriel and his friends have found something of interest there."

Elizabeth frowned. "What could it be?"

A knock sounded on the door. The girl hurried to Charlotte's desk and pretended to be absorbed in reading a primer. Charlotte called admittance and Alfred entered.

"Has Lord Whiddon returned?" Charlotte asked eagerly.

"No, ma'am. But you have another visitor."

"Now? At this hour?"

"Indeed." The footman sounded disapproving. "Miss Mayne insisted on waiting for you in the parlor."

"Good heavens. Harriett?" The last thing she wanted to do when her nerves were so on edge was to deal with her cousin. "Very well," she sighed. "I'll be back up shortly," she told Elizabeth. "Keep working at it."

She followed Alfred downstairs. "Be sure to lock the front door," she told him. "And stick close. Our guest won't be staying long." She gave him a nod and swept into the parlor.

"Oh, Charlotte!" Harriett bounced off the settee. "I simply must speak with you!"

"SOMETHING IS NOT RIGHT." Whiddon spoke barely above a whisper. He held still, pressed against a tree. The moon had just climbed high enough to shed a little light over the clearest spot at the northern edge of the Queen's reservoir.

"He'll be here. He wants his money." Chester crouched low on the other side of the tree. "It's not ten o'clock yet."

"This doesn't make sense. Why choose here? There is no strategic advantage to him here. It's too open. He must have known we would scout the place out ahead of time."

"He didn't know we would have enough men to encircle the whole, wide spot, thanks to Stoneacre."

Whiddon shook his head. "This is not like him. It's too straightforward. It's not sneaky enough."

A long, low call of an owl sounded from the direction of the park gates.

"That's the signal," Chester said with excitement. "Have your pistol at the ready. He's coming."

They waited.

And waited.

The noise came first, a low creaking sound that echoed eerily in the quiet.

Then a short, stout figure came into view, cloaked and hooded and slowly pulling a low, wooden cart.

"That's not Hurley."

"Maybe he's in the cart," Chester whispered.

Whiddon was already striding out into the open. He passed the anonymous figure to peer into the cart. A box lay inside, small enough that it could have been carried. "Where's Hurley?" he barked.

No answer.

Whiddon beckoned. Chester came forward, watching the figure, his pistol held low and ready.

Whiddon reached inside and took up the box. Unlatching it, he tossed the lid open and peered inside—to see it was full of stones.

The stout figure threw back her hood and let loose a cackling laugh. "Your hoity valet always did say my loaves were heavy as rocks!" She creaked with laughter at her own joke.

"Mrs. Prigg," he said in disgust. "Where's Hurley?"

"Where you will never find him," the old woman sneered.

Whiddon turned his back on her and began to move quickly toward the park gates. Around him, men melted out of the dark and the trees. He paused and pointed at Sterne and Chester. "I have to go and check on Charlotte. Divide the men into thirds. Everyone take a group and check on the wives."

"We all have extra men watching our homes," Chester said reassuringly.

"Hurley is sneaky," he shouted back, already moving again. "Go and be sure!"

Fear goading him, Whiddon began to run.

"Good evening, Harriett."

Her cousin approached, running a concerned eye over her. "Are you well, Charlotte?"

"Of course. What can I do for you? I assume you must have an urgent reason for calling. Why are you not out attending a ball or a dinner party? There are still a couple weeks of the Season left."

"How can I enjoy myself when there are such . . . odd . . . rumors circulating about you?"

"About me?"

"Yes. It's not true, is it? Whiddon hasn't harmed you? Physically?"

"Don't be absurd."

"Thank goodness. I am glad to hear you deny it. But that makes it truly odd, the things that people are saying. I don't know where they get such ideas."

Charlotte raised a brow. "Are you sure they didn't get them from you?"

"Now *you* are being absurd. Mama and I are both horrified at the things that are being said. They reflect poorly on all of us, you know. The whole family."

"Fortunately, now you can refute them with a clear conscience. You can tell everyone that you have seen me with your own eyes, and I am just fine."

"It will take more than my word to clean all of this up," Harriett said, disapproving. "Mama and I spent all afternoon coming up with some ways to combat the ugly talk. In fact, I think you should come home with me now. We can share our plans and make new ones."

Charlotte was surprised by the invitation. There truly must be some dreadful gossip out there for Harriett and her mother to willingly invite her into their home. "Thank you. I do appreciate your efforts, but I must stay in tonight."

Harriett looked around. "Are you sure? You seem to have been left here alone with only the servants for company. You might as well spend some time in the bosom of your family."

Good heavens. Something was definitely afoot. "I've promised to stay in, but perhaps we can meet tomorrow?"

Harriett frowned at her. "Are you afraid to go out, for some reason?"

She sighed. "I've already told you, cousin. I have no reason to fear my husband."

"Fine. Are you perhaps afraid of that man lurking in front of your house? I spotted him when I came in." Her eyes narrowed. "Is someone threatening you?"

"No, Harriett. That is just the watchman. There are reasons why we are being careful, but I cannot disclose them. Whiddon has merely hired some extra men to keep watch over the house."

Her cousin shrugged and went to the window. "Watchman, you say?" she asked, peering out.

"Yes."

"Are you sure he's not a drunkard? I should like to know what he expects to see, stretched out on the pavement?"

"What?" Charlotte moved to her side to look out.

"See? Right there. Good heavens, he must have fallen and hit his head." Harriett sounded disapproving. "Is he bleeding?"

Charlotte whirled away and ran out to the entry hall. Alfred was there, in his nook. "The watchman is knocked out. Guard the door." She ran to the green baize covered servant's door, opened it and called out. "Margie! Mr. Flemming! We'll need help!"

Harriett had followed her. "What are you waiting for, you imbecile?" she snapped at Alfred. "There's a man out there, bleeding to death! Bring him in!"

She brushed past the footman and unlatched the door.

"No!" Charlotte called, turning in time to see what she was doing.

The door pushed open instantly. Hurley stalked in. He held a gun pointed right into Alfred's face.

"Well done, my dear," the former steward said to her cousin. He grabbed Alfred and struck him hard on the head, behind his ear. The footman dropped to the floor.

Hurley reached back outside the door to lift a leather bag. He tossed it to Harriett. "Get back in there and get the jewels."

"She called for help."

Charlotte fell back as the former steward strode right up to her. Smirking, he grasped her arm. "I should have expected no less. You are, as ever, a damned nuisance, my lady." He dragged her into the parlor behind Harriett, locked the door, then pulled her over to the window. He parted the curtains and threw up the sash. "Nothing yet."

He pulled her over to the settee and flung her onto it. Tucking the pistol into his coat, he yanked a knife from his boot. Charlotte cringed. "Don't move," he ordered, lifting the knife high. She cowered into the corner as he plunged the knife into the seat next to her.

"Hurry," he ordered Harriett. Her cousin had pulled a knife from the leather bag and was sawing at the matching chair. "Dig down deep, past the stuffing."

He was already digging into the batting of the settee. With a grunt of satisfaction, he lifted out a long set of smokey grey pearls. They shone, rich and lustrous in the parlor's bright light.

Charlotte gaped. The jewels. They had been here all along.

Raised voices and the sound of running footsteps sounded in the entry hall as someone discovered Alfred.

Hurley snagged the leather bag and dropped the pearls in. Harriett had exclaimed in triumph. Now she pulled out a necklace of gold filagree, with a heavy cross pendant. "Toss it in," he told her, opening the bag.

He reached into the settee again and pulled out more treasure. Charlotte saw diamonds, gold and a necklace crafted entirely of pink topaz blooms.

"Keep going." He barked the order at her cousin. "There should be sapphire earrings and an entire set of garnets in there."

He pushed Charlotte onto the floor. "Move. You are sitting on a diamond tiara and more pearls."

The commotion outside grew as more servants became aware of the tumult. She heard Mr. Flemming's deep tones. Someone rattled the latch on the parlor door. "My lady! Are you in there?" It was Margie, and she sounded panicked.

Hurley's knife suddenly pointed at her eye. "Don't answer," he whispered. "Where are the keys?"

"I have them."

"Good."

He went back to digging out jewelry and she eased the keys from her pocket and tossed them under the settee. Whatever happened, he wouldn't be getting them from her.

"Move. Let me in." Elizabeth's voice sounded just outside the door. "I can pick the lock."

Harley cursed and stood. "Toss in everything," he hissed

at Harriet. "If you find more before they get in, hide it away. Hunker down in the corner. You were too afraid to stop me. Get away as soon as you can. Your carriage is outside. I have a hack waiting."

Charlotte watched, sickened, as Harriett nodded.

"I'll see you shortly," he said. Reaching down, he hauled Charlotte to her feet and forced her to the window.

"No!" She fought him every step. "I'm not coming with you!"

"You are. You are my ticket for free passage away from London."

"No!"

He sneered down at her. "I confess, I've never struck a woman before, but if there must be a first, then I'm exceedingly glad it is you."

He raised his hand and Charlotte's head exploded in pain. The light in the parlor tunneled into darkness and winked out.

CHAPTER 21

She woke to the smell of vinegar and yeast. Groaning, she clutched her head. It felt like someone was hammering at her skull from the inside. After a moment, her awareness extended beyond the throb, and she understood she was lying down. Her hair, neck and clothes were sticky and wet on one side. Blood, she realized. Her own blood. She rolled over, but nausea and pain gripped her and threatened to drag her back into the dark.

Time passed. She had no idea how long she lay in sick misery, but eventually the world stopped spinning. She tried to take in her surroundings.

It was a tiny space, dark and shadowed, except for the small light of a burning candle on a crate, next to a door. Beside the crate sat the leather satchel of jewels. She reached out. She lay on a straw mattress, thick with blankets. Beyond it was flagstone floor.

A strange, intermittent rumbling hung in the air. She could almost feel it. She didn't know what it was, but she was grateful for it. Silence would have been so much worse.

Slowly, holding her head steady because it felt as if it

might roll off, she moved to a sitting position. Swallowing against the nausea, she braced herself against the wall—and cringed when the door swung open.

Hurley. Only darkness loomed behind him, but the noise intensified.

"Harriett?" she croaked. Her tongue felt thick.

"She's late," he said shortly. "I'll wait a short time, but if she doesn't return soon, we'll have to go. There are other spots we can hide."

Charlotte shuddered at the thought of moving even an inch and he laughed when he saw it. Leaning against the door, he shook his head at her. "I suppose you were shocked when you realized she was working with me?"

She closed her eyes. She didn't dare shake her head.

"You likely know she hates you." He gave a short laugh. "I'll wager you don't know why."

Her eyes opened.

He snorted. "The golden swan never sees how she outshines the plain duckling."

Charlotte's mouth twisted. "*She* has everything."

"It does look that way on the surface. She has the money, the titled father, and from what I hear, a remarkably easier life. But there is more going on beneath the surface—and isn't that always what they say about ducks?" He shrugged. "I imagine she heard one too many times how pretty you are, how charming, how well-read and well-behaved. How you face your hardships with fortitude. It starts to twist in your gut after a while. I understand all of that. It's why she was so easy to convince—although our shared hatred of you made it easier than anything."

She closed her eyes again, thinking. Did Hurley resent Gabriel in that way, or had it only been William? And why?

He sank down to sit with his back against the door. For a

while he was silent. The rumbling was the only noise between them.

"They did everything together, you know," Hurley said suddenly. "My father and the old Marquess. They were like brothers, that's what my mam said." He spoke as if he was reminiscing over a pint. "The great man. That's what they call him in Broadscombe. He was always around our small cottage. In and out. I didn't understand, for a long time, that that's why my da was so bloody hard on me. Why I could never do good enough. Be good enough. Not until I grew old enough to understand the whispers. Such good friends they were, my da let the great man have a go at my mam, whenever he wanted. That's what they said. I fought them all, when I heard it, at first. But then I realized the truth. I was the cuckoo in the nest. I wasn't John Hurley's son at all, just the great man's bastard."

Charlotte said nothing. Was it true? She'd never noticed a resemblance between him and Gabriel. Never noted any similarity at all.

"Didn't mean anything, did it, though?" he sneered. They were the golden ones in our pond. Lord Whiddon and young Master William."

"They didn't have it so easy," she said quietly.

"A damned sight easier than I ever had it," he spat. "They had the schooling, the horses, the fine clothes. The bowing and scraping and 'Yes, sirs.' All I got was another cuff on the head."

"You killed William."

His head jerked up. Even in the dim light, she saw the uneasiness in his eyes before he blinked it away. "Nonsense. I wasn't even at the tavern that night."

"You set it up."

Grudging respect crossed his face. "He figured that out,

did he? It's just as well. William got what was coming to him. So will Whiddon."

She stiffened and he laughed. "You don't like that, do you? Well, don't worry. I'm not going to kill him. At least, not yet. I'm going to make him miserable first." His gaze glittered. "I'm going to kill you."

She refused to show fear. Glaring, she projected all the fury that his madness deserved.

"I didn't think you were going to be of so much use, at first. Sure, he'll trade free passage for you. Or he thinks he will. But now I hear he's grown fond of you. So much the better. He'll lose you, just like he lost his first love."

There could be no hiding her reaction to those words. He saw her shock and chortled at provoking it. "Oh, he didn't tell you, did he? I'm not surprised. I don't think he ever got over the whole thing. He always looks pained whenever someone mentions Abigail's name."

She frowned. "Abigail was *William's* betrothed."

"He really didn't tell you!" Hurley looked delighted. "I'll tell you the whole truth of it, then. It was Whiddon who fell head over heels for the dark and sultry Abigail first. He loved her, and she was happy enough to have snagged the interest of the heir—until she met William. There was no denying the attraction between them. It was clear as day to anyone who saw them together. Even Whiddon saw it eventually. He gave up his love to his brother."

The pain spiking in her heart put her head's agony to shame. Was this it? The missing piece? The thing that kept Gabriel from fully trusting her? She'd heard the dark emotion in Gabriel's voice when he spoke of his brother's betrothed. She'd understood that the betrayal of his brother had helped fuel Gabriel's general mistrust of marriage, of himself, of everything related to love. She just hadn't understood how personal that pain had been.

He hadn't told her.

"It will be a trio of wounds for poor, dear Whiddon. He sacrificed for love. Then he and his brother both suffered her betrayal of love—though I confess, it did take quite a bit more convincing than I expected."

Her eyes widened. "Convincing?"

"Oh, yes. While William was still in his sickbed, I whispered in Abigail's ear. I told her how difficult it was going to be, married to a cripple. The stares. The whispers. The constant care he would require. The anger and resentment he would always feel. Eventually, she agreed it would be so much easier to wed a whole man, and a wealthy banker to boot."

"You are truly evil," she whispered.

He laughed. "And you are inordinately naïve. But you will also be the third spike in Whiddon's heart. Tragic loss. Harder to bear after the untimely loss of his brother. He'll be alone." He stood, carefully wiping his trousers clean. "With any luck, it will be enough to break him. Perhaps he will never find it in him to trust in fate, to marry again."

Hurley nudged the satchel at his feet. "The great man," he scoffed. "I'll never see an acknowledgement from the old Marquess. Never a kind word, a helping hand or a penny of his fortune. The title will never be mine, but I'll have the damned jewels and one way or another, I'll see his line wiped from the earth."

Charlotte pulled in a slow breath, willing anger and worry to coalesce into something harder and more ruthless. Hurley was more than greedy. He was fixated on Whiddon's destruction. She must do everything in her power to thwart him. He'd mentioned a time constraint and he'd already stood in preparation to leave. She would do what she could to slow him down.

A particularly loud rumble sounded in the room. He didn't react at all. Very well, then.

"Aaargh." She dropped her head into her hands. "It won't stop! Why won't it stop?"

He eyed her, coldly puzzled.

"You don't hear it? The noise? The rumbling?" She gave him a panicked look. "You hear it too, do you not? Or am I going mad?"

The confusion cleared from his expression. "Oh. Yes. That. I hear it. It's just traffic, you foolish girl. Blame your uncle for living on top of a busy street instead of within the quieter confines of a square."

Her uncle's house? That's where they were? She summoned a look of horror. "Traffic? Do you mean that we are *under* the street?"

"Yes. The noise is so constant, I scarcely notice it now, myself."

"Are we in the *sewers*?" she asked with disgust.

"Don't be an idiot. Do you think I would hide, even temporarily, in the sewers? You stupid girl. We are in your uncle's beer cellar. This tidy little room was once likely used to hide untaxed, unstamped brandy casks." He chortled. "I'm not the first smuggler your family has consorted with, clearly." He sighed. "But it does seem as if your cousin is not coming. They must have detained her. She'll play the victim, of course. It will be believable, because she'll likely believe it herself. But we should head to a safer spot."

"I cannot."

"It wasn't an invitation. Get up."

"I cannot. My head. The nausea." She shook her head and groaned. "I am ill."

"I don't care." He crossed to her and tried to wrestle her to her feet. She hadn't been lying, however. As he jostled her, she retched and was sick all over the mattress and floor.

She'd been aiming for his boots.

Cursing, he gave her a shake. "Go on, then. Get it all out. You are coming, sick or not."

She choked and heaved several more times, but at last he got her to her feet. "Come along." He took her by the wrist and pulled.

She stumbled after him and leaned against the door when he stopped to take up the satchel of jewels.

"Let's go. Get out of the way." He shoved her aside and pulled the door open. The smell of vinegar intensified, and she gagged again.

"You disgust me," he snarled. "I'm not sure I believe Whiddon feels anything for you. Come on, there's fresh air just through here." He shut the door behind them and the darkness was instant and absolute. She heard the slide of a cask, felt the movement as he shifted it. He must be hiding the door latch from sight.

He took her wrist again. "Let's go."

Her fingers trailed along the rims of several large casks as they moved forward. She'd just made out the thinnest line of light ahead, a door frame perhaps, when a hand suddenly closed on her elbow and yanked back hard, releasing her from Hurley's grasp. A hand closed over her mouth, and she was dragged back and pushed down against a wall. "Stay here." Lips pressed close to her ear. "Don't move. I'll deal with him."

Gabriel! He was gone in an instant, but Hurley was cursing her roundly.

"You hellishly stupid girl! There's a lantern outside. You cannot hide from me." Exasperation filled his tone. "I should just shoot you now. You are more trouble than you are worth."

She could hear his footsteps, but nothing else. The outer door swung open and flickering light showed outside. She shrank down. The street noise grew. The cellar must open onto the passage to the servant's entrance, below street level at the front of the house.

Hurley turned to face back into the room. He held the satchel in one hand and his pistol in the other. "Come out now," he ordered. "It will go harder on you if I have to fetch the lantern to find you."

Suddenly, Gabriel stepped out of the shadows and grabbed the pistol. Leaning back, he kicked out with a booted foot, hitting Hurley in his middle, and sending him sprawling backwards into the open. "That's enough." He leveled the gun at his former steward. "It's over."

Spewing foul curses, Hurley scrambled to his feet. Clutching the satchel, he turned and ran.

Gabriel went after him. Charlotte stumbled to the doorway and saw Hurley pelting for the stairs to the street level. He was halfway up when Chester appeared at the top, his large form looming, blocking the way.

Hurley hesitated only an instant before turning to the wall and reaching up to grab the railing that separated the pavement from the open space of the stairs. Moving awkwardly with the satchel hampering him, he scrambled up and over the railing. Gabriel was right behind him, however, and he grabbed onto the leather satchel and pulled.

Hurley fought him for it, but Gabriel had gravity and all the weight of his lower position on his side. Hurley was forced to let go.

For a moment, he stared daggers at Gabriel. Charlotte lurched up the stairs behind her husband and saw Chester moving in on Hurley from one side and Sterne from the other.

He saw them, too. He looked wildly about and decided to risk the traffic of the street. He jumped in front of a lumbering night wagon. The driver yelled and kept on coming. Hurley dodged and continued. The light from the houses didn't carry so far and he disappeared into the shadows.

Gabriel and both his friends gave chase. Charlotte made it to the top of the stairs and sank down, wracked with disappointment and fear. She strained to see anything. Suddenly a shout sounded followed by a horse's scream of alarm. Chaos broke out in the street.

"Gabriel!" she gasped. The ordered traffic had become a snarl. Shouts and orders and accusations rang out. Pedestrians rushed out to see what had happened. On the top step, Charlotte gripped the railing and sobbed.

She was still crying, shuddering with grief and shock, when she felt warm arms go around her. "It's all right, my love. It's all right."

"Gabriel?" She looked up and pressed both hands to his face. "Thank God! Thank God." She sobbed still, unable to break free of the hold her emotions had on her.

"Hurley's dead. He ran in front of a coach and four. He was trampled. The others are fine."

She nodded and sobbed. He gathered her into his arms. "Come. Let's get you inside."

WHIDDON GATHERED HIS WIFE CLOSE, so incredibly grateful she was safe. He'd been frantic when he found her snatched away from home. He'd been merciless with Harriett, who tried to play innocent, but cracked quickly in the face of his relentless rage.

Thank all the saints, they'd been in time, although the sight of the blood on Charlotte and the feel of her trembling set off his fury all over again. Her sobs quieted at last, but he kept her in his arms as he entered her uncle's house.

Lord and Lady Burchan stepped out of the drawing room to meet him in the entryway. Harriett, tearstained and disheveled, huddled in the doorway. Tensford stood behind her, watching them all carefully.

"Good heavens, it was true?" The baron looked back at Tensford. "This villain has been hiding here, beneath our noses? How could this happen?"

"I think you need to direct that question to your daughter," Whiddon told him, disapproving.

"Harriett? Don't be absurd." Lady Burchan looked bewildered.

"She was in the beer cellar?" the baron asked.

"Locked in the room behind the beer cellar."

"*What* room behind the beer cellar?" The baroness was beginning to sound hysterical.

"How would such a man have got a hold of the key?" the baron demanded.

Whiddon raised his brows in the direction of his daughter.

"Harriett?" The baron growled, asking a number of questions in just her name.

"Father! You heard Mother. Don't be absurd!" The girl wiped her tear-streaked face and wrung her hands. Looking at Charlotte in his arms, she started forward. "Charlotte, dear! We are so glad you've been found safe—"

"No!"

Whiddon nearly jumped as his wife spoke, her tone ringing unexpectedly loud.

"Let me down." She wriggled in his arms. "I want to be on my feet."

She stood but leaned against him while she pointed a finger at her cousin. "I will stand for no more of your lies, Harriett. And no more of your cruelty." She looked up at him. "She should be searched. She might have some of the jewels hidden on her person. She tore up the furniture right alongside Hurley. She was the one who unlocked the door and let him in."

"Charlotte!" Her aunt sounded shocked and angry. "What are you going on about? Stop this at once!"

Charlotte ignored her. "You know what my husband gave me, before we wed," she said to her cousin. She turned her glare onto her uncle. "As do you. I chose to keep it quiet—and this is the thanks I get." Her gaze narrowed. "I could have ruined you, Harriett. Did you have to do me one better and try and have me killed?"

Harriett burst into tears, but Charlotte continued, implacable. "Enough! I have the proof. A few others already know the truth. Lady Tremaine is one of them."

Harriett blanched.

"Lord Stoneacre knows," Whiddon added. This time it was the baron who flinched. "Likely the entire Privy Council, by now."

"I am done with you. All of you." Charlotte still sounded fierce. "If you cross me, or anyone I care about, if I hear of you tormenting anymore young ladies or anyone at all, Harriett, then I will release the proof to the papers. I will tell my story. *Both* of my stories. The scandal will be endless. You will never be received in polite society again. Women will cross the street to avoid you and men will spit on your skirts as you go by. Am I understood?"

Harriett drew a breath. She looked as if she might argue.

"Am I understood?" Charlotte shouted. Her voice echoed in the marble hall.

The baroness still looked bewildered, but Lord Burchan knew when he'd been beaten. "You are understood, Charlotte. We will not trouble you again."

"It's more than you deserve," Whiddon snapped. "Unfortunately, it is going to take some time for traffic to begin moving again. Perhaps I might take my wife to a quiet room where she can rest and begin to recover."

"Show her upstairs," Lord Burchan told his wife. Turning, he moved away, his shoulders drooping, his step heavy.

Whiddon held his wife close to his side as they followed Lady Burchan upstairs. "Please send some hot water," he asked as they were shown to a room. Remembering when Charlotte had tended to him, he added, "And hot tea, with sugar, if you please."

He sat his wife in a chair. She'd gone quiet, as if that shout had taken all of her reserves. She stared, saying nothing while he pulled a blanket from the bed and draped it over her, and all the while he washed the blood from her face and neck. When he finished, he sat and tried to rub some warmth into her cold hands.

"Your gown will have to wait," he said softly. "Will you drink some tea?"

She took the cup from his hands and looked into it. "I want to go home."

"We will. Chester hared off after the magistrate. They will send for a coroner to tend to Hurley. Sterne is trying to unsnarl the traffic. We'll get you home as soon as we can."

"To Dorsetshire," she said clearly. "I want to go home to Hoverstoke."

His hands fell away from hers. His heart clenched. "Charlotte," he began hoarsely. "I know I failed you. I should have caught Hurley at that damned tailor's shop. I should have known he would lie about meeting me tonight."

"I didn't know where you were tonight. I had no idea what was going on. You didn't tell me."

"I should have. I should have expected—"

"No," she interrupted. "That is not why it was a mistake." She met his gaze, finally. "When you said it was easier to allow others to think ill of you, I didn't think you meant me, as well."

"I didn't!"

"You didn't include me today because you don't trust me. Not truly."

He tried to protest, but she continued.

"You shut me out because it was safer. Safer for me—that's what you tell yourself and your friends. But I know the truth, Gabriel. You are protecting yourself. You are still waiting for the other shoe to drop. You are still waiting for me to hurt you."

He wanted to deny it, but a horrible truth rang in her words.

"I know there is more to your hurt. More layers that you have not shared." She shook her head. "You will always be circling, just out of reach. And I will always be waiting, trying to coax you to let me in. It will be an endless cycle and we will come to resent each other." She drew a shuddering breath. "I will be miserable without you, but it will be worse if I stay. For both of us."

She was right. He'd been waiting. Now the moment was here, and the worst of it was the certain knowledge that he could have prevented it.

"I think I will take Elizabeth with me. She can change identities on the way and reenter her real life after a nice, long stay with me."

His shattered heart was dropping pieces with every beat. But he nodded. He reached for his old cloak of numbness, only to find it didn't fit anymore. His wife had filled it with holes. He turned to go and check on the traffic and he let all of his defenses drop, as he went. With each step he welcomed and accepted every shard of well-deserved pain.

CHAPTER 22

H overstoke had never seemed so small.
Fortunately, Charlotte was warmly welcomed back. Anne and George were ecstatic to see her, of course. Aunt Bernadine was gentle and sympathetic. The villagers hailed her as a returning heroine—a poor, young girl who had snagged herself an earl for a husband.

Things were better here than they had been when she left. Her uncle had kept his promises and food was plentiful. Both of her siblings had new shoes. And her aunt had hired a cook/maid to come into the house to help her on several days of the week.

Eli was gone and Lady Elizabeth had become instant, bosom friends with Anne. Each had knowledge or experience the other lacked and they set about sharing it all, although Charlotte forbade Elizabeth to teach anyone how to pick locks or gamble with dice, vices Eli had picked up in Town.

Two weeks passed. Charlotte visited friends. She wrote letters to Julia and Penelope, sending them flowers pressed from the garden. She set up an easel in the study and began her portrait of Aunt Bernadine. Two weeks stretched into three and Charlotte began to realize that the aching hole in her heart was a condition she was going to have to grow accustomed to.

"Will Lord Whiddon visit us, do you think?" her aunt asked one day while Charlotte painted.

"I don't know. He's from home right now. Julia writes that he and Stoneacre have gone to Devonshire."

"How nice. Perhaps he will stop here when he has finished his visit. I know Anne and George are mad to meet him."

Charlotte had no reply.

She found herself alone in the cottage one afternoon. Anne had taken Lady Elizabeth to meet Herr Adlung. Her aunt had taken George into the village to buy a length of nankeen, as he'd outgrown another pair of breeches. Charlotte donned her smock and set her easel at an angle, so the light would fall on both the canvas and the curio cabinet she was trying to depict. She'd been at it a while and was lost in the shine on a bronze coin when she felt a prickle go down her spine. Looking up, she found Gabriel standing just inside the room, holding a box and staring raptly.

She gasped and began to set down her brush and palette, but he objected. "No. Stay just as you are for a moment. I want to remember you like this."

"With my hair a mess and paint on my smock?"

"And with a smear across your nose," he agreed.

Blushing, she wiped her face clean. She had to fight the urge to rush into his arms. She clasped her hands before her, instead.

"Welcome to Hoverstoke, Gabriel. The children will be beside themselves at the chance to finally meet you."

"I feel the same." He lifted the box. "May I come in?"

"Of course! Come." He looked so strange here. Too large

for the cottage and so splendidly handsome. She cleared a chair of her aunt's needlepoint and bade him sit. 'Should you like some tea? You will have to take my own poor offerings, as today is not a day for Mrs. Whips to come in."

"Margie will be devasted to hear you have replaced her."

"No one could replace Margie," she said firmly.

"She misses you."

She wanted to launch into a thousand questions. About Margie, and the rest of the staff. About the house. His trip to Devonshire. His father. How he felt, without her in his life? Had he missed her half as much as she'd missed him?

She looked down into her lap, instead. "I heard you went to Broadscove?"

"Yes. Stoneacre has been a huge help. He gathered testimony against my father. Eyewitness accounts and formal complaints. We took a page from your book, told him what we had, and laid out the exact trouble that would come to him if he didn't immediately disband the smugglers."

Her eyes widened. "He must have been furious."

"Utterly," he agreed. "I quite enjoyed it."

She laughed, but it faded quickly. "Did he argue on behalf of the families who count on the income?"

"Of course he did, although that has no real meaning for him. He can increase production at the quarry or invest in the fishing fleet, if he cares to make up the difference."

"Perhaps you can donate a flock of Rambouillets to the estate?"

"If I thought he would take them, I would."

She hesitated. "If I may ask, did you mention to your father what I told you about Hurley?"

"Yes. He denied any possibility of being his father, of course. Even if it was true, he would never claim a son who committed such misdeeds—and more importantly—was caught in the midst of them."

They both grew silent.

"I brought something for you," he said, after a moment. "Will you take a look at it?"

"Of course."

He opened the box, took out a stack of papers between two pasteboards and passed it over.

She settled the stack in her lap and lifted the top board. "Ooohh."

Underneath was an engraved and printed copy of the sketch she'd done of Madame Calas' amethysts. She lifted another page, and another. All of the heirlooms she'd sketched were here. Towards the bottom of the stack, one page made her breath catch. It was the quick sketch she'd done of Madame Calas. The older woman looked proud, but distant, as if she stared into the past. "Oh, how well it's all turned out."

"Chester and I knew an artist who needed some work." He nodded toward the sketch. "Madame Calas loves it. She's written the piece she wants to accompany it, but she refuses to give it to us until you've read it first."

"Oh." She frowned.

"She wants you back in London. We all do."

She met his gaze while her heart thumped painfully. "All?"

"Yes. All. Margie has learned three new hairstyles and how to clean mud from dancing slippers. Flemming has perfected a new dish in your honor. One and The Same wander the house, looking for you, crying for you to toss ribbons for them. Julia and Penelope will scarcely speak to me. Chester wants to buy you a dog, Sterne has vowed to dance with you at every society event and Tensford and his wife want us all to come to Gloucestershire for a house party."

"And you?"

"I realized you were right. I was terrified. I thought I was going to make a colossal mistake and you would lose your regard for me. I would turn to you, and you wouldn't be there. You'd realize what a sham I was and have nothing to do with me. And then it happened, and it was so much worse than I ever imagined it would be. I've been a wreck. A horrid, cranky, lonely wreck. And I brought it on with my own fear."

He took the stack of prints from her and knelt before her, taking her hands. "But I'm not afraid of that anymore."

"Why not?" She held her breath, waiting for the answer.

"Because Tensford and Sterne and Chester sat me down and told me all of the incredibly stupid mistakes they have made, and their wives still love them."

She chuckled and he kissed the back of one hand and then another. "Because I trust you. I do. Fully and completely. You had already witnessed the shaking out of all the terrible skeletons from my closet and my family's—and you were still there, helping to clean the mess. I was a fool. I already trusted you, I was just afraid to admit it."

She sucked in a breath. "Do you trust me enough to tell me about Abigail?"

He frowned. "I have done. We spoke of it when I told you all about William's death. And again, when Elizabeth—"

"You didn't tell me that you loved her."

His face went blank with surprise. He stared at her for a long moment. "Is that what this is about?"

"Part of it," she admitted. "Hurley said she broke your heart."

"She didn't."

"She wasn't your first love?"

"Only in that giddy, schoolboy infatuation sort of way. Oh, it smarted when she preferred William, but they were so right for each other, I couldn't stand in their way. But honestly, my pride was more wounded than my heart."

He chuckled a little and shook his head. "If only I'd

known that was what worried you." He frowned. "But I have to tell you the hard truth, Charlotte. It wasn't Abigail that was the problem, it was me. It was my own fear and ignorance. I chased Hurley and those jewels looking for validation and purpose and meaning for my life. I was too caught up to see it when fate stepped in and gave me all that—in you."

Her breath caught.

"It's so easy to look back and see now. Because you showed me what I was really missing." He moved his hands up and let them settle about her waist. "I never knew what real love was, Charlotte, until you showed me."

Her heart swelling, she closed her eyes and leaned her forehead against his.

"You taught me with your perceptive gaze and your imagination and your laugh. With apple cake and sketches of maids. With kisses and sighs and long nights of love. That's what we have between us, Charlotte. It's real love. You renegotiated our agreement to get it, now I want you to come back and live up to your end of the bargain. You showed me how to love and be loved. And now I cannot live without it. Without you."

"Neither can I. Without you, I mean. These have been the most vile and lonely three weeks of my life."

He drew her down for a kiss. It was several, long minutes later that he drew back. "Fortunately, we have all of our lives and a thousand ways to make up for these best-forgotten weeks."

"A thousand?"

"A million."

"Shall we keep score?"

"Only if we change the game. I don't want points for shocking you any longer. I want a point for every new and inventive way I can conjure to show you how much I love you."

"Oh, good," she sighed. "Let's race to see who gets first to one hundred."

"What happens when we reach it?"

"Then we keep going."

And so, they did. Forever.

EPILOGUE

Charlotte glanced over her shoulder and gave a shy smile to the crowd gathered behind her. Smiles of anticipation and her husband's encouraging nod bolstered her. She lifted the latch and pushed wide the door to the finally-complete library.

It had been a daunting task. In the end, she'd broken her heart, throwing away all the old books, but they had been too damaged by damp and mold. She'd restored her spirits and had a grand time, though, choosing an entirely new catalogue of books. She'd felt like the richest woman in the world, gifted it with such an opportunity. Elizabeth and Anne had been a great help, though George had been far more interested in touring Tattersalls and the Tower with Gabriel. The ladies had carried on without them and a wide variety of many sorts of books now graced the new shelves, all bound in buttery leather.

The bindings went well with the sage and rich creams she'd chosen for the rest of the room. A substantial desk of cherry wood sat before the tall windows and new shelves lined the walls. The sighs and exclamations of delight as everyone surged in were a balm to her soul. She'd thrown herself into this project. She wanted it to be a legacy—a room of welcome and learning for years to come.

Gabriel gave the large globe a spin and came over to take her hand. "The room is lovely, but not half so beautiful as you." He leaned in to press a soft kiss to her lips.

"Keep that up and you'll be needing our donation sooner rather than later."

Lady Tensford had come to London with her husband for this trip and brought their son with her. She'd also brought a crate of books for the library, all suitable for children.

"I wouldn't mind that a bit, now that I've seen your little man," Gabriel told her. He shot Charlotte a grin. "We'll just have to keep practicing until we get it right."

"Charlotte," Julia, Lady Chester called from across the room. "This Caradec is delightful, but when will we see a piece of your own art featured here?"

"Soon, I hope," she answered. "I finished the portrait of my Aunt Bernadine and it turned out well. It's hung in the parlor at the cottage in Hoverstock. I have begun a portrait of Gabriel, however."

"It's slow going," Gabriel said. "She's so easily distracted."

The dowager Lady Chester cackled and Charlotte blushed. Everyone else smiled indulgently.

"Another visitor, ma'am." Alfred stood at the door. "Madame Calas."

The small Frenchwoman moved into the room. "Forgive the intrusion," she said quietly. "But there is one more book to be placed on these shelves." She advanced to stand in front of Charlotte and held out an oversized volume.

Tales of the Displaced: French Émigrés in London

"Oh, it is finished?" breathed Charlotte. "How lovely it looks."

"You and your husband have given us back our treasures,

but more importantly, you've given us back our voices. You honor us and we thank you."

Charlotte blinked rapidly. "We thank you for sharing. I will give your stories a place of honor here." She moved to an empty shelf and set the volume there, face out.

"That's enough sentimentality," Chester proclaimed. "I wish to know if Mr. Flemming has prepared those tiny, delicious pigeon pies?"

Charlotte smiled at him. "With you and Gabriel in attendance he would not dare to neglect to include them—or apple cake, either."

"Excellent!" Chester rubbed his hands together.

"The buffet is set up in the dining room and seating has been arranged there and in the parlor. Let's all go and do Mr. Flemming proud, shall we?"

Everyone trooped out. Spirits were high and laughter and loud conversation filled the rooms. After a while, Charlotte stepped outside to consult with Mr. Flemming for a moment. When she came back, Chester pulled her aside. "I just wanted to thank you, Charlotte."

"You are very welcome," she said with a grin. "For the pigeon pies?"

Chester nodded toward her husband. "We had been worried about him for a while, you know. He'd been growing more remote and his heroics felt more reckless. But then he stepped in to rescue you and you saved him right back." His expression softened. "You've made him happy, Charlotte, and that is a miracle I didn't know if I would ever see." He nodded toward the spot where Gabriel stood with Sterne and Tensford. "We all wanted you to know how grateful we are."

She refused to cry. Not today. But her voice sounded thick when she answered. "Thank you, too. There is much I don't know about your friendship, but I know what it means to him. I think you all saved him some time ago—and I am grateful, as well."

Chester looked as if he might say something else, but suddenly his eyes widened and his mouth dropped. "Kes," he said hoarsely. He abruptly pushed past Charlotte, heading for the wide doorway. "Kes!"

Charlotte whirled to see a couple standing at the threshold. A tall, handsome man stood grinning, his arm wrapped protectively around a diminutive woman, holding a tiny infant in her arms.

Chaos erupted. Tensford, Chester, Sterne and Gabriel rushed to surround the newcomers. There was a flurry of words, embraces and shoulder slapping. Lady Tensford pushed her way in to cling to the woman, smiling through pouring tears. "Glory! Look at you! Both of you! All *three* of you! Why didn't you tell us?"

Eventually the commotion subsided. Keswick laughed, for it was he and his wife, returned at last from Ireland. Guests greeted them, then began to filter out, until, at last, there were just the five gentlemen friends left, with their families. Keswick took the opportunity to introduce his tiny daughter, Faith.

"I know! I know!" he said. "We have been gone far longer than we expected. But we had a wonderful time touring all of the grand stables in Ireland. At first we were delayed, waiting for the birth of a special foal." He lit up. "Wait until you see him go," he told his friends. "I'm going to train him up right. He'll be a sensation on the track and then I'll build my stud around him—"

"Kes!" Lady Tensford objected. "Less horse talk for now, please!"

He looked sheepish. "Yes, yes. In any case, we discovered Glory's news just as we meant to leave. There was some difficulty, early on. It scared us right through and we were advised to stay until this little nugget had safely arrived." He ran a hand over his daughter's head.

"It was my fault," Lady Keswick confessed. "I didn't want to tell anyone, not while we still faced the danger. We didn't know what might happen and it was easier on me, knowing that no one was worrying, over here." She sent her sister a look of apology.

"I'm sure I'll be vastly annoyed once I've had time to think on it." Lady Tensford sat close to her sister with her husband on her other side and her own infant asleep in her lap. "Right now, though, I'm just so glad to see all of you . . ." She squeezed her sister's hand. "I want to hear everything! Everything you never wrote."

The talk continued, and eventually the group separated. The men stood in a corner, drinks in hand and smiles on their faces. The women clustered around the sisters and their children. Charlotte listened to the talk of babies with half an ear, but found her attention straying to her husband.

How relaxed and happy he looked. He caught her eye and gave her a smile of happiness and promise. And she felt something inside of her shift.

Chester was right. Gabriel had suffered. All of these men had. She thought of how pressed and desperate she'd felt when she arrived in London. They had all struggled to reach this point. There would be hardships ahead. Life remained a balance. But they all had each other now, and she counted herself among them.

They had struggled. They had survived.

Now, at last, it was time to thrive.

The coquettish look she tossed back at her husband was just the first step.

ALSO BY DEB MARLOWE

A Series of Unconventional Courtships

Love Me, Lord Tender

Nothing But a Rakehell

Kiss Me, Lady, One More Time

A Cup of Cheer

Why Do Earls Fall in Love

The Half Moon House Series

The Novels

The Love List

The Leading Lady

The Lady's Legacy

The Lady's Lover

The Novellas

An Unexpected Encounter

A Slight Miscalculation

A Waltz in the Park

Liberty and the Pursuit of Happiness

Beyond a Reasonable Duke

Lady, It's Cold Outside

The Earl's Hired Bride

The Castle Keyvnor Pixies

Lady Tamsyn and the Pixie's Curse
Lord Locryn and the Pixie's Kiss
Miss Penneck and the Pixie's Poem

Writing as D.M. Marlowe:
The Eye of the Ninja Chronicles
Eye of the Ninja
Obsidian's Eye
The Fire in the Ice

ABOUT THE AUTHOR

USA Today Bestselling author Deb Marlowe adores History, England and Men in Boots. Clearly she was destined to write Historical Romance.

A Golden Heart winner and Rita nominee, Deb writes Regency Romance and Young Adult Fantasy Adventure.

A proud geek, history buff and story addict, she loves to talk with readers! Find her discussing books, movies, TV, recipes from Deb Marlowe's Regency Kitchen and her infamous Men in Boots on Facebook, Twitter, Instagram, and Pinterest.

Connect with Deb
www.DebMarlowe.com
Deb@DebMarlowe.com

Made in the USA
Coppell, TX
09 September 2021